THE SECRET RUNNERS OF NEW YORK

Also by Matthew Reilly

THE SECRET RUNNERS OF NEW YORK

MATTHEW REILLY

HOT
KEY
BOOKS

First published in Great Britain in 2019 by
HOT KEY BOOKS
80–81 Wimpole St, London W1G 9RE
www.hotkeybooks.com

A CIP catalogue record for this book is available from the British Library.

ISBN: 978-1-4714-0795-6
also available as an ebook

2

Typeset in Sabon and Arial by Post Pre-Press Group
Internal illustrations by IRONGAV
Printed and bound in Great Britain by Clays Ltd, Elcograf S.p.A.

Hot Key Books is an imprint of Bonnier Books UK
www.bonnierbooks.co.uk

This book is for everyone
who went to high school . . .
. . . and survived.

**If you have enough money and a good name,
you can do anything.**

CORNELIA GUEST
THE DEBUTANTE'S GUIDE TO LIFE

Why do we remember the past but not the future?

STEPHEN HAWKING
A BRIEF HISTORY OF TIME

CENTRAL PARK, NEW YORK CITY

PROLOGUE
BECKY'S LAST RUN

NEW YORK CITY
2:35 A.M. DATE: UNKNOWN

The girl in the torn bridal gown ran for her life through Central Park.

Thorny branches slashed her cheeks as she charged headlong through the undergrowth. It was late, well after midnight. The park and the city around it were dark and silent.

Becky Taylor's normally pretty seventeen-year-old face was smeared with blood and dirt. Across her forehead written in red lipstick were the words:

HEAD GIRL

The crimson letters were streaked with desperate sweat.

Becky ducked her head as she rushed frantically through the brush, leading with her forearm. Amid all the bloody scratches on that arm were some marks near the wrist.

Four vertical lines: IIII

Rising above the trees behind Becky, black shadows against the night-time sky, were the iconic buildings of Central Park West: the colossal Museum of Natural History and some of the most famous and expensive apartment buildings in the world, the San Remo, the Majestic and the Dakota. Not a single light glowed within them.

Her heart pounding, her lungs burning, Becky kept running as fast as she could.

She could hear them behind her—running, grunting, hunting.

And then she pushed through a final thicket and suddenly the ground dropped away in front of her and Becky pulled up with a lurch, narrowly avoiding falling down a seven-foot drop.

In her ripped bridal gown, Becky Taylor risked a smile.

She'd reached the 79th Street Transverse.

She was almost there.

She quickly lowered herself down the seven-foot wall that flanked the sunken roadway and dashed across it.

Of course the road that had once allowed vehicular traffic to cross Central Park was now empty. Like the darkened city around it, it was eerily deserted.

Weeds, grass and ivy had grown up through the bitumen, cracking it, warping it. Abandoned cars lay at all angles: the weeds had simply engulfed them.

Not a soul could be seen.

It was just Becky in this dead, empty city . . . and her pursuers.

Around her left wrist was a ring of torn, bloody skin. Becky had awoken here bound to a streetlight, her hands tied behind her back with rope. After some very painful struggling, she had managed to wrench her left hand free of her bonds and begun this frantic run home.

Becky sprinted across the roadway and clambered up the stone wall on its opposite side.

A minute later, she rounded a corner and saw it: the Swedish Cottage.

The Swedish Cottage is a strange brown wood-walled gingerbread-style house that was actually built in Sweden in the 1870s and shipped to the US soon after as a gift from the government of Sweden. It sits in Central Park beside the Shakespeare Garden, out of time, out of fashion and out of place.

It wasn't the cottage that Becky was after, but what lay behind it.

She dashed around the brown building and came to a dirt clearing on the other side.

There she saw the low stone well.

Becky hurried over to the well and leapt straight into it, pressing her hands and feet against its close walls and lowering herself down the tight vertical shaft.

Twenty feet later, she emerged inside the mysterious tunnel at the bottom of the well. She dropped the last few feet and hurried down the tunnel until she saw the ancient stone doorway . . .

. . . and stopped dead.

The exit wasn't open.

She couldn't get out.

'Misty, Chastity, you bitches,' Becky said to no-one.

A bloodcurdling male scream from outside made her spin.

And there in that cold underground tunnel in that wretched version of New York City, Becky Taylor realised that she was going to die.

This day wasn't supposed to end like this.

Only hours earlier, she had literally been the belle of the ball, stunning in her Vera Wang gown, outstanding at school, with a handsome date and the world at her feet.

And now she was here.

In this horrible place.

Trapped and alone.

Soon its cruel inhabitants would find her, and when they did, they would kill her in the slowest and ugliest of ways.

And with those grim thoughts, Becky Taylor—in her torn bridal gown and lipstick-branded face—dropped to the floor, closed her eyes and quietly began to sob.

At that exact same moment, in Becky's room in her family's apartment in the Majestic building—a regular seventeen-year-old girl's room in the regular New York City of today—her parents found her phone and, on it, a final text message written but unsent.

It read:

> DEAR MOM AND DAD,
>
> I JUST CAN'T TAKE IT ANYMORE: THE PRESSURE, THE EXPECTATIONS, THE BURDEN OF THOSE EXPECTATIONS.
>
> PLEASE DON'T COME LOOKING FOR ME, BECAUSE YOU WON'T FIND ME. I WILL BE AT THE BOTTOM OF THE RIVER, AT PEACE.
>
> I LOVE YOU.
>
> BECKY

PART I

THE SCHOOL WHERE
NEW GIRLS GO MISSING

**They were careless people, Tom and Daisy—
they smashed up things and creatures and
then retreated back to their money . . .**

F. SCOTT FITZGERALD
THE GREAT GATSBY

NEW SCHOOL, NEW LIFE

It was my first day at school in a new city but I don't think you'd find many people feeling sorry for me.

On paper, my life was the ultimate fantasy of the average American sixteen-year-old girl.

I was living in New York City on the Upper West Side, in the historic San Remo building, in an enormous apartment that overlooked Central Park. The San Remo is one of those imperious twin-towered art deco co-ops that were built in the 1930s which are now occupied by movie stars, Wall Street Masters of the Universe, Saudi princes, and anybody else who can afford to pay $20 million in cash for an apartment.

But as far as I saw it, my life sucked.

Wrenched from my childhood home in Memphis, I had been transplanted at the age of sixteen into the most fearsome milieu of teenage bitchiness imaginable: that of ultra-wealthy New York.

Enrolled at a new school in a new city, away from the father I loved, living with a mother I despised and a stepfather who tolerated me, I hated it. The only plus was that my twin brother, Red—ever calm and easygoing—was in it with me.

The first day of school didn't start well.

I dressed in my uniform: an utterly sexless white

button-down blouse under a navy-and-green tartan dress. The white shirt was long-sleeved with stiff buttoned cuffs. A racing-green ribbon was the only hair accessory allowed. In a school as well-to-do as Monmouth, jewellery can be a serious issue—girls can get competitive about this sort of thing and it was entirely possible for a female student to wear earrings worth a few hundred thousand dollars. So all jewellery was forbidden. The only other accessory permitted was a watch.

I didn't mind the plainness of it all, or the sexlessness for that matter. At my old school in Memphis—an all-girls school—there had been no dress code, so the student body had worn whatever they liked, and as the girls got older, every day became a fashion contest. And as hips became curvier and breasts became larger, the waistlines of jeans got lower and the necklines of tops plunged further. In the stifling heat of the Tennessee summer, the amount of skin on display was outrageous.

One hot summer's day, as I saw two male gym teachers ogling the asses of three seventeen-year-old girls in short shorts, I overheard a female teacher say, 'Are you kidding me?'

But this was not the case at The Monmouth School (never forget to include the 'The'; they will correct you). It was a learning institution and uniforms—for both boys and girls—were one of the ways it kept its students' eyes on their books and not on the opposite sex.

As I said, I didn't mind this. For my own reasons, I especially liked the long-sleeved shirt. And I always wore a watch on my left wrist: a chunky yet very practical white Casio G-Shock.

My mother, on the other hand, had all sorts of iss⌐ ⌐ with the school's uniform policy.

She positioned me in front of the mirror in our entry hall and began redoing my hair from behind me. She twirled a couple of mousy brown strands down around my temples.

'Don't yank your hair back off your face like that, Skye, darling,' she said. 'You could be pretty, you know, if you tried a little.'

I bristled inwardly, but I didn't let it show. I'd heard a thousand comments like this before.

Why don't you wear something a little more flattering?

Stop slouching, pull your shoulders back, push your little titties forward.

Eyes up, child. Honestly, how will you ever get a boy to notice you if you never look up?

And most cutting of all: *You know, Skye, I really think you could stand to lose a little bit of weight.*

Of course, my mom was fully made-up even though it was 7:30 in the morning.

She had already been up for two hours by then, and in that time she had run six miles on her treadmill, done a hundred sit-ups and a twenty-minute mindfulness meditation. My mother was forty-five with the body of a twenty-five-year-old and today her sleek form had been poured into a perfectly fitted Prada dress. Her long auburn hair, as always, had been professionally done, every curl and wave carefully arranged. (Our live-in maid, Rosa, in addition to being my mother's personal servant, confidante and informer, had once been a TV make-up artist, which no doubt had secured her the job.)

Oh, and my mother wore heels, even in our apartment at that hour.

'Skye,' she said, 'this is a hard truth that nobody wants to admit, but you have to learn how the world judges women: it's not what is in our heads that matters. It's the package. How else do you think I won your stepfather?'

A quick little disappearing act under the table at the restaurant on your first date? I thought uncharitably. I'd overheard Mom revealing that to her best friend, Estelle, one night on the phone after she'd had one too many cosmopolitans.

My mother, Deidre Allen (née Rogers, née Billingsley)—one-time Belle of the Memphis Ladies Auxiliary's Debutante Ball and second runner-up in the Miss Tennessee beauty pageant—had only a high-school education to her name, but that hadn't stopped her rising to the peak of New York society and adopting a daily ritual of shopping, lunching, yoga and cocktails.

Thankfully, at that moment, Red came down the stairs, dressed in his Monmouth blazer, tie and trousers, and said, 'You ready, Blue?'

I loved my twin brother. His real name was Alfred, but since time immemorial everyone had called him Red. With his carelessly tousled copperish hair and his elfin face—which matched mine—he somehow managed to make his private school uniform look cool.

I don't know how he did it.

Hell, sometimes I didn't know how he and I had shared the same womb.

A bare two minutes older than me, Red was everything

I was not: chill and all but unflappable. Nothing could rattle him. 'It's that extra level of maturity I possess,' he'd tease me. 'Since I *am* a little bit older than you.'

He made friends easily, effortlessly. You could throw Red into a room full of strangers and within twenty minutes, he'd be chatting and laughing with a bunch of them.

I wished I could do that.

I liked to think that I was pretty good at small talk and felt that I could get along with most people.

The problem was the intro.

I was painfully shy when I met people for the first time. I just had to *get to* the conversation. Once there, I was actually okay, but it was getting there that was my problem.

Blue had been my dad's nickname for me—my real dad's—as in sky blue. (I actually couldn't remember him ever using my real name.) Get it? Red and Blue. And since my dad's name was Dwight, he had loved to say, 'Look at us three: Red, Dwight and Blue!'

Dad jokes. You hate them when you hear them every day, but trust me, you sure do miss 'em when he's gone.

I said, 'Ready as I'll ever be, I guess.'

I yanked myself from my mother's grip and got out of there as fast as I could.

Our new school was directly on the other side of Central Park, maybe half a mile away, so Red and I walked there.

I have to admit, despite all the other things I hated about my life, I liked that walk.

Our building was on Central Park West, not far from the Museum of Natural History, and Monmouth was over on the East Side, on Fifth Avenue near the Met, so we walked along the lovely tree-lined paths that swooped over and beside the ever-busy 79th Street Transverse.

At that time of the morning, it was quite delightful.

Delightful, that is, except for the crazies and the religious weirdos who had become regular sights on the sidewalks near landmarks like the Met and most of the major entrances to Central Park, holding up their signs and bibles.

The happier nutjobs wore tinfoil hats and danced around like idiots. They carried signs like:

**THIS ST PATRICK'S DAY
IS GONNA BE THE BEST ONE EVER!**

YOU SHOULD HAVE ASKED HER OUT.

**<u>FORNICATE! SPEND! LOOT!</u>
AFTER MARCH 17
IT AIN'T GONNA
MATTER ANYMORE!**

The religious ones were older and more serious. They held their placards silently and stoically. Their signs were less colourful:

**LUKE 21: 25–26
1 JOHN 5:19**

THE WHOLE WORLD LIETH IN WICKEDNESS!
AND HE SHALL DESTROY THE SINNERS! ISAIAH 13:9

THIS IS GOD'S VENGEANCE
FOR ALLOWING GAYS TO MARRY.

GOD HATES FAGS AND JEWS.
WELCOME TO THE RECKONING.

I didn't care much for the St Patrick's day stuff. It had been all over the news when that old scientist had first made his announcement a year or so ago, but March 17 was still seven months away and after the initial media fervour, people had got bored with it, and soon the whole thing had acquired the standing of just another Y2K, Comet Hale–Bopp, or 2012 apocalypse. It blew over.

Many people, like my mother, compared it all to that crazy Christian dude who had convinced his followers to sell all their possessions because the world would end on May 21, 2011. When it didn't, many found themselves broke and still very much here.

And so Red and I just walked right past the ragtag group of sign-wavers and entered our new school, where my own personal hell would take place.

ASSEMBLY

The Monmouth School is located inside a 19th century Astor family mansion on Fifth Avenue. Above its aged stone entry arch is a coat-of-arms and the Latin motto: PRIMUM, SEMPER.

First, always.

That about sums it up.

Monmouth is not your standard high school.

Its students are rich. Really rich. Their parents are the kinds of people you see at White House dinners. Situated on the Upper East Side of Manhattan, over-looking Central Park, the school is one of the most exclusive high schools in America. Everyone who is anyone wants their progeny to go there and they do whatever it takes to make that happen.

But with one of the biggest endowment funds in the country behind her, the famous headmistress of Monmouth, Ms Constance Blackman—she has been headmistress for twenty years—cannot be bought. As she puts it, there are *other elements* that make a child 'Monmouth material'.

Those other elements can be anything, really, but they usually pertain not to the student but to the student's family. They might include a sustained contribution over many years to the cultural life of New York City or being the winner of an old and highly-regarded prize (read: Nobel or Pulitzer), but in the end, one asset trumps all others.

Breeding.

When I arrived there, the school boasted four students who were direct descendants of *Mayflower* families and three who had ancestors who had signed the Declaration of Independence.

Monmouth disdained the children of modern celebrities and the nouveaux riches. Ms Blackman, a lifelong spinster of modest tastes who lived in a cosy apartment on the premises, delighted in turning down bribes. She had once famously declined an invitation to attend the Met Gala with a prospective parent, saying, 'Why on Earth would I want to attend a function put on by a magazine?'

Her job, she maintained, was simple. It was to retain Monmouth's number one standing in the dual worlds of education and society.

First, always.

That said, there was one thing about The Monmouth School that Ms Blackman did her very best *not* to talk about.

The missing girls.

Over the last two years, three students connected to the school—all girls, all new, one sophomore, one junior, one senior—had gone missing.

Just *poof*, gone. Without a trace.

Never to be seen again.

There was the smart girl, Trina Miller: a sophomore with a 4.3 Grade Point Average and an exceedingly bright future. She'd disappeared in January of last year, only five months after starting at Monmouth.

Then there was Delores Barnes, the special-needs student. A moon-faced angel with Down Syndrome, Delores had been part of the 'My Little Sister Program', a program that paired students at Monmouth with kids from nearby special schools.

Even though it was designed to show them how fortunate they were, the students from Monmouth mocked the program relentlessly. But they did it anyway, for that all-important 'community service' line on their college applications. Delores had been a junior and had disappeared in December last year.

And finally, the most recent disappearance, that of Rebecca 'Becky' Taylor.

Becky's disappearance had been the most shocking of all.

A vivacious and outgoing girl, within a year of arriving at Monmouth, Becky had become one of its most popular students. Everyone had thought she would be named Head Girl this school year. But then, back in March, on the very night she had been crowned 'Belle of the Ball' at the East Side Cotillion—the most exclusive debutante ball in New York—she had disappeared.

Just vanished into the night in her snow-white debutante gown, never to return.

Alone among the missing girls, Becky had left a note—a text—saying that, overwhelmed by the pressures facing her, she had thrown herself into the river, presumably weighted down so that she would never be found.

It shocked many that a student as bubbly and popular as Becky could have been harbouring suicidal thoughts. You just never know, they said. She became a lesson taught in self-esteem classes.

Of course, in all three cases the NYPD had been called and detectives assigned.

Ms Blackman had even hired a former FBI investigator to look into the matter. The police, she said publicly, 'fine public servants that they are, might not give this task the time and effort it deserves.' In private, she put it another way: 'Regular people use the police. We pay for, and get, a better service.'

But neither the police nor the ex-FBI guy found anything that could lead them to the missing girls—no phones, no fragments of clothing, no bodies.

Not a single thing.

The FBI man investigated the possibility of kidnap in all three cases, but those efforts also came to nothing.

It was puzzling, he said, that in this age of CCTV cameras, credit card records, and Find My iPhone, these three students could vanish from the face of the Earth.

Nasty girls from nearby schools never missed an opportunity to goad Monmouth students about it, and I had only found out about the missing-girls issue when I had casually told someone about my new school.

And as I walked under that old stone archway on my first day, I did it acutely aware that at the school where new girls go missing, I was the new girl.

The 280 students of The Monmouth School gathered in the school's theatre-like auditorium, a sea of blue-and-green tartan uniforms, murmuring quietly.

I must say that, seeing it en masse, I liked the uniform thing even more, chiefly because it allowed me to remain anonymous. I didn't want to stand out and in a uniform I could hide in plain sight.

The girls, I saw, sat in tight cliques that had no doubt been formed long ago. The sophomore boys slouched up the back, watching the girls. Teachers stood in the aisles by the walls, chatting casually with each other.

And then silence—sudden and powerful—as Ms Blackman took the stage.

'Ladies and gentlemen,' she said, 'welcome to a wonderful new school year at The Monmouth School.'

The usual platitudes followed: about how privileged we were to be attending such a fine institution; how Monmouth would make us the leaders of tomorrow; an exhortation to the new senior class to provide the leadership that was expected of them; yada yada yada.

And then Ms Blackman said a few things that actually interested me.

'Do not let these times of hysteria distract you. Over the course of my life, I have seen many foolish people claim the end of the world is coming and I am still here.'

'Not even a nuclear warhead could kill that old battleaxe,' a handsome boy with wavy blond hair in the row behind me snickered. 'When it's all over, it'll just be her and all the cockroaches.'

A nearby teacher hissed: 'Mr Summerhays. *Shh!*'

Ms Blackman then said, 'I will now call upon your Head Boy and Head Girl, Mr Bo Bradford and Ms Chastity Collins, to address you.'

Two seniors sitting in the front row of the auditorium stepped up onto the stage.

I didn't mean to do it, but at the sight of them I did a double take.

To call them 'good-looking' would be to oversimplify the matter. They weren't just blessed with good genes. No, they had something more than that. These two high school seniors had been professionally *styled*.

The boy filled out his racing-green blazer perfectly. He even made his garish tartan tie look sharp. With his exquisitely shaved square jaw, symmetrical cheekbones and laser-parted sandy hair, Bo Bradford looked like a guy who rowed crew for Harvard and modelled for Ralph Lauren in his spare time.

Some girls beside me whispered breathlessly:

'Oh my God, he is so hot, I can't . . .'

'He is a dime. I'd literally let him do anything to me . . .'

'Good luck, he was practically betrothed to Misty Collins in pre-K . . .'

The Head Girl looked about seventeen and she was similarly attractive and well-presented: tall and statuesque, with blonde hair, light freckling, blue eyes and a thousand-watt smile that seemed to me a little too practised. Her school uniform fit her like a glove, as if it had been tailored to her exact measurements, which I actually think it had.

She spoke first, her voice perky and bright.

'Hi everyone. If you don't know me, I'm Chastity.'

A light-skinned African-American girl with a gorgeous mop of curly bronze hair sitting to my left snorted. 'Well, there's the first piece of false advertising I've heard this year.'

'Shut up, Jenny, you bitch,' another girl whispered.

The black girl named Jenny shrugged. 'I mean, *Chastity*. Really? We all know Chastity loves to get all up-close-and-personal with the boys.'

'I'm going to punch you in the uterus, Jenny,' one of the other girls hissed.

'Like you ever could, Hattie.'

'How's your *job*, Jenny? Still waiting tables?'

'Ladies . . .' a female teacher whispered from the aisle. 'Miss Brewster. Miss Johnson. That's enough.'

I was so enthralled by the little battle going on in the cheap seats, I had tuned out of Chastity Collins's speech.

She was saying, '. . . and let us not forget our departed friend, Becky Taylor. God rest her soul.'

The girl named Jenny snorted again. 'Chastity *should* be thanking God. She wouldn't be Head Girl if Becky Taylor hadn't hopped off the planet.'

'*Miss* Johnson! You will report to my office when assembly is over!' the teacher in the aisle whispered.

Chastity Collins continued, '. . . so sad to lose someone so talented and so promising so young.' But then she transitioned brilliantly, her 'sad face' suddenly brightening.

'On a lighter note, this year promises a *very* exciting social season. Monmouth has no fewer than three girls debuting at some of the most prestigious debutante balls in the city, including—and forgive me for being a little biased here—my sister, Misty, who will be attending both the International Debutante Ball and the East Side Cotillion *as a junior*, which is a very rare honour indeed.'

The two girls who had exchanged barbs with the girl named Jenny patted a third girl on the shoulder.

This girl was a younger, more compact version

of Chastity Collins, with the same blonde hair, light freckling and blue eyes. But she had a harder face, a more serious aspect.

I'd seen this kind of kid before. The younger sibling of the golden child, who, known only to herself, was destined for even bigger things.

The girl named Jenny couldn't resist a gibe. 'Smile, Misty. Gotta work on that RBF.'

The blonde girl named Misty turned to Jenny and unleashed what could only be described as a winning smile.

'Thanks, Jenny, I appreciate the advice,' she said.

I saw Jenny frown for a microsecond, thrown by the fact that her taunt had not got a rise out of Misty.

In the space of a few minutes I'd seen a taunt about sluttiness, a threatened punch to the uterus, some humble-bragging by the Head Girl about the school's social status and a dose of good old-fashioned mean-girl passive-aggressiveness from Misty. School, I reflected sadly, was school no matter how high the tuition fees were.

Shortly after, Chastity ended her speech and the handsome Head Boy said some bullshit. Then Ms Blackman retook the microphone and went through a few administrative issues and I kind of switched off until she said something that made my blood run cold.

'. . . thrilled to welcome two new juniors who are joining us from Memphis, Tennessee . . .'

Oh, God, no.

'. . . Mr Alfred and Miss Skye Rogers . . .'

At the sound of my name echoing through that auditorium, I shrank into my seat. I wanted to shrivel up and die.

Please don't make us stand up. Please don't. Please don't.

Ms Blackman smiled kindly at Red and me. 'Why don't you come up on stage so we can all get a look at you.'

Of course, Red sprang out of his chair at the invitation and bounded up onto the stage, waving cheerfully at the student body.

I edged out of my row and stalked up the steps, head bowed, shoulders hunched, trying to create the tiniest silhouette possible.

At which point I tripped on the top step and went sprawling onto the stage like the biggest klutz in America.

Red—God love him—caught me inches off the ground but the damage had been done.

Giggles rippled through the audience.

Blushing with mortification, I regathered myself and gave the audience a weak half-nod.

Ms Blackman gestured for us to vacate the stage and I was off it in a flash.

As I resumed my seat, I heard them:

'Did you see her trip? How *embarrassing* . . .'

'Oh my God, I would just want to die . . .'

Then there came a voice directed at me. 'Nice faceplant, Memphis.'

More giggles.

Damn, I hate girls.

The assembly ended.

And as I watched my fellow students filing out, talking and yammering, high-fiving and pointing, I thought, *Even in a tartan uniform, school is a jungle.*

THE COMING END

I should probably explain the whole St Patrick's Day end-of-the-world thing that was going on.

Long story short, no-one knew what to think.

It had all started in August the previous year when an ageing scientist from Caltech named Dr Harold Finkelstein had written an article in an academic publication called *Astrophysical Journal* about a phenomenon he had spotted in space.

He called it a cloud of high-density ultra-short-wave ionised gamma radiation which the world soon shortened to 'the gamma cloud'.

It was basically a cloud of electromagnetically charged energy that had wafted into our solar system. When Dr Finkelstein spotted it, it was passing Jupiter and, according to his calculations, the Earth—as it swept around the sun—was going to pass through it on March 17 next year.

It was what would happen to the Earth and everyone on it when this event occurred that became the subject of intense debate in the scientific community, on morning TV shows and among the general population.

It was Finkelstein's position that it would be an extinction-level event.

And it would not be pretty. It would be twenty-four hours of terror and misery.

For gamma radiation would not be kind to the fragile human body. It would hurt it in several different ways.

First, electrically. That would be the real killer, Finkelstein said.

Almost every cell in our bodies relies on electrical impulses to survive. The human brain uses electricity to send signals to the rest of the body. When struck by the gamma cloud, the average person's brain would fry and that person would literally drop dead where they stood.

That would knock out 99.5% of the global population.

But the gamma cloud was not, Finkelstein said, of a single uniform level of strength: it would be denser in some places and more diluted in others.

This meant that different locations on the Earth would be hit with different levels of exposure, which meant some people—perhaps because they were hit by a lower level of gamma radiation or perhaps because they possessed a natural resistance to it—might survive the wave of death scouring the planet.

That said, those survivors wouldn't have a great world to keep living in.

Because the same electromagnetic forces that would scramble the brains of most of the people on Earth would also have a devastating impact on every electrical circuit on the planet.

In short, the gamma cloud would cause all electrical devices—TVs, computers, lights, power plants—to snuff out. Power would be lost. Mankind would be plunged back to the Stone Age.

It was all pretty dire stuff.

Twenty-four hours of death and suffering plus catastrophic power loss, which was why all the crazies—religious and otherwise—had got so lathered up about it.

Of course, the media latched onto it.

The late-night comedians had a field day, especially with the date Finkelstein had pinpointed for the coming apocalypse: St Patrick's Day. It was an Irish conspiracy, Stephen Colbert joked, designed to allow Irishmen to drink more beer.

Every network morning show brought on an expert, astrophysicists from around the world who had aimed their telescopes at the sky. Many agreed with Finkelstein, but almost as many didn't.

Even those who concurred with him argued that the cloud might simply miss us. It happened with comets all the time.

But Dr Finkelstein stubbornly maintained that his calculations were correct.

And, of course, the seventy-two-year-old scientist came under intense personal scrutiny himself.

Every scholarly paper and article he had ever written was dissected. A plagiarism accusation from his undergraduate days fifty years earlier was dug up. A sexual harassment complaint—he'd been exonerated—was also found.

Rival astrophysicists accused him of being a sad old man looking for attention in the sunset of his career.

And then, maybe because of the intense media attention and speculation, Dr Harold Finkelstein did the most unexpected thing.

He died.

He'd just finished an interview with George Stephanopoulos on *Good Morning America* and was taking off his lapel-mike when he suddenly clutched at his chest, his face twisting in a rictus of pain, and collapsed to the studio floor. Dead of a heart attack.

The cameras didn't catch his fall but images of him lying on the floor went around the world within minutes.

And with the chief proponent of the end-of-the-world theory gone, and with enough naysayers stepping forward to take his place, the theory itself drifted out of the news cycle and became just another crackpot thing and—tinfoil-hat crazies and religious doomsday proponents aside—the world moved on.

At least until March 17 came within sight, and then people began talking about it again, just in case Finkelstein had been right.

My own feelings about the end of the world were mixed.

Was it true? Was it a crock? By the time the media was through with it, the average shmuck couldn't tell. When *The New York Times* suggests you weigh up all the possibilities and *The National Enquirer* tells you to buy an underground bunker and line the walls with twelve inches of lead, who are you going to believe?

Like many people, I had been leaning toward the it'll-all-be-okay side of the argument until I spoke to my dad about it—my real dad, that is.

Dr Dwight R. Rogers had formerly been the Dean of the School of Medicine at the University of

Tennessee—his area of expertise: nuclear medicine—and on my last visit to Memphis, he had told me he'd looked at Finkelstein's work and concluded that the man wasn't nuts. He was correct.

Dad told me that you could survive the plunge through the gamma cloud if you were inside a vacuum-walled chamber or if you had a naturally or artificially boosted immune system that protected the body's electrical conductivity, especially in the brain.

'Load up on calcium and phosphorus,' he said to me in his ultra-precise, earnest way. 'They are vital to nerve-impulse transmission in the body and the brain, which is what gamma radiation affects. But mainly calcium, not too much phosphorus. Whole milk, yoghurt, sardines—yes, yes, lots of sardines—and any kind of calcium supplements you can find at a pharmacy. Ease up on sodas, because they'll retard your calcium uptake. And maybe get your hands on some antipsychotic medication, something like Risperdal or Zyprexa, which also affect neurotransmitters. ADHD meds or antidepressants would work, too.'

He was starting to babble, his brain moving faster than his mouth, as it often did. I just nodded encouragingly.

Beside me, Red rolled his eyes.

He was a lovely man, my dad, a brilliant one, too, until the nervous breakdown.

I understood Red's point of view: it's hard to take advice about surviving the end of the world from a resident of a mental asylum in Memphis, Tennessee.

NEW YORK, BITCHES VS
NEW YORK BITCHES

After the horror of that initial school assembly, I tried to forge my way through life at Monmouth with maximum invisibility.

For a time that plan worked remarkably well and I have to say I learned a lot, both academically and about the laws of the New York high school jungle.

Red, of course, made friends instantly.

Within three days, he had found a group of buddies from the school's lacrosse team, which he himself joined a few weeks later. Among them was the captain of the team and Head Boy, the gorgeous Bo Bradford.

I myself got to know the warring factions of the females in the junior year of The Monmouth School.

The first thing I learned about them was that they were defined by who their parents were.

Every time I was introduced to someone, it was followed by, 'Her father is on the board at Goldman Sachs' or 'Her mother is the chair of the Met Charity Luncheon Board' or 'Her mom is on the advisory board of the New York Ballet'.

It created the pecking order: as a general rule, the richer the parents, the more powerful the student.

The curly-haired black girl from the assembly was

Jenny Johnson. Her father (see what I mean?) was Ken Johnson, a white billionaire hedge-fund owner who had made his fortune during the 2008 financial crisis by betting against the market. He was vice chairman of one of the most important boards in the city: the Board of Trustees of the Metropolitan Museum of Art.

His wife was black and had been a model back in the day, hence Jenny's beautiful cappuccino skin. This made Jenny technically the richest kid at Monmouth. *But*—and it was a big *but*—her family's money was considered new, which brought her down a few pegs.

I liked Jenny.

We shared a few classes and she had been very welcoming to me, and not in that nervous I-haven't-got-any-friends-of-my-own-so-I'll-befriend-the-new-girl kind of way.

We had also bonded in rather unique circumstances.

It happened one day in the girls' restroom. I'd been washing my hands when Jenny came out of a cubicle behind me and stepped up to the next basin.

As always, I was wearing my watch. I never took it off. That was one of the advantages of the G-Shock: as well as being virtually unbreakable, it was waterproof.

What I hadn't counted on was the new brand of make-up I'd bought the previous day. I wore it on my left wrist, *under* my watch's band. The foundation had run under the flow of water, creating an ugly nude-coloured splotch on my watchband, and I hadn't noticed.

Jenny had, but instead of saying anything, she just grabbed a paper towel, came over, and dabbed the band clean.

'Gotta be careful with make-up on the wrist,' she said. 'Need a good thick foundation that won't run.'

I noticed then that Jenny also wore a sizeable watch. She smiled kindly at me. 'I've been there, too.'

There.

I hadn't always been a timid high-schooler. In fact, back in Memphis, I'd been the exact opposite: popular, outgoing, confident, and vice president of my freshman class at a prestigious all-girls private school. I had happily campaigned—buttons, badges, balloons, and smiles—alongside my best friend, Savannah, a classic southern belle from a prominent family who was running for class president.

We won, our clique was the most envied in the school, and all was right with the world. I was someone.

And then I'd blown it.

I caught Savannah and some of our friends at the mall one day teasing a disabled girl named Tilly Green. Tilly had a funny walk caused by some rare bone disorder. She dragged her left foot.

'My God, Tilly,' Savannah said. 'You are such a *spastic.*'

I'd seen Savannah make hurtful comments before, but for some reason something about her taunts that day affected me. I mean, the kid was disabled. It was too much.

When Tilly started crying, I stepped in front of her and said, 'Hey, Savannah. That's enough. Leave the poor girl alone.'

Savannah glared at me. 'I didn't ask for your opinion,

Skye. I think you'd better go now. We'll meet you later.'

And that was my Rubicon: the moment I could have walked away and left Tilly at the mercy of Savannah and the other girls and kept my life.

But I stood my ground. 'No, Savannah. I mean it. That's enough.'

It was a mistake.

Savannah's wrath was as swift as it was savage.

From that day on she made my life a living hell, both at school and outside it. I was excluded from her table at lunch. I wasn't invited to parties. She even stripped me of my vice presidency on some technicality.

And I learned that when your friend is the pack leader, part of the deal is *remembering* she is the pack leader. I had questioned the natural order of things and had to suffer for it.

(My mother, amazingly, urged me to beg for Savannah's forgiveness. 'Savannah comes from a very influential family *socially* in these parts, darling. Say you're sorry. Swallow your pride. Don't throw your life away because of some crippled girl who doesn't matter anyway.')

I actually tried to talk with Savannah, but she wouldn't even see me.

The social ostracism, the former friends who passed me in the hall as though I was invisible, the complete loss of status: it took a toll.

I fell apart.

I started eating badly and hiding at home. Going to school became an ordeal. I was fourteen, overweight and overwrought, lonely and catastrophising about everything. And then, after some final casual taunt from my mother about my weight, I got *there* . . .

. . . and did it.

The thing was, I regretted it as soon as I made that first cut to my left wrist.

But the damage was done. My wrist had bled uncontrollably and I'd had to go to the emergency room with, of all people, my mom. Months of therapy followed as I desperately tried to prove my sanity. School became even worse. The looks I received from Savannah and her followers were beyond cruel.

I moved to New York eighteen months later with my mother and my brother, having learned a harsh lesson: never rock the social boat.

'You've been there, too?' I said to Jenny.

My cut had left a scar, hence the Casio watch and the make-up I wore underneath it (and my admiration for Monmouth's long-sleeved uniform).

In reply, Jenny Johnson showed me her own scar.

It was on her right wrist, hidden beneath one of the world's ugliest watches.

'A moment of despair,' she said.

'Nice watch,' I said. It was truly unfashionable, plain and black.

Jenny grinned, flipping her wrist like a fashion model. 'It was a gift from my dad. It's made by the same company that makes Swiss Army knives. It's not exactly the height of fashion, but it's got a kick-ass secret feature.'

Raising her eyebrows theatrically, she slid a small retractable blade from within the watch. It was maybe two inches long and it slotted perfectly into the body of the timepiece.

She explained: 'My dad is paranoid about kidnapping or, rather, somebody kidnapping me. He made me take a "kidnapping awareness" class. He also bought me this hideous watch: the hidden blade is for cutting a rope around your wrists or a gag in your mouth.' Jenny shrugged. 'It also hides my scar.'

I smiled. From that moment on, we had a quiet understanding.

Beyond that, one of the things I really liked about Jenny was that, despite all her father's wealth, she had a job.

'My dad's entirely self-made,' she said to me once as we ate lunch together on the school's rooftop basketball court. 'He didn't inherit a dime. He says a dollar earned is more valuable than a thousand dollars inherited, so even though he's got gazillions, he told me that if I wanted to buy something, I'd have to get a job and earn the money to get it.'

Jenny worked weekends as a waitress for a company that provided additional silver-service waitstaff for high-end private events: gallery openings, charity dinners, that sort of thing. It was good money, Jenny said, as much as fifty bucks an hour, because she would often be called in at late notice, when other waitstaff companies were caught short of personnel.

Jenny also had a brash confidence that I admired, like the time she'd traded barbs with the mean girls at the assembly.

Ah, yes, the mean girls.

Every school's got them, especially—I discovered— private schools with female *and* male students. Great white sharks are not as territorial as rich white girls are about their boys.

The two girls who had hurled insults at Jenny at the assembly were as follows:

One, Hattie Brewster—chunky, dark-haired, rich and bullish. Her mother was a Carnegie. She'd been the one who had threatened to punch Jenny in the uterus.

And two, Verity Keeley—skinny, auburn hair with highlights, huge almond eyes but a slightly horse-ish nose. Her father co-owned an oil company that went back to the days of John D. Rockefeller.

By themselves, Hattie and Verity were your standard teen bitches who just happened to live in upscale New York City. While pretty, Verity wasn't pretty *enough* to be an alpha and Hattie—bigger, broader, with more masculine features—was basically a female thug. Both were beta-types, followers.

And all followers need someone to follow.

That was Misty Collins.

She was something else entirely.

At sixteen, she was the younger sister of the Head Girl, Chastity, and if girls coalesce around queen bees, then she was their empress.

Misty Collins ruled the junior year at Monmouth.

Her father was Conrad Collins, a direct descendant of a *Mayflower* pilgrim and one of the largest property owners in New York. Her mother Starley was a prominent socialite who came from another *Mayflower* family. The Collins pedigree was as gilded as it got in America, their money old and untarnished by the stain of modern commerce.

'American royalty,' I once heard another girl say in a hushed whisper as Misty sauntered by, trailed by Hattie and Verity.

She had similar features to her older sister—honey-coloured blonde hair, blue eyes—but she wasn't as classically beautiful as Chastity. For one thing, she was shorter, but mainly it was her eyes. Chastity Collins had bright and wide blue eyes while Misty's eyes were anything but bright.

She had heavy eyelids and a lazy right eye that seemed to always be looking upward. It forced her to tilt her head forward to look at you and gave her a kind of permanent dull-eyed scowl.

This, I learned, was the source of Jenny Johnson's barb about Misty's RBF.

An RBF—I Googled it—was a Resting Bitch Face, and I had to admit, Misty had one.

But it didn't affect her standing in New York society. While the headmistress Ms Blackman might have chosen not to attend the Met Gala, Misty had gone to it . . . *as a sixteen-year-old.* That had been back in May—before I had arrived in New York—but she and her clique were still talking about it in September.

'Rihanna's outfit was *unbelievably* dope,' Misty said one day as we were sitting in English class waiting for Mrs Hoynes to arrive. 'But nothing beats seeing Ryan Reynolds in the flesh. I mean, like, whoa.'

Or on another occasion, in the junior common room: 'You know none of those models and actresses actually pay to go to the Met Gala? It's $17,000 per ticket. Some of them can't even afford the plane fare. The sponsors pay for them, sometimes on Anna's orders.'

Anna was Anna Wintour, the famous editor of *Vogue*, who sat on a charity board with Mrs Collins and often dined at their home.

The home of the Collinses.

Allow me to digress for a moment, because I should mention this, chiefly because it was directly related to how I came to enter Misty's orbit and that of the secret runners.

You see, like me, Misty lived in the San Remo building.

The San Remo is 28 storeys tall, but at the 18th floor its lower podium divides into two towers, the north and the south. Each tower is capped by a weird multi-stepped pagan-like temple like the one in that movie, *Ghostbusters*. I have to admit they're pretty cool—but, so far as I've seen, there are no sexy female gods dressed in bubble wrap up there; you can, however, host a kick-ass outdoor party with awesome park views on them.

My family lived on the 20th floor of the north tower—average price: $19 million—while Misty lived on the 21st floor of the south tower where the prices were slightly higher since the apartments there were larger and received more sun.

(Misty's friend, Hattie Brewster, also lived in the building—hence their long friendship—but in the lower 'podium' section: a grand address by anyone else's reckoning but a step down in the building's pecking order: peck, peck, peck.)

In short, the San Remo is one of the most sought-after addresses in New York. It boasts residents like Steven Spielberg and Donna Karan, and the popular but fiery right-wing radio host Manny Wannemaker, whom my mother loved. Manny waltzed around the atrium, his obese frame draped in his signature black overcoat with purple sleeves, pontificating to anyone who stopped to listen.

More recently, to my mother's disgust, a few Saudi princes had bought apartments high up in the towers. They hadn't even bothered to negotiate.

('Saudis,' she said derisively. 'No class, no culture, just *vulgar*. They've never actually built anything, you know. If they didn't have oil in the ground, they'd all be beggars on the street.')

It was interesting that my mother would say this, given that it was not she who had worked to acquire the money to buy our apartment in the Remo (as the cool kids called it). It was my stepfather, Todd Allen, Wall Street titan and New York identity. My mother had never worked a day in her life, unless you counted the hours she spent working out and glamming herself up in the mirror every day, which I think she did count.

One final thing.

While Red and I walked to school, Misty didn't. Every day at the tick of eight o'clock, she swept out of the south lobby—trailed by her younger brother and often accompanied by Hattie—and dived into the back of a waiting black Escalade to be whisked off to school eight hundred yards away on the other side of the park.

American royalty.

MISTY

It was in the juniors' common room that Misty reigned.

While the seniors had a common room up on the top floor of the school, the juniors had to make do with one in the basement. With a small kitchen, an espresso machine and our own personal server named Ramona, it would have been any high school girl's seventh heaven if it weren't for the general atmosphere of fear, judgement and contempt.

Misty and her lieutenants, Hattie and Verity, had their own booth by the door—everyone learned very quickly that you didn't sit in it, even if they weren't there—and it was from here that they issued their judge-ments: on the hairstyles, make-up, skin-care regimes, or just general appearance of all the girls who entered. (Boys were usually greeted with hair-twirling coos of 'Hi, Hunter . . .' or 'Hey, Palmer . . .')

I was not exempt from their evaluations, especially after my tumble at the assembly.

'Morning, Memphis,' Hattie said one day as I arrived during a free period. 'Managing to keep it upright today?'

'That was *so* embarrassing,' Verity said in a low voice that I could hear clearly.

Misty had been sitting with them, reading something on her laptop (she had stuck a Louis Vuitton sticker over the Apple logo). She looked up at the comment.

'Come on, ladies, give the girl a break. It was her first day,' she said, smiling at me. 'Besides, she's my neighbour. Lives on the other side of the Remo.'

She nodded to me and I nodded back in thanks and kept walking. I wasn't quite sure what to make of this act of social rescue. Sure, it was nice, but somehow it *wasn't*. It felt like there was something behind it: having Hattie and Verity say something nasty allowed Misty to step in and look all sweet and friendly. Of course, maybe I was overthinking all this. Maybe she was just hedging her bets until she sized me up and figured me out.

This is how it usually went: a girl would walk in with, say, a new Birkin bag.

'That's cool,' Misty would comment.

Or a giant zit.

'Did you see her *face*? How embarrassing,' Hattie would whisper.

Or the time one girl came in with a huge swollen jaw after a trip to the dentist.

'Oh, God, like, mortification,' Verity said.

Or if one dared to show enthusiasm for something, especially something geeky, quirky or retro. Like the day Jenny said to one of her friends that she'd bought tickets to an ABBA tribute band concert.

'Lame,' Verity said.

After a time, I began to see the pattern. Any act or thing could be judged with one of three adjectives: *cool*, *lame* or *embarrassing*. (That said, I never saw Misty use the word *lame*. She was liberal with *cool* and selective with *embarrassing*. Again, this confused me.

If she was the good cop, she was still allowing this to happen. Except on rare occasions—like mine—she didn't *stop* the other two from saying the horrible things they said.)

Having said that, as I watched these one-word judgements occur over and over during those first few months, I started to see it less as mean-girl cruelty and more as a sign of a lack of vocabulary. Misty was smart, but Hattie and Verity—who were not that attentive in class to begin with—literally didn't have any other words to describe things.

When they talked about their own lives, it ranged from the superficial to the downright nasty.

One day, Verity turned sideways as she looked in her handheld mirror, assessing her nose. 'Oh, I hate my nose. My mom has said I can get surgery on it next summer. Yay!'

Hattie complained constantly about her household staff. 'They are *such* lazy fucking Mexicans. Consuela never cleans my bathroom properly; the toilet is always filthy. My mom hates her, too—gives her hell, makes her start all over again. But then, last week, Consuela found my stash of weed in my dresser and told my dad. He grounded me for the whole weekend. Fucking cow.'

Often they were joined in their booth by a male student named Griffin O'Dea.

The son of a well-known theatre producer, Griff had the build of a linebacker: six feet tall, stocky but not fat, strong but not muscly. He had a mop of frizzy orange hair that tested the boundaries of Monmouth's male grooming policy.

He was gregarious and flamboyant, the life of the

party, or maybe he just had ADHD. Whether he was in the gym bench-pressing with the jocks or in the common room with Misty and her entourage, he was always going a thousand miles an hour. He'd been friends with Misty since elementary school. Word was, he had been to rehab twice, but for what exactly I didn't know.

In the common room, Griff happily joined in the judging and name-calling with Misty and her gang.

His pronouncements on the boys entering the common room included: 'Hey Cameron, how's life in the closet, dude?' 'Morning, Thatcher, love those new glasses. No, really, I do.' Or one whispered recommendation: 'Girls, make a mental note of Roland. I saw him in the locker room yesterday: he is hung. It's always the quiet ones.' Then he'd laugh uproariously.

The cruellest thing I ever saw Misty's friends do in the common room involved a shy chubby girl named Winnie Simms.

It was lunchtime on a rainy day and the common room was full when Winifred Simms entered, only to have Verity guffaw, 'Winnie! Christ! I saw you naked in gym class yesterday. For the love of God, please wax your pussy. You need a Weed Whacker down there it's so bushy! *Damn*, you traumatised me. I cannot unsee what I saw.'

Winnie's face went beetroot red and my heart went out to her. She was a quiet and studious girl. I also happened to know she was an only child who lived with her father. Older sisters and shallow moms help a girl in this department. Winnie had probably never even contemplated this kind of personal grooming. She scurried out of the room.

Anger surged through me and for a fleeting moment, I thought of standing up and saying something, but then I had a flashing memory of my incident back in Memphis.

And I bit my tongue.

I can't say I was proud of myself, but I'd been burned before. Badly.

A few minutes later I saw Misty approach Winnie in the corridor and place a comforting arm around her shoulder—again, the others tee up the meanness and she follows through after with the niceness—and I convinced myself that it was all okay.

In the end, I guess you'd say that my first couple of months at Monmouth were pretty standard for a new kid: stay under the radar, try not to anger the mean girls or stray too close to the orbits of the weirdos, and make a few tentative connections, like I did with Jenny Johnson.

Jenny and I had several classes together: math, physics and English lit. If the world didn't end, Jenny wanted to be a computer programmer and app designer, while I harboured desires of becoming an engineer, so we both worked hard on math and physics, often getting together to work on homework problems.

I told her about the Winnie incident.

'That's Misty's genius,' Jenny said. 'She never says a bad word about anyone. Her two bitches do it. Then she sidles in after and acts all nicey-nicey. It's brilliant passive-aggressive shit. But don't be fooled, she can drop the axe with the best of them. She was friends for a while with that sophomore who went missing a couple of years ago, the first one, the smart one, Trina Miller.

'But then just after Christmas, around the time Trina started tutoring Bo Bradford, Misty barred her completely, just stopped talking to her, froze her out. Trina became *persona non grata* around here. A few months later, she was gone. Disappeared. I think she just couldn't take it anymore.'

'Is that right? Frozen out?' I knew all about that.

Jenny said, 'I heard that the FBI investigator even questioned Misty about Trina's disappearance but nothing came of it.'

'Are Misty and Bo Bradford a thing?' I asked.

'She seems to think so, but I'm not sure he does.'

I looked at Jenny. 'You really don't like them, do you?'

'I don't like their attitudes,' she said. 'This school is already white enough. But those girls, they're white on the outside *and* the inside, their blank minds completely untouched by the real world. They think that just because they are rich they're *better* than everybody else.

'Yet their parents' wealth has actually hurt them. It has deprived them of any kind of ambition or direction. Any *hunger*. They're modern dilettantes, like those party-girl heiresses you see on Snapchat going out to nightclubs every weekend.

'I don't know what your stepdad's like, but my dad's old-school. He's got more money than God, yet he doesn't even give me an allowance. That's why I got a job. "I have to let the world rough you up a little," he told me.'

For the record, my stepdad, Todd, gave my mother a six-figure monthly allowance and out of that she gave Red and me a couple of hundred bucks in cash to cover standard teenage incidentals (back in Memphis, I'd topped it up with the odd babysitting gig). I seriously doubted Todd even knew how much she gave us. He was a strange guy, Todd, smart for sure, but quiet, detached. There was nothing mean about him, don't get me wrong, but it was like he was surprised whenever he saw Red and me in his home. We were simply the baggage that came with our hot mom.

Jenny went on. 'But those girls, their dads give them black Amex cards and limo rides to school, so all they do is gossip and shop, gossip and shop. And if you asked them what they're going to do with their lives, they'll tell you: gossip and shop. Find out for yourself. Next time you're chatting with them, ask them what they plan to do when they finish school. See what they say.'

'All right,' I said. 'I will.'

BOYS AND BEEMERS

As November came around and the days turned colder, I was feeling pretty good about myself and Monmouth. The place was starting to feel a little less alien.

And then came the day when Ms Vandermeer, the school counsellor, politely interrupted my physics class and asked to see me in her office.

Feeling every eye in the class zero in on me, I rose from my desk and hurried out after her.

'So, Skye,' she said when we had both sat down in her office. 'How are you settling in?'

Ms Vandermeer was an older woman with a soothing voice and no discernible interest in fashion whatsoever except for the pair of bright red reading glasses that she wore perched on the end of her nose and which she peered over to look at you.

I gazed around her office. There was a poster on the wall behind her desk: *COOL KIDS DON'T SMOKE.* It looked like it came from 1992; the kids in it looked about forty and they did not look in any way cool.

'Okay, I guess.' I shrugged.

Ms Vandermeer assessed me over her red reading glasses, as if searching for signs of discomfort or distress.

She held up a manila file with my name on it. 'Skye, as school counsellor, I've been privy to your medical history, so I know about the . . . incident . . . when you tried to harm yourself.'

So that was it.

I rolled my eyes. 'Ms Vandermeer, I swear, I'm *fine* now. School is fine. Life is fine. I do not feel like hurting myself. I haven't since that day.'

I could hear the testiness in my voice and I took a breath, trying to calm down.

Fuck. A suicide attempt was like a scarlet letter on your record and it followed you everywhere.

Ms Vandermeer flicked through the file. 'These notes from your old school in Memphis mention that the . . . self-harm . . . stemmed from a falling-out you had with the class president there. How are you getting on socially here?'

'Good,' I said tightly. 'I mean, so far so good.'

'Well.' She smiled kindly. 'I'm glad things are going okay. If you ever feel down or just need someone to talk to, my door is always open.'

'Thanks,' I said through gritted teeth, and I got out of there at rocket speed.

Truth be told, I was doing well in my classes: in math and physics, of course, but also, to my surprise, in English.

I liked our English teacher, Mrs Hoynes. She was young, bespectacled and newly married to a cute male teacher at a nearby school. Fresh out of Columbia, she was energetic, enthusiastic and idealistic. She spoke a lot about 'taking on the world' and 'being our best selves'.

One day, as she was handing back some creative-writing stories we had done, she asked me and Dane Summerhays to stay behind.

So when the class ended, as the other students dispersed, I waited with Dane. Handsome and carefree, with the wavy blond hair of a California surfer, Dane Summerhays looked like he'd stepped out of an Abercrombie & Fitch ad. I imagined that, outside of school, he probably wore boat shoes a lot.

Even in the short time I'd known him—which included his snide remark about Ms Blackman at the opening assembly—I'd noticed that Dane had a habit of checking himself out in mirrors or windows; always a quick admiring glance. He was on the lacrosse team with Red and Bo. Girls swooned over him. High school was heaven for guys like Dane Summerhays.

When all the other students had gone, Mrs Hoynes said, 'Skye, Dane. I thought your stories were simply marvellous work. Dane, I felt your piece about a day at the polo showed real insight.'

'Thank you, ma'am,' Dane said, grinning.

'And Skye,' she said, 'a ghost story. I thought it was fabulous; genuinely frightening. Where did you learn to write like that? Did you do a course at your school back in Tennessee?'

I shrugged. I'd never done any kind of writing course. 'I just enjoy reading novels, I guess.'

She smiled knowingly. 'I see. Edgar Allan Poe? Or did I detect some Mary Shelley in there?'

'Er, Stephen King, ma'am. I've kinda read all his books. He's my favourite author.'

I didn't say that he was my *absolute favourite* author.

I had all his books on my shelf, arranged in order of publication.

'Oh,' Mrs Hoynes said. 'Well, with your permission, I'd like to post both of your stories on the school's internal website and include them in the yearbook. What do you say?'

Dane nodded casually. 'Sure. Why not? Cool.'

Mrs Hoynes turned to me. 'How about you, Skye?'

I stood there frozen, unable to speak.

The school website. And the yearbook. It terrified me beyond words to even contemplate having my story published openly. What if people hated it? What if they thought it was just the silly, juvenile work of a teenage girl?

I looked at Dane. I envied his calm acceptance of Mrs Hoynes's invitation. How did boys do this? And so easily? Write something, accept praise for it and just happily put it out there for all the world to see? Was it a boy/girl thing? Boys didn't seem to fear failure or any kind of humiliation or embarrassment.

Yet that was all I could think of.

'Skye?' Mrs Hoynes said. 'Earth to Skye. What do you say?'

I shook my head quickly. 'No, no, I don't think so. I don't think I could do that.'

I could hear myself as I said it and I died a little on the inside. I sounded like my father.

'Okay,' Mrs Hoynes said, disappointed. 'I guess I thought—well, no problem.'

I left the classroom, hating myself.

★ ★ ★

There was one other incident with Mrs Hoynes that warrants mentioning, if only because it saved me from following up on Jenny's challenge.

It was the final period of the day on a Friday in mid-November and nobody wanted to be there.

Mrs Hoynes was discussing *Pride and Prejudice* (which I liked) but Hattie, Verity and Misty, huddled at the back of the classroom, were talking. Sitting a few desks in front of them, I could hear what they were talking about: fashion and boys.

It was clearly getting on Mrs Hoynes's nerves. Her eyes kept darting toward them until finally she snapped and said, 'Miss Brewster, Miss Keeley, Miss Collins. Have you no interest at all in what we are studying today?'

'Not really,' Verity retorted tartly. 'It's just a stupid book.'

Mrs Hoynes froze.

The rest of the class fell silent. A line had been crossed.

Mrs Hoynes said, 'You don't think you might learn anything that will help you in later life?'

Verity snorted. 'I'm absolutely certain of that, ma'am.'

'Excuse me?'

'Ma'am, I plan to marry a young man with name-value and a whopping great trust fund, punch out a couple of munchkins for him, hire a fulltime nanny, drive a big BMW SUV and lunch in the city every day. Reading *books* doesn't feature in that plan at all.'

Hattie high-fived Verity. 'And there you go.'

Mrs Hoynes—young, energetic and hopeful—just stood at the head of the class and her mouth fell open.

★ ★ ★

As the days got colder, Central Park became greyer.

The trees became more skeletal, the paths more muddy, and our morning walk across it became more of a stoic trudge.

Every day, Misty would be met by her chauffeur-driven Escalade. If we emerged from the lobby around the same time, I would subtly wave or nod to her.

I also saw her brother.

His name was Oscar but everybody called him Oz. He was fifteen, a sophomore at Monmouth and even though he was a year younger than Misty, he stood a head taller.

He was also kinda weird.

Oz had ruddy red cheeks and a buzz cut, and if he was outdoors, whatever the weather, he always wore a grey beanie. A little overweight, he stood with a hunched-over stance, as if trying to minimise his height. Whenever I saw him, he was perpetually bent over his cell phone. I thought he was guaranteed to have neck problems later in life.

On the rare occasions when he looked up from his precious phone, I noted that he had the same droopy eyes as Misty. One morning, as we passed on the sidewalk, he glanced up and I smiled at him and said, 'Hey, Oz,' but he just ducked his head and didn't utter a word.

I mentioned it to Jenny.

'Misty's a bitch, but Oz is just plain odd,' she said. 'I heard he's got ADHD so bad that he's on the highest possible dose of Ritalin. Word is, when he was thirteen, his mom found a bunch of dirty searches on his smartphone, so she sent him off to military camp for the summer. Misty told everyone about it. Ah, the three Collins kids, Chastity, Misty and Oz: loose, bad and mad.'

I had one other interesting encounter with Oz Collins.

It was just after the school's annual talent show. You know the kind of event, every school has one: students volunteer to perform in front of the entire student body and their parents. It's either a moment of wonder when you discover that one of your classmates has an up-till-then unknown God-given talent . . . or some poor soul gets humiliated when they discover they're not as talented as they thought they were.

The Monmouth School's annual talent show followed that pattern: one cute freshman girl named Jeanne Black had a voice like Adele; a couple of juniors could rap pretty well; two sophomore pranksters got halfway through a striptease before they were yanked off the stage, and Oz Collins performed a magic act.

The thing was, it was great.

Dressed in a full Mandrake the Magician outfit (black-and-red satin cape, top hat), young Oz performed his act flawlessly: a couple of linking rings tricks, one disappearing rabbit, and then some exceptional card tricks including a final one that involved getting Ms Blackman to sign a card which he then magically reproduced. (It was also the first time I actually heard him speak and I noticed he had a slight lisp.)

I thought his act was excellent.

The problem was, it wasn't edgy enough to satisfy an auditorium of jaded teenagers. It was too PG-13.

The tepid applause that followed was cruel.

Someone called out, 'Boring!'

The next morning, as I was walking down a corridor, I saw a couple of big sophomore boys shove Oz against his locker. 'Hey, Collins. Loved your Dracula costume. Do you wear it to Homos Anonymous meetings?'

His back to his locker, Oz bowed his head and averted his eyes. But he was trapped.

The two callow youths moved in for the kill when—

'I thought his outfit looked hot,' I said loudly.

The two bullies stopped and turned. Oz snapped up in shock.

'And it was Mandrake, not Dracula.' I looked the two thugs up and down. 'Let me give you a tip, boys: girls like a man who's good with his hands and last night this guy showed that he's got the touch. Maybe instead of dissing him you should be asking him for pointers.'

I nodded at Oz. 'Loved the act.' And then I did my best twirl-and-depart.

Even as I did all this, I was surprised at myself. Why was I doing it? And now? I hadn't stepped in to help Winnie and yet here I was intervening on behalf of Oz. But then, I thought, maybe it was *because* I hadn't helped Winnie. I think a quiet fury at the fact that I had let this shit go before had been building up inside me.

As I strode away, out of the corner of my eye, I saw the two bullies skulk off and I have to say I felt pretty good about myself.

Somewhere around that time, pre-season training for lacrosse began. At first, it made me sad because it meant seeing less of Red, but it turned out to have an entirely unexpected and very pleasant consequence.

The boys' team trained after school at an indoor facility on the west side and sometimes, invited by Red, a group of them would come back to our apartment after training, sweaty and parched, to hang out.

Now, let me get this out of the way up front: lacrosse uniforms, with their shoulder pads and helmets, are hot.

I always made sure I was home on training days because when Bo Bradford and Dane Summerhays came in, it was a sight to behold.

Of course, I ensured I appeared entirely absorbed in something else when they arrived: homework, study, watching TV or flicking through a magazine. (I think Red knew what I was doing but if he did, he never let on. What a great brother.)

But I always sneaked a peek at them or 'accidentally' arrived at the fruit bowl in the kitchen at the same time Bo did, causing a brief but always thrilling conversation. My greatest artifice was creating some reason to enter Red's bedroom while they were all hanging there (delivering his clean laundry to him was my all-time best excuse; I'd *never* done that before).

Red's room, I should add, was the embodiment of my brother: a carefree mix of weird stuff and pop culture arcana that he somehow made cool.

It started with his bedroom door. On it hung a thin wooden shield that supposedly came from some tribe of headhunters in Borneo. Carved into its front side was the snarling face of a supernatural demon. It looked like a bad souvenir from Waikiki Beach to me.

It got better inside his room. It was a man-boy's

nirvana, from the life-size R2-D2 droid from *Star Wars* that was actually a refrigerator, and the cherry-red couch made out of the winged tail of a 1950s Cadillac (the brakelights worked, bathing the room in a soft red glow), to his pride and joy: a bronze-coloured 'Graceland' baseball emblazoned with a picture of Elvis.

That baseball was, Red said, the cheesiest thing in the world, which was why he loved it so much. (There might have been another reason: my dad had bought it for him during a visit to Graceland when we were six; Red had cherished it ever since.)

Whenever they hung out there, the guys variously sat on the car-couch or on the bed while Red relaxed in front of the window in the large Balinese rope hammock he'd brought back from a tropical vacation. It was suspended from hooks in the ceiling.

It was on one of those occasions—as I approached Red's room from the hallway with some fantastic new excuse—that I heard them talking and I stopped to listen just outside the open door.

Bo said, 'So, Red. How's it going with Verity Keeley?'

Verity Keeley? I thought.

Red said, 'She's cool. Got a little overly friendly the other night at Dane's.'

Dane had held a party the previous weekend while his parents had been away at St Barts. Red had been invited. I hadn't.

'She's got a smoking hot body, dude,' Dane said. 'Chick works *out*. And Tony says she's great for a little mmm-hmm in a dark corner of a party, if you know what I mean.'

And she's also a bitch, I thought. Once again, didn't guys see these things? Didn't Red?

I was also thinking about Verity's stated goal in that English class of finding a young man with a good name and money. I wondered if my brother fit that bill. Given our stepfather's sizeable name-value and wealth, he probably did.

Having said all that, if I was to be brutally honest, I was probably more hurt than concerned: hurt that Red hadn't told me about any of this.

Even though we still walked to and from school together most days, I hadn't known he'd had *any* inter-actions—amorous or otherwise—with Verity Keeley. I'd always felt we were close, and that Red would share something like this with me. It made me sad that perhaps we were growing apart.

Red said, 'A gentleman never tells, guys.'

Over the following month, Red and Verity became official and Red started hanging out with her and the cool kids on the East Side after school, leaving me to walk home alone. (It's funny, around this time, I noticed that he'd started smoking pot; I could smell it on his clothes and detected it in his stare some nights when he came home. He had even gone out and bought a new Zippo lighter to enhance the experience. Not that I'm judging or anything.)

It was strange for me to see Red rolling with the in-crowd, especially having once been there myself. I found myself wondering if this was my future: destined to be separate, an outsider looking in.

But ultimately I was happy for him, in my bitter and abandoned kind of way.

Beloved, cool and enlightened as he was, I had to accept that Red was still a sixteen-year-old human male—and thus beholden to all the hormones, desires and stupid decision-making (like smoking weed) that went with that. So I wished him all the female attention he could get, even if it came from Verity Keeley, and even if it meant that I had to walk home by myself across Central Park in the chill of a New York winter.

I suppose I just missed my brother.

But then as November became December, the girls in the common room and the boys at their after-training hang-outs began talking about one topic above all else.

The Season.

THE SEASON

The debutante ball season.

Growing up in Memphis, I had been dimly aware of debutante balls. They were high-end formal events in which young girls between the ages of sixteen and twenty-one were 'presented' to polite society.

In the old days, it had been about rich families putting their daughters on display for potential suitors, hence the virginal white bridal dresses and the elbow-length white silk gloves. But in the gauche, anyone-can-get-rich world of the 1980s and 90s, such balls fell out of fashion.

And then in the 21st century, something happened to change all that.

Social media.

And in this Instagram-fuelled era of conspicuous consumption—or, more importantly, conspicuous displays *of status*—debutante balls came roaring back.

They became the hottest tickets in town.

They became so exclusive that the modern ball was less about presenting bright young women to polite society than it was about *who* got an invitation and which designer they got to make their bespoke dress.

It carried so much weight in the social milieu of The Monmouth School, that Chastity Collins had mentioned it in her opening-day speech, when she had highlighted the fact that Misty would be debuting at not one but two balls at only sixteen.

The unspoken marvel of Misty's feat was that few girls debuted at such a young age, let alone at two separate balls. That only happened if the girl in question came from a seriously powerful family.

(Apparently, the linguistic anomaly of *debuting twice* was lost on just about everyone in New York society. Rather than an oxymoron, it was considered an achievement.)

And lest you shed a tear for those poor modern maidens who did not garner an invitation to any ball, fear not. Most of the balls had pre-parties, rehearsal dinners, afterparties and *after*-afterparties that friends, acquaintances and boyfriends could happily attend (a girl's escort at a ball—her *cavalier*—was not necessarily her boyfriend). Arguably, with all the booze, cocaine and Molly available at them, these additional parties were considered far more fun than the parent-chaperoned balls themselves.

In any case, the gossip about the Season began around mid-November.

It started when Bo Bradford flew off to Paris to escort the daughter of a prominent Viennese family with Habsburg roots to Le Bal des Débutantes.

'Le Bal is cool but it used to be better,' Misty said in the common room, surrounded by Hattie, Verity, Dane and Red. I sat a short distance away, ostensibly studying but in truth listening.

'It used to be discreet royal families like the Ludovisi, the Bourbon-Parmas and the Auersperg-Breunners.

And the cavaliers were gorgeous young counts and marquises. But somewhere along the way, the organisers started allowing rich Arabs and Chinese to essentially *buy* tickets for their daughters. Now any old nouveau bourgeois who can afford to buy his little girl a Dior haute couture dress can get in. And once you let *them* in, it defeats the purpose of the ball altogether.'

'And what is that purpose?' Jenny asked from nearby. It appeared that she, too, was listening.

Misty smiled that wan, indulgent smile of hers.

'To establish who is polite society and who is not,' she said. 'To establish, publicly and clearly, the social strata of a given country or region.'

Jenny cocked her head in disbelief. 'Seriously? You honestly think that those people who attend deb balls are being announced as the leaders of society?'

'You wouldn't understand,' Misty said. 'Because you'll never go to one.'

The French ball had started the chatter but it heated up significantly when the Season officially commenced at home with the National Debutante Cotillion and Thanksgiving Ball in Washington, D.C.

A senior from Monmouth—Grace Carmody—debuted at that one alongside the niece of the Vice President.

But the talk reached fever pitch when Misty started dress-shopping for her first coming-out ball, the International Debutante Ball to be held at the Waldorf Astoria Hotel in late December.

Having spent the better part of October sitting with her girlfriends in the common room flipping through bridal magazines looking for a gown (the virgin-white debutante dress is basically the same as a bridal gown, so they are created by the same designers), in early November she began meeting with designers.

She had one stipulation. Misty's dress, I heard her tell her friends, had to complement her necklace.

Her necklace.

Because of Monmouth's strict no-jewellery policy, I didn't see Misty's necklace until I began running into her randomly around the San Remo on weekends.

It was actually one of two. Misty and her mother wore identical necklaces: a gold neckchain from which hung a gorgeous figure-eight-shaped pendant with a striking amber-coloured gem embedded in the middle of it.

It was a beautiful necklace by any standard and clearly old, too.

I complimented Misty on it one Sunday.

She fingered it delicately. 'Why, thank you. It's a family heirloom and very precious to me.'

With this condition in mind, Misty met with Zac Posen, Sarah Burton and Stella McCartney (she flew to London on a weekend to meet the last two). She settled on Sarah Burton: 'She did Kate Middleton's—sorry, Princess Catherine's—dress for her wedding to Prince William.'

Misty's made-to-measure one-of-a-kind dress— featuring English lace, an antique white silk-gazar skirt, and subtle gold thread to match the necklace—would cost $86,000 plus tax.

I saw a sketch of it. It was stunning. It was the most beautiful dress I'd ever seen. Any bride would've died to wear it on her wedding day and every other day of her life.

Misty would wear it once.

She was already looking for another dress to wear at her second debut at the East Side Cotillion in early March because, she said, 'It'd be *so* embarrassing to wear the same dress to two deb balls.'

After-school fittings were arranged. Misty and her friends would hurry out the school gates, slide into her black Escalade and be whisked away.

And Misty hit the gym. Hard. On the night of the ball, she would be sewn into her dress, so she had to maintain both her weight and her body shape. Well, okay, she didn't actually go to a gym. She hired a personal trainer to bust her chops on her parents' home treadmill and in their weights room. In any case, I could see she was getting visibly slimmer.

But even when slim, she still looked severe. Skinniness couldn't alter that dead-eyed stare.

I watched it all with a kind of detached fascination.

This was a new world, one that I was privileged to observe from close range yet never be a part of. And I was happy with that.

But then suddenly that world reached out and pulled me into its vortex in a most unexpected way.

Someone invited my brother to the International Debutante Ball.

RED

The process by which eligible young ladies got selected to attend a major debutante ball was old-fashioned, intricate and largely based on heritage and connections.

The process of selecting the dashing young *men* who would escort those young ladies to such a ball was different.

It was traditional that each debutante would be escorted by two cavaliers: one cadet from a military academy and one civilian lad from a suitable family (if a girl had one, this was often her boyfriend).

For the girls who did not know any local boys, an event called the Bachelor's Brunch was held at a local restaurant. And in a world where it's usually the guy who asks the girl out, it was a rare occasion where the girls got to assess the market and have their pick.

In any case, Red and his lacrosse buddies had gone to the Bachelor's Brunch on a lark. Given their inbuilt social cachet, Monmouth boys were always welcome at it, but Red and the guys had really just attended to watch from the edges. But then Red—cool, easygoing Red—had somehow got talking with a young Texan debutante from San Antonio and before you knew it, she'd asked him to be her civilian escort at the ball.

It caused a happy sensation at Monmouth and

suddenly Red was—to use one of my dad's favourite phrases—cooler than the other side of the pillow.

As a result, he started to get invited to all the pre-parties in the two weeks before the ball.

They were high-end affairs to which only the popular kids were invited. Of course, there was booze, weed and Mol at all of them. They would go deep into the night and Red would often return home to our apartment around 3:00 a.m.

It was soon after the pre-parties began that I started to notice something on the inner forearms of the girls who went to them, girls like Misty, Hattie and Verity.

Discreet vertical strokes, written in black permanent marker just near the wrist.

Misty had seven of the strokes, Hattie four, and Verity three.

Some of the boys who were frequenting the pre-party circuit also exhibited similar vertical markings. Bo had four and Dane Summerhays three.

And then, in the early hours of the morning after the International Debutante Ball, my brother returned home, energised and adrenalised.

He rushed into my room and shook me awake, his white bowtie dangling from his collar, sweat in his hair and on his forehead. I worried that he'd taken some amphetamine-type drug that had sent him off on a hyperactive bender.

'Honest, Blue, I swear, I haven't taken anything,' he said breathlessly. 'No. No. I've done something way better, way cooler than any drug. I'll tell you but you've got to swear—*swear*—that you'll never tell a soul about it. Not Mom, not Dad, not Todd and especially not

Misty or any of the girls at school. They were there and they'd kill me if they knew I'd told you, but *holy fucking shit*, I've got to tell someone.'

I'd never seen him like this. Red was never fazed by anything and here he was babbling like an idiot.

And then I saw his left wrist.

There was a single vertical stroke on it.

'What have you done?' I asked him slowly.

PART II

THE SECRET RUNNERS
OF NEW YORK

To keep your secret is wisdom;
But to expect others to keep it is folly.

SAMUEL JOHNSON

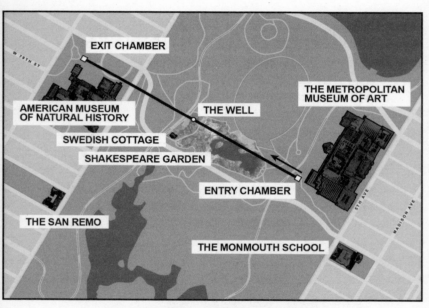

THE TUNNEL UNDER THE PARK

RED'S RUN

Red began by telling me about the ball.

It was a glittering affair. The Waldorf Astoria had been beautifully set up for the event and no expense had been spared.

There were two senators there, three ambassadors, the Lieutenant Governor of New York, plus at least four chairmen of Fortune 500 companies. Wives floated around in diamonds, air-kissing each other, while the debutantes shone in their white designer gowns.

For the parents, the highlight was the formal part of the evening in which the debutantes were presented one by one (the girls viewed this portion of the evening as an ordeal to be survived without tripping over and, as Misty put it, 'being totally humiliated for life'.)

For the girls the real fun would be at the afterparties.

'Geez, Blue,' Red said. 'We went from the Waldorf to the Van Bridens' place, to the Colsarts', and finally to a little basement apartment on the East Side up near the school.

'I don't even know who owned that little place, but there certainly weren't any parents around and it was *pumping*: some girls still in their debutante gowns, others in their after-gowns, cadets in military uniforms and guys like me still in their penguin suits. Hattie and

Verity showed up, plus Griff O'Dea, Dane and some buddies of Bo's.

'It was a dope party. Everyone was drinking, smoking, laughing, having a good time. Beer, shooters, plus a little bit of coke and Xanax going around. Don't worry, I didn't take any.'

'How was it with Verity?' I asked.

Red smiled bashfully. 'We mighta fooled around a little in the bedroom closet. But that's not what I wanted to tell you about.'

Now I was officially intrigued.

Whatever it was that my brother didn't want me to divulge to anyone *wasn't* the fact that he might've got to second base with Verity Keeley in a closet at the afterparty.

I couldn't imagine what the big secret was.

'Anyway,' Red said, 'as the night goes on, the crowd disappears and soon it's just a few of us: Misty, Hattie, Verity, Bo, Dane, Griff and me.

'And Misty says, "What do you say, kids?" And she holds up that necklace she wears sometimes; the one with the yellow gem in the gold figure-eight. "Who's up for a run?"'

Red gave me a knowing look. 'Misty had been drinking all night and had popped a couple of bars, so she was acting pretty loose. Anyhow, Bo glances sideways at me and says, "What about Red? He's never done it before. You think he's—?"

'Misty says, "Red's *cool*. You can be trusted, can't you, Red?"

'"I can keep a secret," I say, although I didn't know what that secret was going to be.

'Misty looks at Bo, who looks at Dane, who shrugs and says, "Hell, yeah."'

Red stood up and, started pacing around my room. It was 5:55 a.m. He shook his head, remembering. His eyes darted manically but I didn't interrupt. I let him get to it in his own time.

Finally, he said, 'So we leave the apartment, cross Fifth Avenue and go into Central Park. I mean, this is 4:00 a.m. It's the middle of the frickin' night. There's no-one around but homeless people and the odd garbage truck.

'Our group walks on for a bit, over the 79th Street Transverse and deeper into the park before we arrive at some fenced-off little garden beside a bend in the Transverse. Bo said it was a "private conservancy garden", whatever that is. In any case, it's hidden deep in the bushes, not far from the back of the Met. Seriously, if you didn't know it was there, you'd never know.

'Anyway, Misty has a key for the gate and we all file into the private garden. In the corner is an old wooden gardener's hatch sunken into the ground. Misty also has a key for that and in we go.'

'And . . .' I said.

Red said, 'Under that hatch is a little miner's cave with a bare dirt floor, and in the middle of that floor is a hole with a ladder going down into it.

'The others, it looks like they've been here before, because they just flick on the flashlights on their phones and clamber down the ladder. I followed after them as Misty locked the hatch behind me.

'Anyway, we go down two levels. It's getting colder as we go down, and we are in, like, old caves now, with walls made of hardpacked dirt or solid rock.

'Then I dropped into the final cave, just as Bo flicked on a couple of portable arc lights attached to a diesel generator, and I stopped and said, "Holy shit."'

'Why? What was there?' I asked.

Red looked at me hard. 'There was this weird ancient stone doorway, like the entrance to an old temple or something. I mean, it was seriously scary. It sort of stuck out from a wall of uneven rock, but it was perfectly cut, with squared-off edges, and it had ancient writing all over it.

'It was just a doorway—no actual doors—and it lay wide open. I could see some kind of tunnel or cave beyond it.'

I nodded. I'd actually studied this. There had been all sorts of native tribes on Manhattan Island long before the Lenape Indians sold the island to the Dutch in 1626, reputedly for $24 worth of coloured glass beads: the famous Manhattan Purchase.

Archaeologists had found evidence of burial grounds, cave-shrines and even some primitive catacombs. There was evidence that meso-American tribes like the Olmecs, Toltecs and Mayans had established settlements this far north. It was entirely possible that a stone structure or burial cave could exist underneath modern-day Central Park.

Red went on, 'On the floor in the exact middle of this ancient doorway is a little stone pyramid. It's maybe two feet tall—barely higher than my knee—but it's made of a strange kind of black stone that, unlike the rest of the doorway, is perfectly polished.

'Anyway, Misty steps forward, pulls the yellow gem from her necklace and places it in a slot cut into the peak of the little pyramid. And then, oh my freaking God . . .'

'What?' I asked. 'What happened?'

'You're not going to believe me.'

'I'll try.'

Red swallowed. 'Some kind of mechanism within the little pyramid initiates, and the gem that Misty placed on its peak tilts abruptly and slides of its own accord all the way down the opposite side of the pyramid, the tunnel side.

'And then—*bam!*—a bright screen of rippling purple-and-black light springs to life from the pyramid and expands to fill the whole ancient doorway!

'It's tough to describe. I've never seen anything like it. The light stretches all the way across the doorway, completely filling it, like a spiderweb or a curtain, a vertical curtain of light.'

'A curtain of light . . .' I said doubtfully. 'Coming from the knee-high pyramid on the floor?'

Red held up his hands. 'I know it sounds crazy but it's true. The others are clearly enjoying seeing my amazement so Bo says, "Go on, buddy, touch it. It won't hurt you."

'So I reach forward and touch the shimmering purple curtain with my finger. It's weird. It's not air but it's not solid either. It has surface tension. My finger made a little indentation in the wall of light, like I was pressing on a rubber sheet. Circles of purple light expanded from the spot where I touched it like ripples on a pond and then—*whoosh*—*my whole hand goes right through it* to the wrist and I jerked back in shock, pulling my hand out. The others laughed at me.'

I cocked my head. 'Red. Are you sure you didn't smoke some bad weed or eat a loaded brownie? Someone didn't slip something into your drink?'

'I swear, Blue, I had one beer and didn't touch any of the drugs. This *happened*.'

I was a little taken aback by his forcefulness.

'Okay,' I said. 'Go on.'

'So Bo nods at the little pyramid on the ground and says to me, "Check out the gem."

'I look through the curtain of light. It's translucent, so I can vaguely see through it. I see that Misty's amber gem is now sitting near the base of the little pyramid, on the flank that's on the *other* side of the curtain of light, out of reach.

'I look at Bo, not sure what he means.

'He says, "There's only one way to retrieve that gem and that's to step through."

'Misty holds up her wrist, the one with those weird marks on it, and says, "This is how you earn one of these, Red. One for each run."

'"Each run?" I say. "Where are we running? Through there?" I nod at the doorway. I'm wondering what stepping through the wall of light might do to me. "It's safe, isn't it?"

'"More or less," Misty says. "You'll have to jump through to find out. Follow us."

'And with that she grabs Bo's hand and she leaps *straight through* the rippling curtain of light. Bo jumps through with her and I can see their vague shapes on the other side.

'Dane, Griff and Hattie go next. They call from the other side and their voices sound distant, muffled, even though they're only a couple of feet away from me.

'"Jump through!" Hattie calls.

'"Don't be a pussy!" Griff yells.

'Then V grabs my hand and smiles at me. "Come on, big boy. I know how you feel. I was like that my first time. Let's go run."

'And holding Verity's hand, I jumped with her through the ancient doorway, leaping through the curtain of rippling purple light.'

THE TUNNEL RUN

Red landed on the other side of the ancient doorway.

He stood in the same tunnel he had seen before. It actually stretched away for a lot further than he'd originally thought.

Now that he was inside it, he could see that its walls were covered in ancient symbols, pictures and hieroglyphics. Creepy.

He turned to look at the doorway behind him.

From this side, the screen of light that filled the portal was a sickly yellow. The powerful beams of the arc lights on the other side filtered weakly through it, dimmed by their passage through the curtain. The immediate area around Red was bathed in a dull amber glow.

'You can't go back through,' Verity said, taking his hand and pressing it against the light-curtain.

This time, Red's hand did *not* penetrate the wall of light. The screen of light bent a little, and he felt resistance against his fingers, but the wall of light did not give and his hand did not go through it.

'You can only go one way through the portal,' Misty said, appearing beside them and extracting her gem from the inside flank of the little pyramid.

A moment later, the entire curtain of light disappeared— retreating into the knee-high pyramid—and Red could suddenly see the entrance cave once again—

—only now it was different.

It was completely dark.

The arc lights were off.

More than that. They were covered in a thick layer of dust and cobwebs.

The cavern looked abandoned, like it had been abandoned for *years*.

Red frowned with confusion and was about to say something when Verity tugged at his arm.

'Don't worry,' she said, 'I'll explain it all later. Come on, there's an exit at the other end of this tunnel. No time to waste.'

Misty and the others had already taken off down the tunnel—running—the lights of their smartphones bouncing away.

Guided by Verity, Red dashed into the tunnel after them.

The tunnel, he saw, was as ancient as the doorway, stone-walled and dead straight. It was as wide as perhaps two cars but low, maybe ten feet in height. Its walls tapered inward—wide at the bottom, narrower near the ceiling—making the whole thing trapezoidal in shape.

It looked almost *ceremonial*.

At regular intervals, reinforced stone arches held up the ceiling, looking like the ribs of some colossal subterranean animal.

After about four hundred metres of jogging—Red deduced later that this was somewhere around the middle of the tunnel—he saw a very strange thing.

A well hole in the ceiling.

An eight-foot-high heap of trash and other detritus lay underneath it, almost reaching the ceiling. The trash mound was made up of all sorts of odds and ends: bicycle wheels, clothing, discarded books, fast food wrappers, sneakers.

Bo, Misty, Dane, Griff and Hattie had all stopped at the trash heap to wait for Red and V to catch up. Bo was poking around at some of the trash.

'Take a look up into it.' Misty nodded at the well hole above the mound of garbage.

Red stepped up awkwardly onto the pile and peered up into the well hole.

The cylindrical shaft was narrow, maybe three feet across. Looking up into it was like looking through a telescope the wrong way, but there at the top of the shaft, Red could just make out the star-filled night-time sky.

'We think that whoever is up there has been throwing garbage down into the well,' Verity said. 'It piles up here.'

Red was peering up into the shaft when suddenly the shadow of a person wearing a hoodie popped into view up there, shocking him.

The figure blocked out the stars and seemed to look directly down at Red!

Red jumped back, ducking out of view. But he knew that whoever it was had seen him, had seen the moving white light of his phone's flashlight at the bottom of the well.

A terrifying bloodcurdling shriek pierced the air as the figure at the top of the shaft cried out in fury. It was the scream of a man, yes, but it was more animal than human.

Adrenaline shot through Red's body.

'What the fu—' he breathed.

'Shit!' Bo said as he and the others took off down the tunnel.

'Go! Go! Don't stop!' Verity shoved Red forward and he resumed running, looking frantically behind him every few seconds.

After another four hundred metres, the seven of them

came to a second ancient doorway, identical to the first.

This doorway also had a black knee-high pyramid sitting in the centre of its maw.

Beyond the doorway was another dirt-walled miner's cave, empty and covered in years of dust, with a ladder leading up out of it.

Misty placed her gem on this little pyramid and once again, by some mysterious mechanism, it moved down the opposite flank and a luminous curtain of purple light sprang up from the pyramid's apex, stretching across the doorway.

The others wasted no time and stepped straight through it. Following close behind them, Red lunged through the curtain of light—

—and emerged inside the miner's cave he had seen seconds ago . . . only now it was clean and normal, unravaged by dust and time.

Misty immediately reached down and removed the amber gemstone from the pyramid, and the rippling curtain of light filling the doorway (seen from this side, it was yellow) instantly vanished and suddenly the ancient doorway was just a dark yawning aperture again.

'Are you, like, totally freaked out right now?' Verity said, grinning.

Red caught his breath as he stared back at the tunnel, trying to wrap his head around it all.

Bo smiled at him. 'Is that not a total *mindbender* or what?'

Red blinked rapidly. 'Sure is.'

In his mind, all he could think of was the creepy hooded figure who had peered down the well shaft at him and shrieked like an animal.

'Who was that guy who screamed at me?'

Bo shrugged. 'We don't know. I've only been outside the tunnel once: I shimmied up the well, pushing my hands and feet against its walls. I emerged just behind that weird Swedish Cottage not far from the 79th Street Transverse. But the area around me was all freaky, so I didn't stray from the well.'

'What do you mean, freaky?' Red asked.

Bo said, 'What I mean is, it's still New York up there: the same Central Park, all the same buildings, *but it's all been trashed and abandoned*. The windows on all the skyscrapers are smashed; that Swedish Cottage has fallen apart. No power, no lights and no people—or at least, no-one besides our friend in the hoodie. It's like . . . *another* New York . . . not ours. A parallel New York of some kind.'

Red blinked. 'A kind of parallel New York?'

At that moment, Misty stepped up to him, grabbed his left arm and with one quick movement, drew a single vertical mark on his inner wrist with a black permanent marker.

'Welcome to the club, Red. You just became a member of The Secret Runners of New York.'

THE REAL WORLD

'A parallel New York?' I said flatly. 'You're telling me that after a big night of partying, you went to a parallel dimension in which New York has apparently been trashed and weird dudes in hoodies scream at you in rage. I think you're right, Red, we shouldn't mention this to anyone and you should seriously think about finding a new weed dealer.'

'I know it sounds crazy, but it's true!' Red said. 'You gotta believe me, Blue. That exit chamber, by the way, was hidden underneath another private conservancy garden out the back of the Natural History Museum not far from here. We had basically run *right across* Central Park, underneath it, from the east side to the west. It was seriously weird, but man it was a rush. Maybe I can get them to bring you along if they do it again.'

'Sure,' I said, rolling over on my bed and grabbing my pillow. 'Whatever. I think you should get some sleep.'

The following Monday morning Red went off to join the cool kids for coffee at a trendy café on the East Side, so I walked to school across Central Park on my own.

As I came to the 79th Street Transverse, I saw a sign:

HISTORIC SWEDISH COTTAGE

I must have walked past that sign dozens of times before, but only now did it actually register on my consciousness.

I found myself recalling Red's tale.

In it, Bo had said that when he climbed up the well shaft, he'd come out of the well behind the Swedish Cottage, not far from the Transverse.

I bit my lip in thought.

Why not?

And so despite my reservations about my brother's sanity and possibly reckless drug use, I took a little detour: I crossed over the Transverse and headed toward the Swedish Cottage.

It is a truly whacky building: an eerie dark-brown storybook house, the kind usually inhabited by wicked witches. It was also located in a somewhat secluded spot, set back from the regular thoroughfares of the park, which meant that, at this hour, there was nobody around: no cyclists or joggers or regular walkers like me.

Stepping around the wooden cottage, I found a dense tangle of bushes, vines and shrubs behind it, separated from the structure by a sturdy wooden fence.

Taking a quick look around me to make sure no-one was watching, I swung myself over the fence and ventured into the undergrowth.

It was no easy task.

Thorns nicked me. Branches smacked my face. Vines tripped me up more than once.

It looked like no-one had come through here since the park had been built back in the mid-1800s. Certainly no gardeners or groundskeepers had. The dense tangle was unkempt and ugly, and had clearly kept out any would-be explorers for at least a century.

Fifteen yards into the thicket, I swore aloud. 'Damn you, Red, making me think I might—'

I cut myself off.

There on the ground in front of me, overgrown with weeds, hidden deep within the thicket, its faded grey brickwork encased in creeping vines, was an old low well.

THE WELL

I examined the well for a good ten minutes. This was worth being late for school.

The many vines that covered the well's circular mouth lay over it so thickly that I could probably have stood on them and not fallen through.

Peering through a small gap in this layer of vines, I looked down into the well and saw only darkness.

I called, 'Hellooo!' and my voice bounced back to me as if from a great distance. This was no simple well. Maybe there *was* a tunnel down there.

What exactly had Red done on Saturday night?

I covered the well with a few extra branches and then retraced my steps through the surrounding scrub, making sure no-one saw me emerge from it near the Swedish Cottage.

(I would show the well to Red the next day and when he saw it he smiled with vindication and exclaimed, 'I told you!')

As I made my way to school, I thought more about his story, about his 'run'.

It sounded intriguing, but sadly, unless I penetrated the inner sanctum of the cool crowd like Red had managed to do and got invited to go on one of their runs, I wouldn't be able to investigate it any further.

THE NEW YEAR IN NEW YORK

Red's popularity with the in-crowd continued through December.

He actually asked me once if I was okay with it and I was. Over the years, we had always had mutual friends and separate friends; these kids were definitely *his* friends.

Mind you, I did start to seriously contemplate the state of my social life when, that New Year's Eve, Red was invited to an inner-circle-only party at Dane's apartment on the East Side and my mom and Todd were invited to a soiree at the Majestic and I was faced with the prospect of spending New Year's Eve alone in our apartment. I came to the sad conclusion that I needed to work harder on social matters. Even my mom had a better nightlife than I did.

And then, two days before New Year's Eve, Jenny called.

'Hiya, Skye. Last Minute needs one more waitress for a gig on New Year's. Want to do it? They're offering seventy bucks an hour for maybe four hours' work.'

Last Minute Staff and Events was the name of the company she worked for, the one that provided extra waitstaff at the eleventh hour.

Lacking anything else to do—and happy to bolster my

own coffers with some quick cash—I said sure, why not.

Dressed in black pants and a waistcoat, it was actually fun working with Jenny. At a vast suite in the Mandarin Oriental Hotel in the Time Warner Center filled with cheerful Canadian businesspeople and their partners, I carried a tray loaded up with champagne for almost four hours and walked out of there at 1:00 a.m. with two hundred and eighty bucks in cash.

Jenny's manager said I'd done well and asked if I wanted to go on their roster for future functions. I shrugged and said sure.

I walked home with Jenny, and as we parted at her building, the famous Dakota, I thanked her for the opportunity.

'Hey, anytime,' she said. 'It's nice to hang with someone who's not too proud to work.'

I arrived home long before anyone else in my family and fell into bed.

I heard Red return shortly after dawn, and when he finally came down to breakfast the next morning, I noticed a newly added black line on his wrist.

Oddly, he didn't talk to me at all about this run. I wondered if Misty and the others had reminded him that runs were not to be discussed outside their circle and thus Red was not going to elaborate on what he had already told me.

I let it go. Good for him, I thought. And good for me. The New Year in New York had been okay.

The coming of the New Year brought with it something else: renewed interest in the end of the world.

March 17 was suddenly only two-and-a-half months away and the media was back on the case. The papers and TV news were filled with animated graphics of the Earth moving around the sun, its elliptical orbit carrying it inexorably toward a billowing cloud of gamma-radiation particles. In most of the animations, the Earth smashed through the cloud, causing many of its particles to cling to our planet like a zillion magnetic insects while others were scattered into space.

But now that the Earth was so close to the cloud, a new feature of humanity's final day was presented to us.

As the world penetrated the gamma cloud it would, of course, be spinning.

This meant that one hemisphere of the Earth would plunge into the gamma cloud first and experience its effects. This would give the other side of the planet a six- to twelve-hour glimpse of what was to come.

New computer models showed that Australia, Asia, India and the Middle East would hit the cloud first. Then as the Earth rotated, Africa, Europe and North and South America would be affected.

Jimmy Kimmel said, 'Expect last-minute ticket sales on Virgin Galactic to go through the roof during those six to twelve hours.'

It was interesting to see people's opinions on the gamma cloud. Politicians, for example, sat resolutely on the fence since if the world *didn't* end, none of them wanted to be mocked forever after as Chicken Little. They called for calm and for people to go about their lives.

Scientists from MIT, Princeton, Caltech and Oxford weighed in, but when all was said and done, the prevailing wisdom was still split fifty-fifty.

Or as one of the experts put it: 'In evolutionary terms, the human brain is not wired to deal with threats like this: existential threats that it has not encountered before. We know to run from lions and tigers because we know from experience that they could kill us. We have no experience with a cloud of gamma radiation, so we just shrug and say, "Oh, well, let's see what happens. Till then, I'll just go about my life."'

This was the view of our fellow San Remo resident, Manny Wannemaker, the right-wing radio host.

He said to his millions of listeners: 'This gamma cloud stuff is all nonsense. It's just more scare tactics from the Left. Climate change didn't work, so this is another grand attempt by the socialist-progressive-liberal elite to redistribute the wealth. Trust me, folks, it'll all turn out to be a whole lot of nothing.'

(Manny famously spoke into a solid-gold microphone. With the mike, his expensive overcoat with the purple sleeves and his apartment in the San Remo, he was not a fan of redistributing anything.)

The usual whackos built hermetically-sealed bunkers in their backyards. Others stocked up on canned tuna and bottled water.

And, of course, the crazies with their placards still gathered outside tourist sites like the Met and the Natural History Museum. I couldn't say there were more of them, but passers-by definitely seemed to take more notice of them now.

Disturbingly, there had been a spike in hate crimes around the world: members of one religion killing members of another, or in the case of Islam, Shiites killing Sunnis, one blaming the other for the coming end of all things.

And then, somewhere around mid-January, came the first hate crime against the rich.

A gang of thugs raided the Westchester mansion of a well-known billionaire whose wine cellar had featured in an article in *Forbes*. They killed the billionaire and his family . . . and then put their feet up and drank his wine while streaming the whole thing live on Periscope.

When a SWAT team eventually raided the house, the TV cameras and helicopters caught it all, in particular, the bandana-clad youth who called from the upstairs window: 'We're all gonna die anyway, so we might as well *live large*!'

And then, live on TV, he drew a gun and shot himself in the head.

Naturally, this incident captured the attention of those souls who till then had not shown the slightest interest at all in gamma clouds, electrical currents in the human brain, science and the end of humanity. In short, people like my mother.

Now she was all ears.

Late one night, I heard her whispering to my stepfather.

'Todd,' she said. 'Is there anything we can do? Surely we're not going to die with everybody else.'

My stepfather answered in his detached, measured way. 'It'll be okay, Deidre. I think the whole thing is just a big scare.'

'But what if it isn't? What if—'

'I got it covered, honey,' he said, assured as always. 'I'll make sure we're safe.'

I had wondered what he'd meant by that. How could anybody make sure they survived the Earth's passage through the gamma cloud?

The answer came in scattered whispers and hushed comments I heard in the schoolyard, in the common room and from my mother on the telephone to her girlfriends.

Four whispered words: *The Plum Island Retreat.*

'—Have you heard about Plum Island?'

'—They're just calling it the Retreat. It's an old high-security animal disease facility, with airlock doors and biohazard-level air seals. They think it can withstand the gamma cloud. It's also an island, which makes it secure—'

'—It was set up by a few Goldman Sachs guys who knew all about this gamma shit ages ago. They found out about it when they were investing in some biotech thing. They bought the whole island from the government five years back and have been kitting it out for habitation ever since. The plan is to stay there till the gamma radiation passes—'

'—My dad's paid for our family to go to the Retreat, just in case—'

'—Starley Collins was telling me it can only hold sixty people, that's it. Once they hit that number, the doors will be closed.'

'—What's the buy-in?'

'—Seventeen mil. Per person. In cash. And you gotta know the right people. It's all very hush-hush. They haven't even told those who are in when they'll move there.'

'—That's a lot of cash to gamble on a never-before-seen cosmic event. What if it all blows over and nothing happens? Everyone who goes there will look like a fool.'

'—And if everybody dies and they survive, what do they do then anyway? Live in an empty world?'

Naturally, my mother heard these things, too, and when she discovered that Todd's cool and measured solution had been to buy four places for us at the Plum Island Retreat—at $17 million each—my mom had rewarded him just like she had on their first date.

When he informed her that he had offset the cost of the Retreat by shorting a selection of specific stocks— meaning that if the world did *not* end as predicted, he stood to make about $200 million—she rewarded him again. Go Todd.

Red's view of it all was typical Red. 'If it really is the end of everything'—he shrugged—'there's nothing I can do about it, so I might as well have fun in the meantime. And that way, if the end comes, I can say I enjoyed the last few months.' My brother was never going to win any philosophy prizes, but in its own way, his logic was hard to fault.

And so, while Red partied, at the end of January I flew down to Memphis to see our dad.

'Have you been eating your sardines?' he asked me as soon as I walked into the ward. 'Taking your phosphorus supplements?'

'Yes, Dad.' I had been, actually. Truth be told, my mind had actually felt sharper for doing so.

'And no sodas?'

'Not a drop.' I didn't add that my stomach looked the best it ever had: no bloating from the carbonated fizz. My dad's end-of-the-world diet was awesome.

'How's your mother?' he asked.

'She's still Mom.'

He smiled sadly. Their marriage had always been doomed. He'd been the brilliant but bookish doctor from a high-standing Memphis family; she had been the local beauty queen determined to marry into wealth and society.

But when the wealth-management company managing my father's family trust ran off with the money and it was suddenly revealed that my father no longer had any fortune, my mother was out of there.

My father—sweet, smart yet totally naive—had been devastated.

The nervous breakdown had come soon after.

I liked to remember him as the man I knew as a ten-year-old kid: the one who would take us on sailing vacations to Martha's Vineyard and Rhode Island and, most of all, to the lighthouses near them that he admired so much.

'Those damn lighthouses,' my mother would say. She didn't like those trips at all because they messed up her hair. But my father came alive on them. His eyes lit up as he gazed at his beloved lighthouses.

His favourite one was Race Rock Light, a storybook cottage built precariously on a tiny island not far from Rhode Island. It looked so incongruous, so out of place, this dainty little cottage perched on a rock above the pounding waves. My father called it his ideal beach house because it had no neighbours.

Eventually Mom stopped going on those trips altogether and Dad, Red and I had an even better time.

Thanks to some grand-uncle I never met, Dad was an associate member of the New York Yacht Club's Rhode

Island clubhouse. ('This is a very famous club,' he told us. 'In 1983, its yacht, *Liberty*, lost the America's Cup for the first time in 132 years.') It was from the New York Yacht Club on Newport, Rhode Island, that we would take out a loaner yacht for a week or so.

We'd lie on the deck of that yacht, anchored at sunset in some bay or near some lighthouse, listening to vinyl records of Dad's favourite sixties bands: The Doors, The Kinks, The Who and, my favourite, Eric Burdon and the Animals.

(It was Dad who gave me my prized 1968 vintage poster of 'Eric Burdon and The Animals at Whisky a Go Go' in all its pink psychedelic glory. I still played their greatest hits—'House of the Rising Sun', 'We Gotta Get Out of This Place', 'Don't Let Me Be Misunderstood'—constantly on my phone.)

They were the best of times.

But that was a long time ago. Another life.

'So, Dad,' I said. 'Do you think it's really going to happen? Do you think the world's going to end on March 17?'

He looked at me and smiled kindly with his milky honest eyes. 'The world will go on, Blue. It survived the asteroid that killed the dinosaurs. It's survived ice ages and heatwaves. It's humanity as we know it that's going to end.'

BOYS

I returned to New York from Memphis feeling oddly ambivalent about the fate of the world.

That TV expert had been right: despite everything I had heard and read, I couldn't bring myself to fear some nebulous cloud of gas up in space. My brain just couldn't compute it as a threat.

On my return, I glimpsed two more marks on Red's inner wrist, making a total of four now.

I also went back to school and the familiar routine.

Trudges across the park—passing Misty, Hattie and Oz on the sidewalk as they waited for their ride to school—classes—essays—return trudges across the park on my own. I teased Red for abandoning me, told him that if an axe murderer killed me on the way home from school, it'd be his fault.

A highlight from that time was an invitation from Jenny to attend a function—not as staff, but as a guest—at the Metropolitan Museum of Art: the announcement of this year's exhibit on the Cantor Roof Garden.

It was an awesome affair.

The Cantor Roof Garden is possibly the best entertaining space in New York: a gigantic patio, it sits on the roof of the Met above the tree line of Central Park and boasts unobstructed views of the park and the city skyline.

At dusk, it is spectacular. Every year in the summer the roof garden plays host to a single-artist exhibition: previous artists have included Jeff Koons, Sol LeWitt and Cai Guo-Qiang (his bizarre pair of crocodiles were particularly memorable; trust me, Google them).

I stood by the edge of the roof with Jenny, nibbling on some finger food and looking out over the railing. The sloping glass side of the Met fell away beneath us at an angle of about sixty degrees. I found myself wondering if you could slide down it safely when Jenny's father joined us.

He smiled broadly when he saw me. 'So this is the famous Skye Rogers! It's nice to finally put a face to the name. Jenny speaks so highly of you.'

I nodded graciously. 'Thank you, Mr Johnson.'

'Please,' he said, 'call me Ken. Now, go and enjoy the evening.'

Shortly after, Mr Johnson—sorry, Ken—introduced the artist of the moment, a talented yet provocative young sculptor from London named Clive Mayhew (although he went by the single name 'Clivey'). Together, they swept a large white sheet off a sample of the artworks to come: a ten-foot-high crucifix made of fibreglass and painted bright pink. Instead of the usual image of Christ attached to it, a life-sized pink sculpture of a woman in a business suit was nailed to it, arms spread wide. It was called THE PRICE OF FEMINISM. Very meta.

The crowd oohed appropriately. Some gasped.

'That's not gonna be controversial,' Jenny said sarcastically.

But I could see that her dad was as proud as punch.

He and the young artist smiled as a hundred flash-bulbs popped.

As January came to an end, Red's lacrosse training picked up. The season was fast approaching (if the world didn't end), but since Red was too cool to walk home with me anymore, I'd lost track of the days when he trained.

Which was how I came to be in my bedroom early one evening with the door half-open, focused intently on my physics homework, my ears covered in noise-cancelling headphones. I was dressed in an old yellow Jake the Dog nightshirt, pink Ugg boots and one of my mother's old green SoulCycle headbands, when a muffled knocking invaded my sonic cocoon.

It was not my best look, but I was home alone on a winter's evening doing homework, so sue me.

You can imagine my horror, then, when I looked up and saw Bo Bradford standing in my doorway, smiling at me and looking gorgeous in his lacrosse tracksuit.

I hadn't known today was lacrosse training and Red had brought the boys back to our place to hang.

'Hey there,' Bo said.

I swallowed, literally unable to speak.

'I was just going to the restroom and, well . . .' He nodded at my nightshirt. 'Jake the Dog, huh?'

I curled my shoulders inward. 'Who doesn't like *Adventure Time*?'

Then, to my total mortification, Bo stepped into my bedroom, strolling casually around it, calmly taking it in.

They say a stranger can see more about your home in one minute than you can in six months. As I suddenly saw my room through Bo's eyes, I knew that to be true.

The books on my shelves: my prized Stephen King collection, a couple of Michael Lewis books, some Philippa Gregory historical novels, and, yes, the *Twilight* saga.

All of them held in place by white woodcut bookends that read: DREAM and LOVE.

On my dresser, my dearest toy from childhood, a gift from my dad that he'd purchased on a trip to Australia: a fluffy pink kangaroo with a heart sewn onto its pouch plus the words: HOPPY THE HAPPY KANGAROO.

Oh, dear Lord . . .

The posters on the walls made a cooler showing, I thought/hoped: Green Day, The Killers, and my vintage pink 'Eric Burdon and the Animals at Whisky a Go Go' poster.

But, then, perhaps all this coolness was negated by the cheesy motivational picture of a basketball under a ring with the shout line: YOU MISS 100% OF THE SHOTS YOU DON'T TAKE. Thank Christ I'd taken down my old 'Hang in there' kitten poster a few months back.

'It's hockey, not basketball,' Bo said.

'I'm sorry, what?' I said.

'That quote: "You miss 100% of the shots you don't take." It was Wayne Gretzky who said that. He played ice hockey, not basketball.'

I shook my head mock-seriously. 'Don't you just hate it when motivational poster companies get it wrong?'

He laughed before nodding at my desk.

'Whatcha studying?'

'AP physics,' I said.

'*Advanced placement* physics?' He gave me a sideways look. 'That isn't normally popular with girls.'

'I am no ordinary girl,' I said with what I felt was my winningest smile.

Then I shrugged. 'My dad told me once that if you want to be big in the twenty-first century, be an engineer. Engineers can go into lots of industries and these days, all the heavy hitters studied some form of engineering: Bezos, Brin, Bloomberg, even the Koch brothers.'

'Is that so?' Bo said.

'Uh-huh,' I said, but the look he was giving me made me suddenly fearful I'd said the wrong thing, made some kind of social mistake.

I plunged on anyway. 'And if I want to study engineering at a good school, I have to do well in physics. That is, of course, if we don't all die in March.'

He laughed at that. Then he jerked his chin at my textbook. 'What're you working on today?'

'Increasing electric current in a circuit.'

'Ah, yes, Ohm's Law,' Bo said.

'You know it?'

''Course I do. I love physics. I'm good at it, too. But, alas, when I get out of school, I won't be becoming an engineer.'

'Why not?'

'Let's just say—again, assuming we don't all die—that my father has grand plans for me.' The way he said it made it sound more like a death sentence than a grand plan. 'Go to Yale, like he did. Study law, like he did. Be a Bonesman, like he was. Then go into politics, like he never did.'

I was vaguely aware that Bo's father was a player in the Republican Party. Not a congressman or anything like that, but a donor, a behind-the-scenes kingmaker.

'Last year, Father invited Bush 43 to our place just to talk to me about the best way to—'

Bo cut himself off, blushing. 'I'm sorry. Bush 43. That sounded like the name-drop of the century, didn't it?'

He was genuinely abashed, annoyed at himself for performing the drop so effortlessly.

It made me want to jump him then and there.

He rallied well, as smart people do, by turning the conversation away from himself.

He looked out my window at Central Park. 'A lot of the girls around here, they don't want to do anything. No goals, no ambition, no *thinking*. They just want to find a husband and live the life. But engineering. Wow. That's something. Takes dedication, commitment, and smarts.'

He looked at me oddly, evaluating me closely. 'It's nice to meet a girl with those qualities.'

I smiled shyly but on the inside I was exploding with excitement. I liked impressing him.

'Well, that's my grand plan,' I said. 'Right now I just need to answer these problem questions.'

'Here, let me help you . . .' he said, pulling up a chair.

He brushed against my shoulder as he casually sat down beside me. I felt almost naked in my flimsy nightshirt; hot, flustered and thrilled.

After helping me with a few questions, Bo excused himself. 'I'd better go. The guys'll be wondering where I got to. See ya round.'

'You bet,' I said. 'See ya round.'

He left and for a few moments I stared like a dumb-struck fool at the empty doorway.

Then I saw myself in the mirror: pink Ugg boots, yellow Jake the Dog nightshirt, green SoulCycle headband.

'Great look, Skye,' I said to my reflection.

As it happened, being abandoned after school by my brother wasn't all bad.

I was leaving Monmouth one afternoon in late January—alone—when I spotted Bo crossing Fifth Avenue on his own and hustling up the steps of the Metropolitan Museum of Art.

Curious, and a little jazzed by our recent interaction in my bedroom, I decided to follow him.

After a little bit of searching, I found him sitting on a bench in the Egyptian Wing of the Met. He was facing the Temple of Dendur, the awesome ancient Egyptian temple that had been transplanted brick-by-brick from Aswan in Egypt to New York City in the 1970s, but he wasn't looking at it.

Bo's head was buried in a book—a math text-book—while on his ears he wore top-of-the-range Bose noise-cancelling headphones to block out the world. Rising high into the air behind him was the enormous bank of glass windows that encased the ancient Egyptian temple.

I debated whether or not to go and speak with him. This was clearly his personal study space, somewhere he went to be alone with his work and his thoughts.

Would he be upset if I interrupted him? Or would he—maybe—like it?

I didn't know. I couldn't know. I felt paralysed with indecision, terrified of being rejected.

But then a strange resolve materialised inside me and I thought to myself: *Go on, Skye. Be brave. Give it a try.*

And so I went over there and tapped Bo gently on the shoulder.

He turned, removing his headphones, and as his eyes met mine they widened with genuine delight.

'Hey! Skye! Hi,' he said. If anything, he seemed a little tongue-tied, which kinda delighted me. 'I'm just studying here. Want to join me?'

And that was how I came to visit the Met on nine glorious occasions to study with Bo Bradford, Head Boy at The Monmouth School and all-round sublime specimen of manliness.

Sometimes we sat in the Egyptian Wing while at other times we sat in the American Wing, with its soaring ceiling, enormous faux façade and café.

It was kinda awesome.

I'd get him a coffee, he'd get me one. I'd flirt mildly with him and he'd flirt with me. I particularly liked it when we worked at a table facing each other and our feet would inadvertently touch underneath. Bo knew it and I knew it, but neither of us moved our legs apart.

We took breaks to look at the various art exhibits. I adored a visiting collection of Monet paintings but recoiled at a gruesome modern-art display of bear traps titled *THE EVOLUTION OF CRUELTY*: it was comprised of six spring-loaded bear traps, each older than the last; they ranged from a rusty 130-year-old iron model to a modern steel trap. To think of the spring-loaded jaws crunching through a poor bear's leg made me ill.

But most of all Bo and I talked about stuff, all sorts of stuff, from school politics and real politics to novels and engineering and the end of the world.

'What do you think?' I said as we stood in front of the hideous bear traps. 'Do you think everything is going to end on St Patrick's Day?'

He looked away into the middle distance, thinking. 'I hope not. Because there are a lot of things I'd still like to do. See the pyramids, hike to Everest, you.'

I almost didn't hear that last part, with the unexpected double entendre. I'd followed his faraway gaze and when I turned back to face him I found him looking right into my eyes.

He took my hands, moved forward and gently pressed his lips against mine.

Adrenaline flooded through me. His kiss was electric. If this was what the gamma cloud was going feel like, I thought, bring it on.

He pulled away and we were left standing there, facing each other, awkwardly holding hands.

He looked confused, surprised at what he had just done.

'I'm sorry. I honestly don't know why I did that. I just . . . had to.'

'That's okay.' I looked down shyly and he laughed gently, released my hands and turned back towards the café.

'We should get back to studying,' he said.

I paused as he walked away from me, thinking about the feel of his lips on mine, the spark in his eyes, the end of the world and one other thing.

As I'd held his hands and looked down, I'd seen the collection of marks on his left wrist: nine parallel slashes.

January became February, and as the world swept toward its destiny—and I walked on cloud nine whenever I thought of Bo Bradford—the gossip at Monmouth turned to the last and most exclusive debutante ball of the Season, the East Side Cotillion, which would take place on Saturday, March 3.

Misty Collins, as we all knew, was going, as was a senior named Donna Abrahamson.

Misty's squad gossiped about the pre-parties that were scheduled and the night itself, which promised, they said, to be totally snatch.

I listened wanly, knowing that I had more chance of going to the moon than I did of attending any of those parties or the Cotillion.

And then came the day I lingered in the girls' locker room, a day that would change my life.

AN UNEXPECTED FAVOUR

It happened after gym class, which at that time was held during the final period on Wednesdays.

For the record, I should mention that, for a girl, gym class is as horrible at an elite private school as it is at any other school.

No-one enjoys changing in the locker room with twenty other teenage girls or putting on tight white gym shorts, tube socks and a navy polo with a collar patterned in the school's signature green-and-navy tartan.

Nor does anyone enjoy the running, jumping, climbing and throwing of balls. I'm naturally fast but put any kind of ball in my hands and I'm completely useless.

Anyway, after another pointless and humiliating session in the school's indoor gym, we had all showered and changed and were leaving for the day.

As I always seemed to do, I'd left my housekey in my temporary locker and went back to get it after everyone had gone.

I only just heard her.

Heard an ever-so-faint sniffle coming from the row of toilet cubicles adjacent to the shower room.

Someone was in there. I peered under the door, but whoever was inside the cubicle had raised her feet so no-one would spot her.

I edged toward the cubicle and knocked hesitantly.

The sniffling ceased immediately, as if the person doing it had frozen instantly at being caught.

'Hello?' I said softly. 'Are you okay in there?'

Pregnant silence.

And then a husky voice. 'Please go away.'

It was Misty.

Eventually, I coaxed her out and saw her dilemma.

Oh, God.

It was every high school girl's nightmare.

That time of the month . . . an extra heavy flow that came unexpectedly early . . . during gym class . . . in tight white shorts.

Misty's eyes were puffy and red from crying. She sat in the cubicle, pantless, holding her bloodstained gym shorts and underpants in her hands. She'd been hiding in the cubicle—as I certainly would have done myself—waiting for all the other girls to leave, after which she would make her escape.

And for someone whose friends had made an art of passing snide judgements on others—from nose jobs to the awful incident with Winnie Simms—there would be no coming back from this.

Live by the sword, die by the sword.

And yet as I stood there looking at her, I couldn't help but feel sorry for Misty. Maybe I was a softy, maybe I was a sucker, but despite her imperfections, she was still just a girl who lived like I did at the mercy of her anatomy.

'It's okay,' I said. 'Let me help you. And don't worry, I won't tell a soul.'

★ ★ ★

The following day, Misty Collins added me on Snapchat.

That small act of kindness in the locker room would change the course my life, no matter how much longer it lasted.

THE PLAZA, THE DAKOTA
AND THE CARLYLE

It was like I had been knighted or damed or whatever the hell the female equivalent of being knighted is.

Both at school and outside it, Misty ushered me into her inner circle.

I was *in*.

The first thing she did was wait for me one morning in her Escalade outside the San Remo and ask me if I wanted to ride to school with her. Of course, I jumped straight in the back of the car with her, Hattie and her beanie-wearing brother, Oz.

She showered me with praise in the hallways, and in the junior common room she would not tolerate an unkind word said about me, not from Hattie or Verity or anyone.

Red was both impressed and confused. 'What *did* you do?' he asked me one morning as I gleefully left him to walk to school across the park by himself.

'Nothing,' I said, skipping away. 'We just bonded on a female level. You wouldn't understand.'

Misty asked me to accompany her to her 'bouquet fitting' for the Cotillion. (Unlike other balls, for the Cote, the debutantes get to choose their individual bouquets of flowers. This, naturally, creates an expensive competition of its own.)

I hung out at her place after school with her, Verity and Hattie. We talked about the usual stuff: school, fashion, hair, boys.

(One conversation that I will never forget involved Hattie saying that she thought the world was flat, like some rapper I'd never heard of. 'I mean, look at the horizon, it's *flat*,' she said. 'And, hello, if the world was round, wouldn't the people at the bottom fall off? Until I see it for myself from space, I just won't believe it.' Seriously. She said that. I wanted to ask her if she believed in gravity.)

One afternoon at Misty's apartment, I went to the restroom. This meant walking past her brother's bedroom.

Oz was in there studying. His room was a shrine to the New York Rangers: the walls were covered with red, white and blue Rangers paraphernalia, including framed jerseys, posters, pennants, hockey sticks and even a goalie's facemask painted with the American flag and signed by Henrik Lundqvist.

I suppose a kid's gotta have a hobby, I thought as I kept walking.

Misty even invited me along to one of her fortnightly afternoon teas with Griff O'Dea at The Plaza Hotel, a rare honour that even Verity and Hattie prized very highly.

Now, I should be clear about this. There is The Plaza and there is *The Plaza*.

Towering over Central Park South, with its steeply slanted Parisian mansard roof, The Plaza is an icon of New York City. It is also one of the most expensive hotels in the world. Its commanding location affords it unobstructed north-facing views of the park.

Now, your standard well-to-do lady of leisure might do high tea at the hotel's Palm Court, a lavish garden-like space encased by a stained-glass dome. This impresses most.

We, however, went to The Plaza's *private* tearoom up on the 14th floor. It is not advertised. If you do not know it's there, you're not invited. It was quietly added to the hotel during its $400-million renovation in 2008. A plush little salon, it has panoramic views of Central Park, a gorgeous fireplace and its own dedicated butler. Access is permitted only to owners of the private residences in the building and to people like Misty Collins.

Misty and Griff sat beside the fireplace—their usual spot, I learned—sipping espressos and nibbling éclairs as they gossiped.

Griff said, 'So my dad tells me that he wants to get me a car for my eighteenth birthday in April. I said "Awesome, I want a Porsche 911 Turbo." But then he says he's already bought it: a Jaguar convertible. I mean, Jesus, do I look like a forty-year-old wage slave suffering a midlife crisis?'

He threw his head back, laughing, sending his mop of frizzy orange hair bouncing wildly.

In my time since starting at Monmouth, I'd discovered that the rumours about Griff going to rehab twice were true. He'd gone for substance abuse.

But it was actually more complicated than it appeared.

When he was thirteen, Griff had been hit by a drunk driver while crossing 69th Street. Both of his legs had been broken. He was living in constant pain so his doctor prescribed him several different pain-relief meds including Vicodin. Griff, already on Ritalin for ADHD, got hooked. Twice. He stole a few of his dad's watches and pawned them for money for drugs. Hence, rehab. Twice.

'Where are you going to keep it?' I asked.

Griff's family lived in the Majestic building. Garage space in Manhattan is priceless, especially near old buildings like the Majestic since, because they were built in the 1880s, they don't have any internal parking.

Griff said, 'My dad took a leaf out of Jerry Seinfeld's book: he bought a townhouse a couple of blocks behind our place, gutted it, and turned it into a garage. It has an internal elevator, fits four cars.'

That townhouse, I figured, was probably worth about sixteen million dollars.

No wonder regular people despised the wealthy. While the homeless lived on the streets and the middle class struggled to make ends meet, people like the O'Deas were gutting perfectly inhabitable homes in order to store their car collections.

I was reminded of the story of Marie Antoinette, the Queen of France at the onset of the French Revolution.

The poor are starving, Your Majesty.

Then let them eat cake, she'd said, before the poor rose up and cut off her head on the guillotine.

Misty said, 'Oh, Griff. A Jag. You do understand that I am never *ever* going to be seen in that car with you.'

They laughed. I tried to, but I just ended up turning and looking out the windows at the glorious view of the park.

Let them eat cake, I thought.

★ ★ ★

And then, after all this special treatment, came the invitation.

The following Friday, February 16, was Verity Keeley's seventeenth birthday and she was throwing a party at her family's apartment in the Carlyle on the East Side. I'd heard the other girls talking about it for a couple of weeks, but until I'd rescued Misty, I had not been privy to the details. Of course, as Verity's current squeeze, Red had been invited a month ago.

The day after I went to the Plaza with her, Misty elbowed Verity and said, 'Hey, V, you should invite Skye to your party on Friday night. She'll dig it the most.'

I saw a flash of calculation cross Verity's face. It only lasted a millisecond, but it was there: the calculus of social status.

Then she smiled sweetly and said, 'Cool. Sure. What do you say, Skye, wanna come? The theme is Famous Villains.'

In the moment before I answered, a warning bell rang in the back of my mind: if I said yes to this, would I be stepping into a social scene like the one that had broken me in Memphis?

I figured I would be, but then I was older and wiser now and this was my new life in a new city. I couldn't hide forever. And, of course, Red and Bo would be there, so I wouldn't be in it all by myself.

'Thanks, Verity,' I said. 'I'd love to come.'

THE PARTY

The Carlyle building is one of the premier addresses on the Upper East Side. John F. Kennedy once lived there, famously sneaking Marilyn Monroe in via a basement entrance. Set back a block from Central Park, at 35 storeys tall it commands superb views of the park and the city.

Red and I arrived at Verity's penthouse apartment at the same time Griff did. We were met by Mr and Mrs Keeley.

'Hey, kids,' Verity's father said. 'The party's up on the roof. You can head up via our private stairs.'

We were guided by a butler through the gorgeous apartment. I'd heard that Verity's dad was a keen hunter and as we passed his den, I saw some deer antlers on the wall, plus a very high-tech-looking crossbow on a display shelf.

Griff nudged us. 'See that crossbow? It's a TenPoint Carbon Xtra. It's a four-thousand-dollar weapon. Best hunting crossbow money can buy.'

'Oh,' I said as we headed up the private stairwell.

Like the San Remo, the Carlyle has an awesome rooftop 'temple' structure which residents can use to host private events and which, I must admit, was a fantastic location for a girl's seventeenth birthday party.

And what a party it was.

Fairy lights crisscrossed the multi-tiered terraces. Hollywood-style spotlights sent shafts of light into the sky. Bow-tied servers carried trays of soda drinks (which the kids liberally spiked with vodka).

Music was pumping. A hot DJ named PhaseOne was working his turntable, headphones on, head bouncing to the rhythm while a couple of girls danced provocatively in front of him.

There must have been fifty kids there, most of them from Monmouth plus a few from other nearby schools.

And then there were the costumes.

For the boys, dressing up as a movie villain wasn't hard. There were the usual Batman villains: a lot of Jokers, both the Heath Ledger version and the Jack Nicholson one (no Jared Leto Jokers; I guess that one never took off); Griff was dressed as the Riddler in a natty green suit covered in question marks; and there were a few Banes (gym jocks wanting to show off their muscles). One Dr Evil, a Darth Vader and a very clever Jigsaw from *Saw* added nicely to the mix.

Dane Summerhays was dressed as Tyler Durden from *Fight Club*: in a red leather jacket and with his already chiselled Brad Pitt–like features, he'd picked an outfit that was villainous but which also made him look good.

Red, with his copper-coloured hair, went as Syndrome, the bad guy superkid from *The Incredibles*. He had gelled up his hair, attached a mask over his eyes and happily went out in public in a cape and spandex. That was my brother.

Bo was there, looking devastating in a navy blue LAPD motorcycle cop outfit, complete with knee-high black boots. He was the T-1000 from *Terminator 2*, not the Arnie terminator, but the sleeker one, the liquid-metal man who'd adopted the body of an LA cop.

Misty's younger brother, Oz, was there too. He was the same age as Verity's kid brother and they were buddies, which must have been how he'd got invited. Oz's costume was detailed, elaborate and easily the scariest thing on the whole rooftop.

He was fully decked out as Pennywise the evil clown from the Stephen King horror novel, *It*. Oz had painted his face white and his lips red, added a skullcap with clown hair and put scary fang-like teeth in his mouth. Tim Curry would have been proud.

As for the girls, they hadn't held back.

They had gone for the villainesses with the skimpiest, sexiest outfits. Or put another way, like Dane Summerhays, they'd gone for the villains who made them look hot.

I counted four Harley Quinns (sequinned hotpants), three Catwomen (sleek bodysuits), two Jennifer Checks (a male-fantasy cheerleader's outfit with a tiny skirt and bare midriff) and two Maleficents (nice horns).

Verity, the birthday girl, was dressed in the distinctive yellow-and-black motorcycle bodysuit of Uma Thurman's character in *Kill Bill: Volume 1*. She even had a samurai sword slung across her back.

The bright yellow costume stood out beautifully among the crowd on the rooftop, and at a party full of villains, it was obviously the birthday girl's privilege to dress as the only heroine: a clever touch.

As I tentatively stepped out of the stairwell onto the Carlyle's roof, I beheld all this saucy villainy with more than a touch of self-consciousness.

My costume wasn't sexy at all.

In fact, it was dowdy; deliberately dowdy.

I had parted my brown hair on the side and pressed it down flat, fixing it in place with hairpins, making it look short and drab. And I wore a rural Appalachian outfit: a colourless flannel shirt buttoned right up to my chin with a plain brown smock-dress over it.

Sure, my villain was a little old, but she was from my favourite Stephen King book. As I looked out over the party, however, I feared that no-one would get it—

'You're the crazy hillbilly woman from *Misery*!' Misty cried when she saw me. 'The psycho stalker of that author, who used the sledgehammer on him. I love it!'

I exhaled with relief.

Misty wore a distinctive crown and a black-and-gold medieval-style velvet dress that narrowed dramatically at the waist, thanks to an internal corset of some kind. Its gold stitching matched her figure-eight necklace perfectly. Her blonde hair rolled down over her shoulders in a pair of long undulating tresses.

I saw who she was instantly.

'Cersei Lannister,' I said. 'The queen from *Game of Thrones*. She's an awesome villain.'

There was more to it than that, a clever subtlety to her choice: even in fancy dress, Misty was the queen of the hive.

Standing with her was her older sister, Chastity, the Head Girl at Monmouth. Chastity wore a sexy nurse's outfit with a white pirate's eye patch. The eye patch had a red medical cross on it. With her long blonde hair, she was the spitting image of Daryl Hannah's female assassin in *Kill Bill*.

'Elle Driver from *Kill Bill*,' I said, nodding. 'She was a great villain.'

Chastity shrugged. 'I just wanted to be a hot nurse.'

Misty guided me through the party and I said hi and happy birthday to Verity. Verity frowned as she looked me up and down. She didn't get my costume at all.

At one point, I found myself standing alone at the edge of the rooftop looking out over Central Park. I could see my home, the San Remo, on the opposite side. The park itself was a rectangle of inky blackness edged by the lights of the city.

'Annie Wilkes,' a voice said from behind me, lisping on the *s*.

I turned.

Oz Collins stood before me in his evil clown costume. He was four inches taller than me. Despite his garish circus make-up, he looked at me with genuine earnestness.

I smiled. 'A few people at this party have guessed that I'm the chick from *Misery*—including your sister, Misty—but no-one has known her actual name till now. Props to you . . . Pennywise.'

His eyes widened with delight.

'You know my character's name?' he asked, shocked.

I shrugged bashfully. 'I'm a big Stephen King fan.'

'Me, too.' His eyes brightened. 'I own every single book he's written.'

I said, 'I have them arranged in order of publication on my bookshelf, including the Bachman books. Yup, King nerd.' I nodded at my hillbilly costume. '*Misery* is my favourite. And just to show how truly King-nerdy

I am, it's not Pennywise the Evil Clown, it's Pennywise the *Dancing* Clown.'

'That's right!' he said.

He stared at me in a strange way—made all the stranger by the fact that he was covered in clown make-up. It was a kind of dazed admiring awe. Apparently, identifying his character's name had scored me many brownie points.

He held that gaze a fraction too long and I began to feel uncomfortable. I recalled his sweet but awkward magic performance. I also remembered Jenny's comments about Oz Collins: heavy Ritalin dosage, porn searches on the Internet, military school over the summer.

Thankfully, at that moment, Bo came over in his dashing LAPD cop uniform, gripping two drinks in plastic cups.

'Mind if I steal this young lady from you, Mr Evil Clown?' he said politely to Oz.

Oz bowed his head shyly. 'Of course, of course,' he muttered, and my heart went out to him. What hope did a lisping sophomore dressed as a clown have against the Head Boy dressed as a motorcycle cop?

But I'd wanted to be alone with Bo since I'd arrived and the chance hadn't arisen till now so I jumped at it.

We eased over to an isolated corner of the rooftop.

'You arrived at exactly the right moment,' I said, extracting some of the hairpins from my hair. I also undid the top button of my hillbilly shirt in the vain hope it somehow made me sexier.

I sipped the drink Bo gave me, instantly tasting the alcohol in it but saying nothing about it.

'You look awesome,' he said.

'Liar.'

'Okay, how about: you picked a great movie villain and you look a lot like her,' he corrected himself.

'At least that's honest,' I said, smiling. 'I knew I should've come as Poison Ivy. We didn't do many movie-villain costume parties back in Memphis.'

Bo nodded. 'I was hoping to get some time alone with you—'

'Hey hey, party people!' Misty sprang between us, grinning broadly and spilling her own jacked-up diet soda.

Bo retreated instantly from me.

'Was my little brother getting weird on you?' Misty asked me.

'He's harmless, but yeah, a little weird.'

'Fucking creepoid loser,' she spat, glaring at Oz a short distance away. Misty may not have been drunk but she was definitely getting there. 'He and V's brother, Quincy, are always doing whacked-out shit. Verity's mom insisted that V invite them to the party, but they're so embarrassing. I mean, shit, an evil clown? Come on! I'll check his room later this week to make sure he hasn't put a photo of you on the wall to jerk off to.'

She turned to Bo. 'Why, hey there, Bo. Haven't had a chance to say hi.'

'Hi, Misty,' Bo said a little standoffishly and I sensed that in some way he'd been here before. *Did* they have a history? Or was he just uncomfortable in the face of her very forthright attentions? Or did he, like me, also detect her subtle possessiveness of him?

'Do you like my costume, Bo?' she asked, stroking her corseted waist sexily.

I glanced again at my own frumpy costume and once again cursed my literal interpretation of the dress code.

'Why, your majesty,' Bo said with a smile, 'of course I do. Queen Cersei is one of the best female villains of them all.'

Misty leaned in close to his ear, and whether it was the alcohol or just because I was so close, I heard it very clearly when she whispered a little too loudly, 'We could always go downstairs to V's room and play Cersei and Jaime . . .'

Bo leaned back uncomfortably, glanced worriedly at me and, as politely as he could, said, 'Thanks, Misty, but I think you might have had one too many "sodas". How about we all go join the birthday girl?'

It was a smooth transition and Misty seemed to take it in stride and in a few seconds we were safely ensconced within a larger group of Red, Verity, Hattie, Dane, Griff and Chastity.

'Safety in numbers,' Bo whispered to me.

I hid my smile, thrilled to know that it took more than a sexy costume to capture his attention.

At length, the party wound down, as even the best parties do, and the crowd thinned out until by about 2:30 a.m. all that remained were the members of the inner circle, which tonight included me.

Misty had sobered up a little by then but she was still energised.

'What do you say, boys and girls? Is it time for a run?' she said.

Verity threw a glance at me. So did Hattie and Griff. Bo waited for Misty to respond, saying nothing.

So did my brother, Red. I looked at him as innocently and incomprehensively as I could—as if to say, 'What does that mean?'—desperately not wanting to let on that I knew full well what a run was.

Misty smiled at me. 'It's okay. She's cool. You're cool, aren't you, Skye? I mean, you can keep a secret, can't you?'

INTO THE PARK

Within minutes, the nine of us were out of the Carlyle and striding/waltzing/spinning down Fifth Avenue at 2:45 in the morning, a gang of joyous teens dressed in our colourful villain costumes—although by this time a few of our outfits had been partially covered with track tops or anoraks, and high heels had been replaced with sneakers.

Misty, ever the ringleader, led the way in her sleek velvet dress, now overlaid with a white Moncler parka.

Hattie called, 'I'm too tired to run tonight. I'll meet you at the other end.'

'And I'm too drunk,' Griff said. 'I'll go with Hattie.'

I watched this exchange with a suitably perplexed look on my face, a look Misty noticed and seemed to enjoy.

'Here.' Misty tossed a keychain with some keys on it to Hattie. 'For the outer locks.'

Hattie caught the keys and then dived into an Uber with Griff, calling out the window, 'See you at the other end!' as the car peeled away.

'The other end?' I said to Bo.

'You'll understand soon,' was all he would say.

I glanced at Misty as we walked up Fifth Avenue, alongside the low stone fence that separated the street from Central Park.

'All will be revealed,' she said mysteriously as we crossed the 79th Street Transverse just short of the Met.

Then Misty veered abruptly, hurdling the stone fence and plunging into the darkened park.

It was all a blur to me as the group swept along in the shadow of the Met and arrived at the private conservancy garden, went down the hatch, climbed down some ladders and suddenly we were in the dirt-walled chamber that Red had told me about, the cave with the ancient stone doorway in it.

Red's description of the door hadn't done it justice.

It wasn't just scary. It was terrifying.

It looked ancient and cruel, like the mouth of a snarling snake.

It yawned wide, a perfectly square stone doorway in the otherwise rocky and uneven cavern. The only break in its symmetry was the squat black pyramid on the ground in its centre.

As Red had said, the chamber was lit by two tripod-mounted arc lights, powered by a generator. If anything, the harsh glare of the lights made the doorway look even more sinister.

Looking through the stone portal, I saw the tunnel beyond it, ominous, long and inky black.

I kept up my act. 'O-*kay*. So this is genuinely creepy. What is it? A Lenape tomb or something?'

'It's a tunnel,' Bo answered. 'I think it's Mayan. I did some research. It matches their stonework and there is evidence that the Mayans ventured as far north as Canada.'

In my mind, I loved that he'd analysed the place, thought about it, and then looked into it. He was inquisitive and I liked that about him.

But I didn't dare say it, not in front of everyone.

Instead, I just gave Bo some serious side-eye and said, 'Where does it go? Across the park?'

'All the way, yeah,' Bo said.

I indicated the ancient inscriptions carved into the lintel of the door. 'What about those? What do they mean?'

'No idea,' he said. 'I wish I knew.'

Misty stepped forward, unzipping her parka to reveal her necklace.

She unclipped the amber gem from it, held it up, and turned to face me.

'Now, Skye. This is our little secret. If you tell a single soul about it, we will *ruin your life*, okay? Ruin it. Never to be restored. Ever. Understood?'

I nodded quickly. I got the impression that what I had gone through in Memphis was nothing compared to the reputational vengeance Misty could unleash.

'Understood,' I said.

Then Misty reached down and placed her gem in the slot in the apex of the little pyramid, and the incandescent curtain of purple-black light that Red had so vividly described to me apparated into place in the mouth of the portal, evidently coming from the pyramid.

I didn't need to fake my astonishment anymore.

It was dazzling, hypnotic, mesmerising. It was chiefly purple and black, but there were other colours in there, too: wisps of violet and thin ribbons of green that slithered and twisted between the dominant patches of light.

I stared at it in awe for a full ten seconds.

'My *God* . . .'

'I'm not sure even He knows about this,' Misty said. 'Come on, let's take you on your virgin run.'

And without any further ado she jumped through the curtain of light and disappeared from view.

Red came up beside me.

'Pretty trippy, huh?' he said.

'That's one way of putting it.'

He took my hand. 'Here. Come with me. I'll take you through.'

And with those words, my twin brother led me toward the rippling screen of purple light filling the ancient doorway.

I gripped his hand tighter as we came near the barrier of light. Standing this close to it, I could see that it was made up of thousands of luminescent particles all swaying and swirling, spinning and curling. It reminded me of the northern lights, the Aurora Borealis, with its swaying ribbons of ethereal luminescence, only this aurora was trapped in a doorway.

I shut my eyes and, for some reason, held my breath as I jumped through the shimmering curtain of light.

VIRGIN RUN

It's funny how hearing about something is never the same as seeing it for yourself.

My mental image of the tunnel, taken from Red's description of it, had not even come close to describing it.

Yes, it was trapezoidal in shape, but it was only when I was standing inside it that I saw how dramatically its slanting walls closed in over my head, creating a very claustrophobic effect.

Red had mentioned carvings in the walls, but he hadn't mentioned that most of the carvings were of *skulls*.

Row upon row of crumbling stone skulls stared at me from the sloping walls, their mouths open in eternal screams.

Each skull, I saw, was unique. This wasn't mass-produced ancient skull-carving. This was precise stuff. Each skull had its own distinct characteristics: a narrow chin, larger eyes, broken teeth or a wider screaming mouth.

My skin crawled.

A few primitive paintings of running men were interspersed between the many skulls. In a few of those images, the running men appeared to be fleeing from large dogs of some kind.

In a few images, men dressed in priestly garments held coloured baubles or gems high above their heads: yellow gems, red gems and green gems.

Without warning, I was shoved roughly from behind and my face was pushed up against a particularly gruesome stone skull.

It was Verity.

'Not scared, are you, Memphis?' she said tartly, before hustling off down the tunnel.

Red just shook his head apologetically and followed after her, totally and utterly pussy-whipped.

'Pretty awesome, huh?' Bo said, coming alongside me.

'You can say that again.' I shivered. It was cold in here, too, really cold.

The tunnel stretched away from me in a dead-straight line, disappearing into darkness.

I turned to look at the curtain of light filling the portal behind me: seen from this side, it glowed a sickly off-yellow, like old stained glass, just as Red had said.

I reached out to touch it . . .

. . . and the wall of yellow light bent against my finger like a stretched piece of rubber, but it would not allow my finger to go through.

Bo appeared beside me. 'One-way traffic only,' he said.

Then Misty crouched and retrieved her gem from the pyramid and the curtain of light vanished. I beheld the entry cave again, only now it was eerily dark and everything in it was covered in dust. The two arc lights and the generator were caked in a long-undisturbed layer of grime and cobwebs, looking old and abandoned. Weird.

'This way,' Misty said as she headed off down the tunnel. 'We get out this way.'

Chastity, Dane, Verity and Red were already running ahead, using the flashlights on their phones to light the way.

I frowned at Bo.

He smiled. 'Come on. The tunnel is about half a mile long. The exit is at the other end.'

He grabbed my hand and I let him pull me down the dark passageway.

It's hard to describe how I felt.

I could see why Red had been so buzzed when he had first come here.

There was something monumentally exciting, thrilling, *exhilarating* about the whole experience—being inside this grim ancient structure with its skulls and cave paintings, cut off from the world, with only one direction to go. It felt dangerous, illicit, like we were trespassing on sacred ground.

I also had one extra feature to my first run that Red hadn't: I was doing it with Bo.

And with all that energy coursing through me, running was all I wanted to do, and gripping Bo's hand tightly, I ran with him.

About four hundred yards down the tunnel, we came to the trash heap Red had mentioned.

This time his description had been accurate.

It was an eight-foot-high pile of garbage, situated directly underneath a well hole in the ceiling. Given that the ceiling was about ten feet high, the pile almost reached it.

Bo and I arrived there to find Chastity, Dane, Red and Verity analysing some of the trash while Misty was crouched over by the left-hand wall, leaning in close to a collection of deeply-cut ancient carvings there.

As Bo and I approached the big rubbish heap, Misty stepped away from the wall and took some photos of the carvings with her phone, every flash strobing like a lightning bolt in the enclosed space.

Red said to her, 'Hey, Mis, do you think you should be doing that?'

Misty shrugged. 'Why not?'

'How about the screaming dude I saw up the well that time?' Red said. 'Someone up there could see.'

'Ooooh . . .' Misty cooed, mock scared.

My eyes were drawn to the trash heap and the well above it.

I saw the random bike wheels, McDonald's wrappers, old books, broken toys and torn clothing forming the layers of the heap.

And then I saw a toy at the edge of the pile, half-hidden by the other detritus.

My blood went cold.

There, looking particularly forlorn and abandoned, faded and dirty, was a fluffy pink kangaroo toy.

My fluffy pink kangaroo toy.

I saw the familiar name stitched across its stomach: HOPPY THE HAPPY KANGAROO.

What. The. Hell?

I checked to see if the others were watching me, to see if they were playing a joke on me, but they were busy chatting or examining the walls of the tunnel. None of them had seen my shock.

I bent down and touched my toy kangaroo, a unique toy purchased by my father in a trashy souvenir store in Australia six or seven years ago.

How on Earth had it got here? I wondered.

Then I saw something stuffed inside its pouch. I pulled it out: a yellow Post-It note. Written on it in messy handwriting were the words:

HE IS WAITING FOR YOU.

I dropped both the note and my kangaroo toy as if they were scalding hot.

Again I looked around myself, and again I saw that no-one was watching me.

My gaze drifted upward, to the well shaft in the ceiling.

Curiously and cautiously, I stepped onto the trash pile so that I could peer up the well shaft.

I saw the night-time sky, half blotted out by a dark round shadow . . . that abruptly moved.

It was a man, a bald man, his face a black shadow, peering down at me.

I leapt back out of sight, slipping and sliding down the unstable trash heap.

A demented cackle echoed down the well shaft.

'*Helloooo, pretty girl!*' he shrieked.

'Go!' Red said urgently.

Everyone bolted, racing away down the tunnel, running for all we were worth. I ran with them, forgetting all about the pink kangaroo I had dropped.

I don't recall much about our sprint through the second half of the tunnel, such was my panic. After running for about four hundred yards, I remember coming to the exit: another ancient stone doorway with another low pyramid. Beyond the stone doorway, I saw a second dust-covered miner's cave.

Misty inserted her gem into this pyramid and the portal filled with purple light, and staying close behind the others, I stepped through the curtain of light—

★ ★ ★

—to find Griff and Hattie waiting in the dirt-walled chamber.

I blinked. They certainly hadn't been in the cave only seconds before, and the cave was now completely devoid of dust.

What the hell . . .?

Even though we were underground, I could hear the distant noises of the night from above: sirens, a car horn.

No sooner were all of us out of the portal than Misty removed her yellow gem from the outer flank of the little pyramid and the curtain of light vanished. The tunnel stretched back into the distance behind me, silent, sombre and—somehow—not as dangerous with the light-barrier gone.

Misty came up to me, smiling. 'How about that for a rush?'

I nodded, breathless. I couldn't find the words to describe it.

Misty took advantage of my temporary muteness to reach forward with a marker and draw a single black line on my wrist.

'Welcome to the most exclusive club in New York, Skye,' she said.

AFTER

After emerging from a private garden attached to the American Museum of Natural History (on the *west* side of Central Park), we adjourned to Misty's place at the San Remo and hung out in her bedroom.

Misty's bedroom was actually two rooms, designed like a hotel suite: it had one room with a bed in it and another sitting room, with a lounge, TV, desk and bookcase. We gathered in the sitting room.

I was still processing the whole experience, which Misty and the others seemed to particularly enjoy.

'I think we blew your sister's mind,' Verity said to Red as she lay across his lap.

Bo smiled at me. 'I know what you're thinking. I know *everything* that you're thinking.'

'What . . . how . . . what is it?' I said. 'What is that light across the doorway? How can the entry and exit caves be normal one moment and then caked in dust the next?'

Misty said, 'We don't know. You put the gemstone in the pyramid, it opens the portal, and you step into another dimension or something. Then the second doorway at the other end of the tunnel brings you back to this dimension. But you can only go one way through each portal. They are both initiated by placing the gem in each portal's pyramid: one takes you there, the other brings you back.'

'Alternate dimensions?' I said.

'At least an alternate New York,' Griff said. 'A parallel New York.'

'I think it's another *time*,' Bo said. 'New York in another time: judging by the junk on that pile, I reckon it's the future.'

'It could be the past,' Hattie said.

'It could *alternate* between the past and the future . . .' Dane said. 'Every time we open the portal, it might be opening up randomly to a *different* time.'

'But what about the trash heap?' Bo pointed out. 'It only ever grows. It doesn't disappear or get smaller. Stuff only gets added to it. I don't think it's random.'

I recalled finding the well concealed in the thicket behind the Swedish Cottage. It was definitely here in our present-day New York.

'Seriously, we don't know what the hell it is,' Verity said, 'let alone *when* the hell it is. Except for that one time Bo shimmied up to the top of the well, looked around for a minute and saw the city in ruins, none of us has ever gone out into the world up there.'

'What about that bald man I saw up the well?' I said. 'The one who laughed at me.'

Bo shook his head. 'I don't know.'

'Have you seen him before?'

Hattie said, 'A couple of times. Sometimes he wears a hoodie. I call him Mr Insane.'

Misty said, 'We have no idea who he is, but he makes it a hell of a ride, doesn't he?'

I blinked hard, taking it all in.

'How did you discover it?' I asked.

'We didn't,' Misty said. 'It got passed down to us.'

'What do you mean?'

Misty held up her necklace, which now had its amber gem clipped back into its figure-eight centrepiece.

'A long time ago, my great-grandmother gave this necklace and another one just like it to my grandmother, who gave them to my mom when she turned fifteen. My mom still keeps one necklace with a similar gem in it herself, while she gave this one to Chastity and me. We share it.'

'Where did the gems come from?' I asked.

'You know about the Manhattan Purchase?'

'Of course.'

'Remember the coloured glass beads that the Indians took from the Dutch in exchange for the island? They weren't just any old beads and they sure weren't worth twenty-four bucks. Some say that the Dutch had *stolen* them from the Indians and were returning them. To get them back, the Indians offered the Dutch the entire island of Manhattan. In any case, those beads somehow made their way to the *Mayflower* settlers in New England: our ancestors. Two amber ones—these two gems—came to my family.'

Misty shrugged. 'Obviously, it's all pretty strange to begin with, but there are a couple of extra things about the portal that are super weird.

'First, it only works between December and April. Why? We don't know. And second, it won't allow anyone younger than fifteen or older than eighteen to pass through it. It *knows* how old you are. Once you turn eighteen, it won't let you pass. The light-barrier just won't let you through, in the same way it won't let you go back out through the entrance.'

Chastity said, 'Which is why the gems get passed down from generation to generation. After you turn eighteen, you can't enter the tunnel anymore. So my mom, like her mom before her—and *her* mom before her—ran between the ages of fifteen and eighteen. After that, she kept the gems and waited until she had children. When we were old enough, she brought us to the two private gardens and showed us how it worked.'

'Your family owns the two conservancy gardens?' I asked.

Misty stood up and went over to her bookshelf. 'Our family and a couple of other *Mayflower* families. Those gardens are held in a very old trust that predates the building of the park and which the Met and the Natural History Museum *wish* they could break open, but that ain't going to happen, not while I'm alive or while any of our future kids are.'

As she spoke, Misty pulled a fat hardback book from the bookshelf, a copy of Tolstoy's *War and Peace*.

I was wondering what she was doing—why grab a classic novel in the middle of a conversation?—when she opened the book and I saw that its pages had been hollowed out.

A rectangular void had been cut into the core of the book.

And suddenly Misty's choice of book became clear to me: *War and Peace* was long, so it was thick enough to conceal the necklace inside it.

Misty placed her figure-eight necklace inside the

book then snapped the book shut and placed it back on the shelf.

Misty smiled. 'It's a trick my mom taught me. Thieves always rifle through your drawers and they can open any safe these days. Mom told me about one rich guy who had a wall-safe: while he was away in the Bahamas, some thieves used a jackhammer to rip the whole thing out of the wall. It took them an entire day, but they did it. This is better. Seriously, there aren't many thieves out there who are going to check out *War and Peace* during a robbery, are there?'

'Good point,' I said.

'As my mom told me, you just have to pick a book that you hate enough to cut the middle out of,' Misty said.

Everyone laughed.

'You know, it's funny,' Chastity said sadly when the laughter had died down. 'I'm going to be eighteen in June, so these'll be my last runs. After that, the portal won't let me through. I have to admit, though, I'm sorta done with running. Over it. It's been fun but I'm happy to pass it on to you guys, the next generation, so to speak.'

She nodded solemnly to the group and they nodded back.

Red grimaced. 'Hey, in three weeks, the whole world might fizzle out, so we may as well enjoy ourselves.'

'Too true.' Misty turned to face me. 'I mean, whatever happens on March 17, you have to admit, this was a total rush.'

THE LAST DAYS OF FEBRUARY

I found it very hard to concentrate on anything the next week. My mind kept drifting back to the run, fixating on the tiny details.

The knee-high stone pyramid.

The rows of carved skulls.

The cave paintings of priests holding coloured gems and men running from dogs—or were they wolves?

The mysterious trash heap.

My pink kangaroo toy, Hoppy, with the note in her pouch: *HE IS WAITING FOR YOU.*

And, of course, the cackling bald figure at the top of the well who had called, 'Hello, pretty girl!'

He was the worst part of it.

He invaded my dreams.

Three times that week, I woke up shouting and breathless, gasping for air and drenched in sweat. His evil laugh echoed in my head.

St Patrick's Day was now only a month away and in some parts of the world edginess was beginning to show: there were protests in France (what they were protesting against, I didn't quite know; I was pretty sure the gamma cloud wasn't listening) and mass prayer events in Mecca, Jerusalem and Rome.

In the States, we did what we always did: repressed our darkest fears and kept buying shit. Apart from a spattering of more hate crimes and some news reports criticising the President and key members of Congress for their plan to hide in a secret underground facility during the gamma cloud ('I'm not doing it by choice,' the President said, 'I'm doing it for America.'), it was, at least for the moment, life and business as usual in America.

In my corner of New York City, that meant everyone was talking about the East Side Cotillion. It would take place on Saturday March 3 whether the world ended a couple of weeks later or not.

That meant a flurry of last-minute activity for Misty: final dress fittings, personal training sessions, lettuce-only meals, formal afternoon teas, rehearsals, two evening soirees and lots of gossip.

Misty had asked Bo to be her primary escort. Her other cavalier, she said, was 'some pleb boy from the military academy who I was forced to invite'. In any case, this had meant that Bo had to attend several of those pre-Cotillion events.

After the kiss I'd shared with him, I must admit I was a little jealous. And at school, in the presence of our friends—were they really my friends now?—Bo kept a careful distance from me.

No matter how hard I tried to justify it all in my mind (I mean, Misty had asked *him* to the Cotillion), and to not be 'that girl'—stupid, needy, and boy-dependent—I still felt a little hurt and confused.

In the end, I figured it was due to Misty. Bo knew of her crush on him—knew how possessive she could be—and didn't want to complicate things before the Cotillion. I gave him the benefit of the doubt, rationalising that he was keeping his distance so as not to make things difficult for *me* with Misty.

I hoped to see him at the Met again after school, if only to discuss the run on the weekend, but he was called away on Cotillion and Head Boy duties every afternoon that week.

I did, however, encounter one new individual.

Mrs Starley Collins, Misty and Chastity's—and Oz's—mother.

I literally bumped into her out the front of the San Remo one morning on my way to school—or more precisely, she bumped into me.

I was coming out the front doors of our building, heading to school on my own that day, when Mrs Collins, walking backwards and scanning the street for her limo, accidentally tripped into me.

She was, quite simply, the prototype for Chastity and Misty: blonde, blue-eyed, and for a woman in her early fifties, impressively fit and slim, almost as buff as my mother. In the early hours of each morning, the StairMasters of the San Remo must have been working overtime.

'I'm so sorry—' she blurted. 'Oh,' she cut herself off, recognising me. 'You're the new girl. Skye, right?'

'Yes, Mrs Collins,' I said. Of course, I'd seen her before but we had never spoken.

'Call me Starley, darling. I feel like an old woman when someone calls me Mrs Collins.' She leaned closer, smiling knowingly. 'Misty told me you've joined her *running club*.'

I returned the smile. 'Yes, ma'am. On the weekend.'

'They do run in a very interesting place, don't they?'

'They do,' I said, enjoying the cryptic nature of the conversation. Secret clubs will do that to you.

'Beats doing laps around the Reservoir with the peasants. I remember when I ran, way back when,' she said wistfully and a little too dramatically.

At that moment, her limo pulled up, the driver leaping to open the door. 'Well, I'm simply charmed to make your acquaintance, Skye. I have to go and join Misty at a fitting. The Cotillion is on Saturday and I want to make sure my Misty makes an impact.'

She slid into the limo and as the driver closed the door, I heard her say to him, 'You're fucking late, asshole. You were supposed to be here at eight.'

I checked my watch. It was 8:03 a.m.

On the Friday of that week—February 23—I left school on my own.

I ventured to the Met, pretty certain that Bo wouldn't be there, and sure enough he wasn't.

I sighed but sat down anyway near the Temple of Dendur and opened one of my books. I'd been reading for an hour or so when abruptly someone put their hands over my eyes from behind.

'Guess who?'

It was Bo.

I smiled broadly, every nerve inside me suddenly alive. 'I thought you'd have other things to do besides studying.'

'Not anymore. My evening function got cancelled. And I didn't come here to study.'

He opened his right hand to reveal Misty's necklace with the amber gem in it.

'I borrowed this from Misty. Wanna go for a run right now? Just the two of us?'

PRIVATE RUN

The sun was setting as Bo led me down the side of the Met and into the hidden conservancy garden near the Transverse.

Even in daylight, it was hard to get to. A fence and a dense cluster of bushes shrouded the garden from public view: you could walk past it every day and never know it was there. The sunken hatch at the farthest end of the private garden might as well have been a myth.

By any standard, it was a sublime time to be in Central Park: the leaves of the trees lit by the dying light of the sun. They shot movies here at this time of day. Romantic stuff.

I couldn't believe we were doing this.

Together. Just the two of us.

My heart thumped loudly inside my head. I was giddy at both the prospect of doing another run and doing it alone with Bo.

All those confused feelings I'd had about him keeping his distance from me in order to save me from Misty were washed away. He could have done this run with any of the runners—especially Misty—and he had chosen to do it with me.

Arriving in the underground entrance chamber—evidently he had also got the keys to all the locks from

Misty—Bo placed the gemstone on the low pyramid and the rippling curtain of light appeared.

'You ready?' he asked.

Even though I was still in my school uniform, he wore jeans, sneakers and a shell jacket. I noticed then that he also had a pack on his back.

'You bet,' I replied, looking from the backpack to his eyes.

Then we stepped through the light-barrier together.

SECOND RUN

Even though it was only my second time inside the tunnel, it felt like my third. I think I'd mentally appropriated Red's initial run as my own.

And this run was actually more of a walk. It was not the late-night scramble that my first one had been with the larger group.

After he removed the gem from the little pyramid and extinguished the curtain of light behind us, Bo lingered near the entrance and took photos of the ancient carvings and drawings.

'I'll share all these photos with you later,' he said. 'I want to look them up afterward. See if I can figure out what this place actually is.'

There it was again, that curiosity. It was one thing to run through here for cheap thrills but, like me, Bo wanted to know what it was we were actually running through.

He peered at the cave paintings of the priests holding their coloured gems and the young men running from the dogs.

'I've been thinking about these paintings. Did some more research,' he said. 'I don't know about the guys holding the jewels, but these images of the running men resemble paintings found in some Mayan ruins in Guatemala. Those paintings are thought to represent initiation ceremonies for young warriors: the would-be warriors had to outrun a pack of wolves through a narrow canyon or tunnel. I wonder if running through this tunnel—in another time, chased by wolves, with only one way in and one way out—was an initiation ritual of some kind. A test of nerves for teen boys. After all, only young people can enter it.'

'Not a bad theory.'

'I haven't even got started,' Bo said.

'What do you mean?'

'I want to see what's up there.'

'You want to go *outside*?' I said, alarmed.

'Don't you? Don't you want to know what's out there?'

I thought of the cackling bald man up there, but I had to admit, I did want to know.

I nodded silently.

We were still near the entrance portal. I looked back into the entry cave and saw the dust-covered ladder leading back up out of it.

'Do we go up that way?' I asked.

Bo shook his head. 'We can't. We checked it on one of our first runs. In this time or dimension, something heavy has been placed on top of the hatch up there. Dane, Griff and I couldn't get it open no matter how hard we pushed. It's the same with the hatch at the other end of the tunnel. We'll have to go out through the well hole.'

A short while later, we came to the trash heap under the well hole and I saw the full extent of Bo's preparation.

He extracted from his backpack a long nylon rope with knots along its length and a triple-pronged steel hook at one end: a grappling hook.

Bo straddled the top of the trash heap, his feet sliding awkwardly against the accumulated litter as he tried to get a stable footing, and then he began throwing the hook up into the well shaft.

It took five attempts—it wasn't an easy throw, even for an athlete like Bo, and every time the hook clattered loudly against the upper rim of the well and fell back, I thought of the bald man hearing it.

Then, with a soft *whack*, the hook caught hold of the rim and didn't fall back.

Bo tested it. It held his weight.

He looked at me with an excited smile. 'Let's go and see what's up there.'

He must have seen my hesitation, because right then he paused and stepped over to me. He held me close in his arms, leaned down and kissed me tenderly on the lips.

If our first kiss had been quick, spontaneous and uncertain, our second one was confident, assured and unhurried. Damn, it was good. I could definitely get used to kissing Bo Bradford.

After a pleasantly long time, we separated.

'It'll be fine,' he said. 'Trust me.'

Then he turned, grabbed the rope and began climbing it, hand over hand, gripping the knots along its length. Within moments, he had clambered up and out of the tunnel. I watched him go all the way up the well until I saw his feet disappear over the outside rim.

And suddenly I was wholly alone in the tunnel and I didn't like it.

It was almost as if I could hear ancient voices screaming.

I looked at the trash heap and noticed that Hoppy the Happy Kangaroo was still there.

I didn't want to stay there by myself, so I grabbed the first big knot on Bo's rope and hauled myself quickly up it.

If the tunnel was claustrophobic, the well was doubly so.

I only just fit inside it. The slick brick walls closed in tightly around me, with barely a few inches to spare on either side.

At length, I reached the top, where Bo was waiting with an outstretched arm and he pulled me up the last two feet.

I stepped out of the well and stood on solid ground beside him.

And then I looked up.

'Oh, God . . .' I breathed.

PART III

NEW YORK REBORN

Nothing is flat or solid. If you look closely enough at anything you'll find holes and wrinkles in it. It's a basic physical principle, and it even applies to time. Even something as smooth as a pool ball has tiny crevices, wrinkles and voids . . . There are tiny crevices, wrinkles and voids in time.

STEPHEN HAWKING

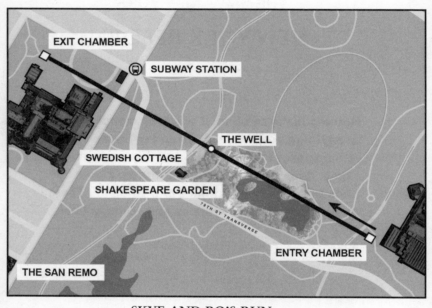

SKYE AND BO'S RUN

THE 'NEW' NEW YORK

We were standing in the same thicket of thornbushes that I had found a couple of weeks earlier . . .

. . . only now the bushes had been cut away, cleared, so that the well stood on a bare patch of open dirt about the size of three car spaces. That bare section of dirt was ringed by thick shrubbery beyond which I could see the outline of the Swedish Cottage.

An abandoned firepit—its embers long cold, its ashes grey—sat on the earth beside the well, as if someone had camped here. The bald guy, I guessed.

Central Park loomed around us.

As far as I could tell, it was exactly the same time of day in this alternate New York as it was in my real New York: a cool February evening, about 5:30 p.m., the edge of sunset.

If we were indeed stepping through a tear in the fabric of time, the days, it seemed, were overlaid on each other.

The same seemed to apply to the season. The weather felt the same and the trees had the same amount of leaves and snow on them as they did back home.

I raised my gaze westward.

Through the skeletal upper branches of the trees in that direction, I glimpsed the taller buildings on Central Park West, including my own home, the San Remo.

I froze.

Giant blood-red letters blazed out from the front flanks of both towers of the San Remo:

KiLL   **WE**
THE   **ROSE**
RiCH!   **UP!**

The letters were enormous, each one perhaps two storeys high, so that the two messages took up the entire front faces of the two towers.

(I couldn't be sure from this distance, but there appeared to be a figure hanging by the neck from one of the windows, too.)

Other buildings had been similarly vandalised.

FUCK THE 1%!
EVERYBODY DiES NOW
YOUR $$ COULDN'T SAVE YOU!

Bo took photos of them with his phone.

I turned slowly, taking it all in.

I was worried about the bald man, but the only sign of his presence were some large bootprints in the dirt by the firepit. He wasn't here, at least not right now.

Eerie silence surrounded us. Nothing moved in the trees.

It took me a moment to realise the really freaky part of it all.

There was no sound.

Nothing. None of the usual noises of the world's most famous metropolis. No honking car horns or wailing sirens: the signature soundscape of New York City.

This New York was deathly silent.

Looking more closely at the buildings overlooking the park, I saw that nearly every window of every building was shattered.

A multitude of vines, unchecked for who-knew-how-many years, snaked out of those windows, while green moss covered whole sides of skyscrapers.

It was like nature had overtaken New York.

'Let's go take a look,' Bo said, stepping away from the well.

I wanted to say, 'Are you kidding?' but I was curious, too, so I just said cautiously, 'Not too far.'

The first familiar thing we came to was the Swedish Cottage.

In this New York, however, the cottage was a ruin. Its roof had caved in. Its walls were bowed and twisted. Its windows were all broken.

It was the same with the Shakespeare Garden. In our world, the Shakespeare Garden was designed to look like an idyllic English country estate: rustic benches, flagstone paths, weeping willows and gorgeous flowerbeds, all of it meticulously maintained. Newlyweds would often get their photos taken there.

Not so here.

The Shakespeare Garden of this New York was overgrown with weeds, derelict in the extreme.

Its flowerbeds had been swamped by invading vines. Its broad walking paths had been so overwhelmed by sprouts and thistles rising up through the cracks that they were difficult to even see.

I frowned, confused and wary.

We ventured toward the western border of the park, crossing a bridge that spanned the 79th Street Transverse.

As we looked down into it, we saw that the Transverse was also overgrown with unchecked plant life. Noxious weeds and a million dandelion stems had risen up through the asphalt, cracking it, warping it and covering it.

I saw abandoned cars parked at odd angles on the sunken roadway, all but consumed by the high weeds.

And in them I saw . . .

. . . rotten skeletons.

I swallowed in horror. 'Oh, God.'

Many of the rotting figures, kind of hermetically sealed in their cars, still had some flesh and clothes on them. Their heads either lolled backwards with their mouths open or rested on their steering wheels as if they were taking a quick nap.

Bo saw them, too. 'Shit . . .'

I took in all the rampaging vegetation. I'd seen a documentary about this once: if mankind were to abruptly die out or disappear from the face of the Earth, it wouldn't take long for nature to reclaim our cities.

'This definitely looks like the future to me,' Bo said. 'New York in the future.'

So this was why he'd come. To settle the argument: was this the future, the past or some other dimension?

'Doesn't look like a very pleasant future,' I said, nodding up at the cruel graffiti on the towers of Central Park West.

The blood-red words practically spat their venom out at the world and for a second it occurred to me that maybe all those giant letters were written in actual blood.

'I don't think we should stray too far,' I said.

'It's okay. I just want to find . . .' Bo's voice trailed off as he eyed the landscape ahead of us. He was on a mission and I, it seemed, was merely tagging along.

We emerged from the park onto Central Park West.

Or what had once been Central Park West. The foliage of the park had grown fully across the wide boulevard and even up several floors of the buildings on the other side. Central Park West was now a cloverfield, a waist-high plain of grass dotted with ferns, spiky bushes and fescue grass.

And it was deserted.

Empty and eerie.

No movement, no sound.

In the soft glow of twilight, the once bustling main thoroughfare of the Upper West Side was silent. Abandoned cars lay strewn along its length, half-concealed by the unstoppable plant growth. Some of the vines and weeds had grown right *through* a few of the cars—and through the human skeletons in them.

But there was no movement.

Not a single sign of life.

What had happened here? I thought.

Directly across the street from us stood the Museum of Natural History.

Its imposing granite façade—with its four colossal columns and triumphal centre arch—lorded over the weed-strewn street. But it was not immune from the ravages of nature: moss and mould covered the lower half of its front face.

The giant statue of the museum's great patron, Theodore Roosevelt—sitting heroically astride his horse, flanked by a native American and an African American—still stood in front of the building, tall weeds climbing up its sides, but with one major difference.

Roosevelt's head had been cut off.

The cut was clean—the work of a blowtorch I guessed—and across the chest of his horse had been spray-painted the words:

ANOTHER RICH ASSHOLE!

And then Bo saw what he was searching for and he suddenly dashed northward up the street and, to my horror, descended into the subway station out in front of the Museum of Natural History, at the corner of 81st Street.

I raced after him and rushed down the stairs of the subway station.

I found Bo standing in near darkness a short distance from the base of the entry stairs in front of a shuttered newsstand, hammering away at its padlock with a length of pipe.

BANG!

BANG!

The newsstand, like the subway station around it, was covered in moss, mould and vines, as if this whole place had once been enveloped in tropical humidity. It looked like a rainforest.

Looking beyond the turnstiles and down some iron stairways, I saw the train platforms.

The concrete trenches containing the tracks were filled with water, right to the edge of the platform. Instead of train tracks, they were now underground rivers.

I'd also heard about this: every day, the city of New York pumped groundwater out of the subway system, about thirteen million gallons per day. If the power went out, no pumps. And no pumps meant the New York subway system became an underground river network.

BANG!

BANG!

The noise Bo was making worried me. It was shockingly loud in the silence of the empty city, and I was about to tell him to stop when he broke the padlock and yanked open the shutters.

He found what he was looking for instantly.

Two small stacks of newspapers, bundled tightly in shrink wrap: the *Post* and the *Times*.

'Newspapers,' I said, realising. 'Oh, that's smart, Bo.'

The shutters had kept most of the moisture out of the newsstand but it was the shrink wrap that had kept the newspapers intact.

Bo tore open the plastic and snatched up a copy of *The New York Post*. Our eyes zeroed in on the date of the newspaper:

MARCH 17, 2018

The date of the coming end of the world.

But in this New York . . .

. . . it had already come.

READING ABOUT THE COMING
END OF THE WORLD

The front page of *The New York Post* blared:

THE END OF MANKIND!

- GLOBAL CHAOS
- TOTAL POWER OUTAGES
- AS WORLD ENTERS GAMMA
  CLOUD, DEATH SPREADS
- AMERICA'S TURN NEXT . . .

SPECIAL FINAL EDITION
MARCH 17, 2018

As our planet entered the gamma cloud late last night (U.S. time) the first reports came in from around the world.

The loss of life worldwide has been catastrophic.

The major cities of Australia and Japan were hit first: Sydney, Melbourne, Tokyo and Osaka.

People just dropped dead where they stood—in the streets, in their homes, everywhere. Planes (of those airlines that chose to keep flying) simply fell out of the sky, some crashing into city centres and taking out buildings. At the same time, all electrical power began to fail.

In some cities, social media networks and closed-circuit cameras managed to operate for a brief period of time after the cloud hit, giving the rest of us a few minutes of footage of what occurred before those phones and cameras winked out.

We may have been better off not seeing it.

Survival rates are low, possibly as low as half of 1%.

Social upheaval has intensified. Fires have broken out. Gangs of survivors roam the streets, overwhelming supermarkets and looting homes.

With only twelve hours till our spinning planet exposes the United States to the gamma cloud, this will be the last ever edition of this newspaper and the editors sincerely wish you all Godspeed and good luck.

May God have mercy on us all.

'This is the future . . .' I breathed. 'We're in the future, but sometime *after* the world ended on March 17.'

'Yeah, but how long after?' Bo gazed at the rainforest-like ecosystem that had consumed the subway station. 'It would have taken years for all this to form.'

I tore open the other bundle and grabbed a copy of *The New York Times*. It was very thin, barely a dozen pages, and was also dated March 17, 2018. It too proclaimed itself to be a special edition.

America Collapses: Total breakdown of law and order across country

It didn't take long.

Once word began to spread on news sites and social media of what was happening in other parts of the world, society as we know it broke down completely in America.

The smattering of hate crimes and other incidents of social unrest that have marred the city for the last week—all of which began with the bloody siege at the University Club on March 9 and which escalated around March 14—turned into an outright society-wide breakdown yesterday.

The police disappeared from the streets and as they did, lawlessness took over.

The last civilised place on Earth

Being the last major country to plunge into the gamma cloud was always going to give America a front-row seat to the end of the world. What a terrifying sight it has been.

This quirk of fate has also, sadly, given us the better part of a day to prepare for our own demise.

Most Americans have spent time with their families, some have left their families, many have gathered in churches and synagogues to make peace with their gods, while, more disturbingly, many more have gone on rampages to settle old scores (we include the recent deliberate crashing of a passenger-filled airliner into the runway at Denver International Airport in this category).

Here in New York, the storming and vandalising of wealthy homes on the Upper East and West Sides of Manhattan—plus suburbs like Scarsdale, Rye and the Golden Triangle—that has appalled so many over the last three days continued. That much of the looting was done not just by the obviously poor, but by middle-class adults and teens, has laid bare the rage that was simmering beneath the surface of our society.

The lottery: Who lives and who dies?

As the effects of the gamma cloud washed like an unstoppable wave across Asia, word spread quickly on social media about who was surviving the invisible cloud of radiation and who wasn't, moments before the writers' accounts went eerily silent.

Short snippets of footage from closed-circuit security cameras—their hacked feeds watched anxiously from overseas—recorded bizarre scenes in streets, parks, prisons and hospitals.

A CCTV camera on a street in Melbourne, Australia, filmed a thousand-strong crowd of people gathered outside a church. One moment, they were all standing, the next all but one had collapsed to the ground. Ten seconds later, the camera itself went off.

And as the power went out in a westward wavelike progression, there came fewer images, posts or tweets.

Just silence.

The accounts and rumours of who has survived are varied.

In Nagasaki, Japan, an entire elementary school survived when practically no-one else in the rest of the city did. In the desperate rush to find out why, it was noted that the school provided meals to its students, meals comprised of locally-caught fresh raw fish.

In a hospital for the mentally ill in Mumbai, India, as their doctors collapsed around them, three-quarters of the patients survived.

The inmates of an entire wing of a maximum-security prison in the southern Chinese city of Guangzhou were said to have been unaffected by the gamma radiation. When their guards dropped dead, they escaped. This has also been reported as occurring in high-security prisons in Japan, Turkey and parts of Russia.

What is the common denominator?

Who are these lucky few to survive?

(Or are they really lucky? To find themselves living, essentially alone, in an empty shell of a world, its population slashed from seven billion to a bare couple of million?)

And does it matter? If eating raw fish will save you—or taking anti-psychotic medication—where will you get it now?

And could you eat or swallow enough of it in time to develop a resistance to the gamma radiation?

Thank you and the end

Today, this usually bustling newsroom is quiet.

Those of us who came to work—mainly the single ones who see this office as our home and our colleagues as our extended family, plus many printers and delivery workers—did so with the sole intention of producing one final edition of this grand old newspaper.

Some newsstands will receive this edition, others will not. It depends on whether your delivery person came in today. The company left it up to each of us to decide.

As the invisible wave of death and electromagnetic annihilation comes across Europe and the Atlantic Ocean toward the United States, we wish you well.

This is *The New York Times* editorial board, signing off.

May God have mercy on our souls.

Bo and I looked at each other.

'People went berserk in the final days,' I said. 'Riots, murders, the poor against the rich.'

'When you've got nothing to lose and no police to arrest you,' Bo said, 'all bets are off.'

My mind spun with myriad thoughts: the end of civilisation, social anarchy, and what would happen to my family during that chaos; a shortened future with Bo; and the simple mind-bending fact that *this hadn't happened yet*.

'Bo,' I said seriously. 'What do we do? Back in our New York, the real New York, it's February 23. It's *three weeks* before all this happens. What should we do?'

Bo shook his head. 'I don't kn—'

A strange sound cut through the air.

A call, like that of a hunter in the wild.

'Eeeeee-oh!'

It had come from outside.

'Did you hear that?' I said quickly.

Bo's eyes were wide. He sure had.

Then a return call came from inside the train tunnels: 'Ooooh-ee!'

'Someone's here . . .' I said.

'Go!' Bo hissed. 'Run! Back to the well! Now!'

We flew out of the subway station.

The Natural History Museum loomed behind us in the half-light of the early evening as we sprinted away from it, across the cloverfield that was now Central Park West.

We hurdled the low boundary wall of the park and landed on muddy ground amid some bushes. Bo gripped in his hands copies of the *Post* and the *Times*.

I risked a glance behind me.

I saw no movement, no pursuers—

And then I saw him.

A figure, a man, standing on the roof of the Natural History Museum, a silhouette against the darkening sky, staring straight down at us.

He stood dead still.

The hoodie he was wearing veiled his face in shadow, so I couldn't see his features. Was it the same man who had screamed at Red and who had cackled down the well at me?

I raced into the park with Bo.

We bounded over the bridge spanning the dandelion-covered 79th Street Transverse, raced past the Shakespeare Garden, and swept around the Swedish Cottage until finally we came to our well with Bo's grappling hook still clutching its rim and his rope dropping into it.

We weren't going to wait around to see if we had been followed.

I went first, sliding quickly down the knotted rope.

When I hit the bottom, Bo unhooked the grappling hook from the edge of the well, jammed it into his belt, and shimmied down the narrow shaft, hands and feet spread wide, pressed against the walls, until he dropped down onto the trash heap beside me.

'Don't stop!' he said. 'Keep running!'

We bolted down the second half of the tunnel, all four hundred yards of it, as fast as our legs could carry us, and my heart leapt with relief when I saw the exit portal up ahead.

I looked behind me as I ran, but I saw no pursuers.

We arrived at the exit portal, panting and breathless. Bo placed the gem in the small pyramid.

The curtain of light sprang to life across the ancient doorway and, together, Bo and I stepped through it—

—and emerged inside the exit chamber in our time.

Bo immediately reached down and yanked the yellow gem from the pyramid in the floor of the doorway and the rippling curtain of light vanished.

All that remained in its place was the empty doorway and the tunnel beyond.

I heaved for breath. Despite the cold, my Monmouth school uniform was damp with sweat.

Bo sucked in air as well, still gripping the newspapers in his hand. He grinned at the adrenaline of it all.

'That,' he gasped, 'was intense.'

I could only nod in agreement. 'Intense doesn't even begin to describe it.'

DEBRIEF AND DECISION

Of course, we couldn't wait to tell everyone about what we had seen.

The next night, Bo invited the whole gang to his place on the East Side and together we told them about our run: about the empty city and the overgrown park, the cloverfield that was Central Park West, the vandalised apartment buildings, the flooded subway station and the mysterious hunting calls.

And then, with a flourish, Bo pulled out the two newspapers describing the coming end of the world. He passed them around the room, their headlines blazing:

THE END OF MANKIND!

America Collapses: Total breakdown of law and order across country

'Jesus . . .' Verity said, reading the future edition of the *Times* with Red. 'This is horrible.'

'It's seriously messed up, is what it is,' Red agreed. 'An "outright society-wide breakdown" before the cloud comes.'

'The plebs started attacking the wealthy,' Hattie said, appalled. 'Honestly, why would they do that?'

Misty was reading the newspaper over Red's and Verity's shoulders, occasionally glancing across at Bo and me.

I detected resentment there: resentment that Bo and I might have gone off together and had a bonding experience.

She'd given Bo her gem but she clearly hadn't anticipated that he would take me along on his exploratory run.

Bo showed the others the photos on his phone of the outside world, of the San Remo defaced by the exclamations:

KILL   WE
THE   ROSE
RICH!   UP!

(His zoomed-in photos definitely showed a clothed figure hanging from a noose from one of the windows.) And the other buildings, also vandalised:

FUCK THE 1%!
EVERYBODY DIES NOW
YOUR $$ COULDN'T SAVE YOU!

Bo said, 'Our world is racing towards anarchy. The *Times* mentions riots and mayhem that start on March 14, riots and mayhem that target people like us. And then, as that professor predicted, the gamma cloud arrives and kills practically everybody on March 17. What should we do?'

'What *can* we do? Misty asked.

'I don't know, tell someone. Tell our parents.'

Misty gave Bo a look. 'My mom might get it because she knows about the tunnel, but what would everybody else say when we said: "Yeah, hi, we went to *the future* and saw what's going to happen." Good luck with that, Bo. We'd end up spending our last days on Earth in a mental asylum.'

She was definitely pissed at him.

Verity said, 'Maybe we can try to convince our families to go to the Retreat early.'

'Or maybe we can leave them to their fates and ride out the gamma cloud safely in the future,' Griff said with a grin. 'Just saying.'

Misty threw a couch pillow at him.

Griff kept grinning.

'Are you guys kidding?' he said. 'This is *so fucking awesome*! I gotta see this. We've all gotta see this. We've only ever run at night and then only inside the tunnel. I say we check this out in the full light of day. Let's all go for a run tomorrow afternoon.'

And so it was decided.

We would all meet at the conservancy garden behind the Met at 1:00 p.m. the next day, Sunday February 25, and run.

I returned home with Red.

As we walked across the park, he shook his head.

'So, let me get this straight,' he said. 'Our two portals and our tunnel would seem to be a bridge between two different times: now and the future, but a future sometime beyond the imminent end of humanity.'

'That's right,' I said. 'And *geographically*, the two versions of New York appear to be overlaid on each other.'

'What do you mean?'

'What I mean is, Bo and I didn't climb out of the well and pop up somewhere in China. We went under Central Park in our time and we emerged from a well in Central Park behind the Swedish Cottage in the other time. So the two New Yorks are overlaid on each other.'

'Right . . .' Red said.

'And on top of that,' I added, 'it would seem that, *temporally*, the two times are also overlaid.'

'Now you're just geeking out, Miss AP Physics,' Red said, smiling. 'Please explain for those of us who are not as academically gifted as you.'

I returned his smile. 'It's a time-travel thing. If it's 6:00 p.m. *here*, it's 6:00 p.m. *there*. Bo and I left here around sunset and when we emerged from the well it was sunset there. It also means that if you're inside that other world for an hour, then an hour passes here. The two times move forward together at the same rate.'

Walking parallel to the Transverse, we passed the Shakespeare Garden and the Swedish Cottage. Both looked as they always did, well tended and normal.

Red turned to face me as we walked. 'You say the whole of New York was overtaken by vegetation and weeds?'

'Yes. Roads like Central Park West and the Transverse were completely overgrown. The buildings, too. The moss and greenery had climbed up maybe ten storeys.'

'Hmm.' Red frowned.

'What are you thinking?'

'I'm wondering exactly how far into the future that alternate time is,' he said. 'For vegetation to grow ten storeys up city buildings would take some time, I think.'

He stopped suddenly.

And turned, his eyes narrowing.

'Come with me,' he said. 'I have an idea.'

We backtracked to a stand of oak trees a short way from the path.

Red scanned the area for onlookers. As he waited for two walkers to pass, he picked up a sharp rock from the ground.

Then when the walkers were gone, my brother started hacking like a maniac with the sharpened stone at the trunk of one of the oaks, gouging out a triangular chunk.

I was horrified.

Then, to my even greater horror, he discarded the stone and took out his Zippo lighter and started *burning* the newly created void in the oak's trunk.

I tried to stop him. 'What are you *doing*?!'

He put his body between me and the lighter.

'Chill, petal. I'm not going to burn it down. I just need to leave a visible wound.'

Wisps of smoke began to swirl from the trunk of the tree as the exposed bark began to burn.

I spun, sure that a passing cop would spot us trying to start a fire in Central Park. But we were alone.

Red managed the little fire, blowing on it gently. When he was satisfied with his bizarre act of arson, he spat on it, putting out the fire.

A sooty black splotch remained in the gouged-out section of the tree trunk.

'There,' Red said. 'Now we'll be able to tell roughly how far into the future our Future New York really is.'

I frowned at him once again, and then I got it.

'Very clever, brother dearest,' I said. 'Tree rings.'

'Exactly,' he said. 'I may not be as book-smart as you are, Blue, but I have my moments. Now, during tomorrow's run, all will be revealed.'

RUNNERS ASSEMBLE

It was a bright and sunny New York day when we all gathered at the conservancy garden behind the Metropolitan Museum of Art the following afternoon.

We went down into the cavern.

I wore hiking shoes and cargo pants and had brought a backpack with some water, snacks and a small first-aid kit in it. Having seen the world we were venturing into, I wanted to be prepared.

Red had brought a rucksack, inside of which was a bottle of water, some protein bars and a small hacksaw.

Misty, Chastity, Verity and Hattie all wore athletic clothing: yoga pants, sneakers and track tops. Misty's sneakers were thousand-dollar Golden Gooses. Verity's were Saint Laurent. Hattie's tracksuit was a black Lululemon one with gold piping and a shiny gold collar. Misty and Verity had also brought along small handheld SABRE stun guns, while Chastity had some pepper spray.

Dane and Griff also carried packs with water and food in them, and Bo had brought his grappling hook and rope.

Red checked his watch. 'Time is 1:02 p.m., local time.'

Misty inserted her gem into the pyramid and the rippling light appeared.

'All right, funsters. Time to rock and roll.'

And with those words, packed and ready for an extended run, one by one, the nine of us entered the portal.

A RUN IN BROAD DAYLIGHT

We made quick progress through the tunnel.

This was no carefree late-night sprint. This was an exploratory mission.

We came to the trash heap and Bo hurled his grappling hook up into the well shaft. It caught on the second throw and we all climbed up its knotted length.

Dane and Griff went first.

I followed behind them.

When I emerged from the well in the other New York, I immediately noticed that while the time of day was the same, the weather wasn't. Whereas back in regular New York it was sunny and bright, here the sky was filled with dark storm clouds and a light rain fell.

When the whole group had emerged from the well and gawped at the vandalised buildings visible through the trees, we made our way out of the thicket and past the ruins of the Swedish Cottage.

When we came to the Transverse, Red hurried to the oak tree he had burned yesterday and pulled out his hacksaw.

'What are you doing?' Misty said.

I joined Red as he sawed away at the oak and extracted a flat chunk of wood from it.

'Figuring out just how far in the future we are,' Red said.

I peered at the flat chunk of tree trunk in Red's hand.

It was about the size of a slice of pizza. He had cut it out of the trunk right at the spot he had burned.

Tree rings ran in fine curving arcs along the chunk's flat surface . . . until they reached an ugly black distortion. At that point, they bent markedly to divert around it.

'That's the part I burned,' Red said, pointing at the distortion.

He counted the rings outside the burn mark.

'Twenty-two,' he said, looking up.

'So this is twenty-two years in the future?' Hattie said.

'The year 2040?' Bo said.

'Give or take, yes,' Red replied. 'Tree rings aren't perfect, but these rings are pretty well defined.'

Misty stepped forward. 'So where do we want to go, people?'

Verity said, 'I want to see my old apartment on the East Side.'

Griff grinned. 'I want to check out the school.'

Misty looked to Bo.

He shrugged. 'We went west last time. Happy to go east this time.'

'Then let's go,' Misty said and away we went, our packs on our backs, into the overgrown park.

We were halfway across Central Park when Hattie stopped suddenly and looked up, scanning the sky.

'You hear that?' she said.

'Hear what?' Verity asked.

'I don't hear anything,' Griff said.

'That's the problem,' Hattie said. 'No birdsong, no chittering of squirrels. No animal noises.'

She was right. The park was eerily silent and in the middle of the day, it shouldn't have been.

I searched the trees for movement—for squirrels or birds or anything—but saw nothing, no movement at all.

Then suddenly a lone bird shot across the sky, a seagull, squawking loudly.

But it was the only animal we saw.

I found myself scanning the area for the one living thing that I knew for a fact was out there, the bald man, but he was nowhere to be seen.

I said, 'I don't think the gamma cloud cares what species you are; so long as there's electricity in your brain, it'll kill you. The survival percentages for birds and mammals—squirrels, raccoons, rats—are probably similar to those for humans: less than 1%.'

We pushed on.

Since we were heading east through the park, we decided to stop at the conservancy garden behind the Met—the one that contained the entrance cave—to see why we couldn't get out through it in this time.

We all frowned when we got there.

A taxi cab—a classic New York yellow cab—lay slumped over the hatch in the garden.

The car was shot through with weeds and ivy. It had clearly been there a long time. Behind the cab, the conservancy garden's gate and fence had been destroyed, evidently flattened when the cab had crashed through it. The broken fence was also covered by many years' worth of plant growth.

No wonder Bo and the others hadn't been able to get out through the hatch.

'Someone crashed a *cab* into the garden?' Verity said. 'How random.'

Bo lay on the ground to examine the derelict cab more closely.

After a few moments he said from somewhere down among the weeds: 'It wasn't random.'

He rose to his knees and looked at us all. 'The tyres have been punctured. Each has been stabbed with a knife, to make sure the cab sits right down on its belly and presses down on the hatch. Someone did this deliberately.'

Disturbed but undeterred, we went to the Carlyle next to check out Verity's apartment. We also went for another reason: to see the city from the building's roof.

As we came to the eastern side of the park and emerged onto Fifth Avenue, it quickly became clear that the Upper East Side had fared no better than the Upper West Side.

Fifth Avenue looked like Central Park West had: it was now a field of waist-high grass that stretched away to the north and south.

And the mansions and buildings here had been defaced, too.

To the north, I saw the Met. It had been trashed. Most of its many windows were shattered. Priceless statues that had once stood inside it now lay out in the street, consumed by weeds and vines.

The nine of us fanned out as we stepped across the grassy thoroughfare.

Looking down the grand old avenue to the south was like looking at a pair of railway tracks receding to the horizon: the buildings on either side of the street stretched away into the distance, gradually converging.

Halfway along it, however, I saw a very strange thing.

The Empire State Building stood at an extreme angle, slanting dramatically out over Fifth Avenue like a supersized version of the Leaning Tower of Pisa.

'The water in the subway system must be causing rust and subsidence,' Bo said. 'The ground around the Empire State is subsiding. It'll fall eventually.'

I stared at the tilted skyscraper. It was a fitting metaphor. Here was the ultimate symbol of New York City, a steel-and-stone behemoth that testified to the city's force of will, its in-your-face bravado, its corporate might, and now it was a half-fallen shell, empty and broken.

We arrived at the Carlyle building.

Since the power was out, the elevators didn't work, so we schlepped up the fire stairs, all thirty-five floors of them.

At length, we came to the roof, the scene of Verity's birthday party nine days earlier (or twenty-two years and nine days earlier).

The rooftop terrace looked awful. It was covered in a slippery carpet of greenish-black mould. The smell was revolting. Sprouts had grown from nearly every seam in the floor.

But it was the view from up here that seized our collective attention.

We all stared dazedly out at the panorama of New York City.

Almost every building was damaged. They either had their windows smashed or showed evidence of fire damage. Black charring scarred many of them.

Some, like the Empire State, teetered at precarious angles. Others had completely fallen. Quite a few had mossy growth high up on their summits, like here at the Carlyle.

Against the grim grey sky, it all looked haunting, eerie.

In perhaps a dozen places—on a few rooftops and on the ground at the northern end of the park—small fires burned, sending up wispy columns of smoke. It was the only movement in the otherwise empty city.

'Fires?' I said to Red apprehensively. 'Who's lighting them?'

Red grimaced. 'Survivors? Or maybe lightning strikes?'

Misty pointed southward at The Plaza Hotel, with its distinctive Parisian roof. All the windows on its upper floors were shattered. A fire burned in one smashed-open room up there.

There was graffiti on the front face of it, like on the San Remo:

GOD
CAME
HERE

'Hey, Griff,' Misty said wryly, 'I don't think they're serving high tea at The Plaza anymore.'

I looked at the once grand old hotel, remembering the afternoon tea I'd had there with Misty and Griff.

Red shook his head. 'You don't get runaway plant growth so high up without a *lot* of rain. After the gamma cloud killed everyone, the city must've been hit by some hurricanes or superstorms like Sandy. I mean, look at the park, it's gone wild.'

That was an understatement.

Below us, Central Park looked like a veritable jungle.

Its various twisting drives and transverses had been completely reclaimed by nature. The forest in the park had started to consume the Met—like a snake slowly trying to eat a large animal, it had crept up the entire western side of the enormous museum. Within a few years, it would encase the whole thing.

'I don't believe it,' Hattie said. 'The whole city. I just don't believe it.'

We descended as a group to Verity's apartment.

I lingered at the back, hesitant.

'You okay?' Bo asked, dropping back to join me.

'We don't know what we're going to find in there,' I said.

'If you're thinking about dead bodies, I wouldn't worry,' he said. 'I think everyone here has a spot reserved for them at the Retreat. Knowing what we know, there's no way any of us would've stayed.'

The front door to Verity's apartment had been forced open. Wind whistled in through a bank of smashed windows.

The place had been ransacked. The couches had been slashed, spraying goose feathers everywhere. The TV had been tossed, its screen cracked. Potted plants were shrivelled, dead.

Cautious yet curious, Verity went into her old bedroom . . .

. . . and froze. She stopped so suddenly, Hattie almost bumped into her.

'What—?' Verity breathed.

I looked past them and saw Verity's bedroom.

It had been ransacked as well—all the drawers hurled open, the mattress thrown off the bed, the posters ripped off the walls.

But it was the writing scrawled on the wall that seized our attention. It was written in thick black marker:

VERITY,
   WE DON'T KNOW WHERE YOU ARE.
   WE HAD TO GO.
   THE POOR STARTED ATTACKING THE
BUILDING.
   WE HAVE GONE TO THE RETREAT.
FIND US THERE.
   WE'RE SO SORRY.
   LOVE,
   MOM & DAD

I looked from the desperate scrawl on the wall to Verity's shocked face and I saw the confusion in her eyes.

Was this her future?

One in which she was separated from her parents during the coming anarchy back in our time? One in which her parents fled from the city to the Plum Island Retreat without her?

Verity blinked, trying, it seemed to me, to absorb the enormity of what she was seeing. And she was seriously struggling. This didn't fit into any of her usual categories of cool, lame or embarrassing. This existed in a category all of its own and it looked like her simple mind had seized up trying to process it.

I had feared finding dead bodies, but as I watched Verity practically shut down before my eyes, I thought that maybe this was worse.

'You shouldn't know this,' I said. 'We shouldn't have come here.'

SCHOOL

After they saw the scrawl in Verity's bedroom, a grim silence descended on the group.

Red put his hand gently on Verity's shoulder. Dane whispered, 'That is not cool.' Bo shook his head. Misty and Chastity said nothing. And Griff just shrugged. Either way, nobody wanted to linger in the apartment.

We returned to Fifth Avenue and, now led by Griff, we headed toward The Monmouth School a couple of blocks north. Alone among the group, Griff still seemed in high spirits, enjoying the grim adventure.

I turned to Bo as we strode up Fifth. 'Any ideas about what to expect at the school?'

He shook his head, his lips tight. The message scrawled on the wall at Verity's had rattled him. 'No.'

We arrived at our old school.

Monmouth's once proud front doors were splintered and broken, smashed in, I guessed, by an angry mob.

'Guys,' I said. 'We've been in this world for about two hours. We should leave enough time to get back to the tunnel before it gets dark. I don't want to stay too much longer.'

Griff wasn't having any of that.

He practically ran inside.

He darted into the administration wing on the ground floor and marched straight toward Ms Blackman's office at the end of a short hall. The door to her office—a brass plaque on it read *MS C. BLACKMAN – HEADMISTRESS*—swung askew on its hinges.

Griff hurried toward it. 'I want to find out what happened to that bitch—'

He kicked open the door and rushed inside, only to stop dead, much like Verity had in her bedroom.

Red, Bo and I caught up, and our mouths opened in horror.

'Oh, crap . . .' Red gasped.

'Whoa,' I whispered.

Bo covered his mouth, gagging.

A heavily decomposed skeleton lay slumped behind the wide mahogany desk, still seated in its high-backed chair. That it was Ms Blackman, there was no doubt: she still wore her severe black skirt-suit with white lace collar.

The office itself was oddly clean. Being on the ground floor, it had wire-reinforced windows and they were still intact. They had protected the office from the elements and whatever few animals had survived the gamma cloud.

Ms Blackman's mouth was open in a soundless scream.

The top rear quarter of her skull had been blown out. A star-shaped blood splatter covered the wall directly behind her, desecrating her diplomas from Amherst and Dartmouth.

A note sat on her desk, held in place by a paperweight from the New York Opera. I recognised her perfect hand-writing immediately.

I read it without touching it:

> *Oh, cruel world.*
> *For some reason that I cannot discern, I was one of the few to survive our planet's passage through the cloud.*

I wish I hadn't.

There is no God. No loving God could unleash such violent wickedness on His followers.

It is better that I end my life now, on my terms, rather than face the monstrous souls now roaming this city of the dead.

And then she'd blown her brains out.

I shook my head. Even in her final moments, Ms Blackman had retained her effortless snobbishness: *Oh, cruel world.*

I gazed at her skeleton, lying limply in the chair.

Red said, 'She survived the gamma cloud only to kill herself. And who are the "monstrous souls" now roaming the city?'

'This is like a bad dream,' I said softly.

Griff snorted. 'Screw that. She got what she deserved, the stuck-up bitch. I hated her.' He stomped out.

I turned to Bo and Red. 'I'd really like to go now.'

'Good idea,' Bo said.

'I agree,' Red said.

We left the office.

Walking back down the hallway, we found Hattie and Misty in the office of Ms Vandermeer, the school counsellor. They were, bizarrely, laughing.

'What are you doing?' I asked.

They were sitting at Ms Vandermeer's desk, under her *COOL KIDS DON'T SMOKE* poster, reading something.

It was then that I saw what they were reading: a student's confidential file.

A bolt of fear shot through me at the thought of my own file—the one Ms Vandermeer herself had shown me—containing evidence regarding the scar on my left wrist and my ostracism back in Memphis.

Hattie held up the file. 'OMG. I didn't know Jenny Johnson's parents were *divorcing*. Look here: just before the gamma cloud came, Jenny's mom cheated on her darling dad with Chad the tennis pro at the racquet club. It broke her dad's heart and that tore Jenny apart. She opened up to Ms Vandermeer about the whole thing.'

Misty held up another sheet from the file. 'You should see Jenny's In-Case-of-Emergency medical file. One suicide attempt and she's been on Xanax for the last six months. Poor little Jenny-wenny is depressed.'

I stared at them in open-mouthed disbelief. 'You're reading the confidential files of the other girls?'

Hattie shrugged carelessly.

'Why not?' she said. 'Jenny's world is going to end in three weeks anyway. What's a little more needling from us gonna hurt?'

She offered Misty a high-five and they smacked hands gleefully.

'We're going back to the tunnel.' I turned on my heel and left.

We made good time heading back through the park to the well.

I stared forward as I walked, trying to make sense of what I'd seen: from the destroyed city to Verity's room, to Ms Blackman's fate and to Hattie and Misty's casual callousness.

I thought about people who wished they knew the future and what it had in store for them.

Maybe knowing the future wasn't such a good thing.

PART IV

THE LAST DAYS OF NEW YORK

It is your thoughts and acts of the moment that create your future. The outline of your future path already exists, for you created its pattern by your past.

SAI BABA
INDIAN SPIRITUAL MASTER

A FOLD IN TIME

The next week went by quickly.

I saw Ms Blackman roaming the corridors at school—ever prim, ever proper, in her black dress-suit and lace collar—and when she nodded politely at me, all I could see were flashes of her skeleton with the skull blasted open at the back.

I studied with Jenny in a free period. A few times I caught her staring off into the space, her mind far away, her eyes filling with tears.

'You okay?' I asked.

She blinked back the tears and smiled tightly at me. 'Sure, I'm fine. Sorry, where were we again?'

'What's wrong?'

'Oh, it's . . . my dad,' she said. 'He's going through a . . . a tough time with my mom.'

But the next day Hattie and Misty stopped her as she walked into the common room.

'Hey, Jenny,' Hattie said. 'I want to work on my tennis game. I hear Chad, that cute young pro at the racquet club, is excellent. I'm told he gives, like, *really* personal attention. Like he *gave it to* your mom.'

Jenny's face fell at the realisation: *somehow they knew about her mother's affair.*

I was standing a short distance away over by the

coffee machine. This was so wrong. Should I say something? Should I step in?

But then memories of my time in Memphis flashed through my mind—the disastrous result of standing up for someone—and I felt the pain of those horrible months anew. I also wondered what I *could* say. Worse, if I did intervene, what if they implicated me in their ill-gotten knowledge?

In the end, it didn't matter, for as I stood there paralysed, dumbly silent, Jenny hurried out of the common room.

I also saw Verity's parents: the ones who would abandon her and flee to Plum Island during the mayhem. They picked her up after school one afternoon, all kisses, smiles and hugs.

It was like I was walking through a ghost world: I knew what was coming, what was going to happen in a few short weeks. Homework, a neat school uniform, Facebook, Snapchat, the East Side Cotillion: they all suddenly seemed completely meaningless.

I thought of calling my dad down in the asylum in Memphis, but Misty's words echoed in my mind: what could I say? That I had seen the future? Not even my father would believe that.

The curse of knowing the future.

Red saw it one evening in the look on my face and he placed a calming hand on my shoulder.

'I know how you're feeling, sis. But, hey, it could be worse. You could be Verity.'

This was true. Her future contained a frightening un-known: her own disappearance. Now that was a mindfuck.

Red was right. It could indeed be worse.

★ ★ ★

Red and I also discussed the tunnel and the other New York.

As was my way, during that week, I had gone to the Public Library to read up on the concept of time.

I searched Google and read a bunch of books on the subject, including a few chapters of Stephen Hawking's *A Brief History of Time*. One quote from that book lingered in my mind: *Why do we remember the past but not the future?*

Guess what, Professor Hawking? I can remember the future.

Anyway, late one night, as we sat together in Red's room, I held up a book I'd borrowed from the library.

'So, I found this,' I said. 'It's called *The Time Mechanic: A Physicist's Guide to Time Travel*. It's by some multiple-PhD genius from Caltech named Dr Kevin Maguire and it's all about concepts of time.'

'Okay . . .' Red said.

'What this guy says is that time is unique in all of physics. It only ever moves forward, never back, and it's *always* happening. The Earth could stop spinning, the sun could explode, but time will always go on.'

'That's deep, sis, even for you,' Red said.

I smiled. 'Smart-ass. But he also mentions weird phenomena, like déjà vu in dreams. Have you ever had a dream and then, a few weeks or months in the future, what happened in the dream happened in real life?'

'Sure, I have. Everyone experiences that. It's weird. It's also entirely unprovable. You never quite know if you really dreamt it or not.'

'Right,' I said. 'But this guy suggests that it *can* be explained, if you think about time in a weird way.'

'Go on.'

'All right, so time is always moving forward, right?'

'Right.'

'Only we tend to think of time as moving forward in *a straight line*.'

'We do,' Red said.

'Well, don't. Don't think that,' I said. 'Instead, think of it as moving in a *spiral*, an upward spiral.'

I flipped open the book and found a page depicting a flat spiral: it looked like the up ramp in a parking lot.

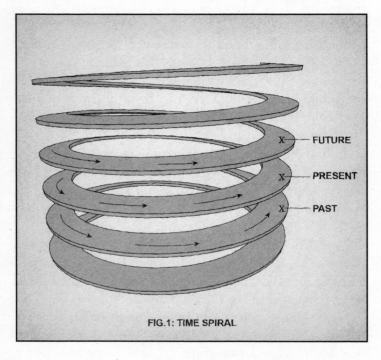

FIG.1: TIME SPIRAL

'This is time,' I explained. 'The lower layers are the past, the upper ones are the future. And time is always moving, up and up, round and round, ascending the spiral in these parallel layers. But'—I held up a finger—'occasionally, randomly, the layers sag or fold.'

I turned the page to reveal a second drawing, this one with an upper layer that sagged down into the one below it.

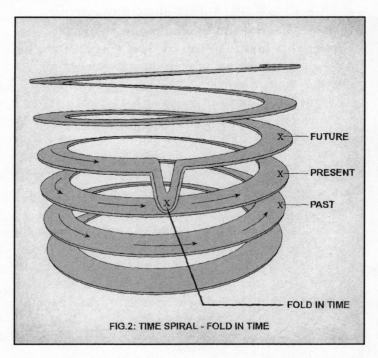

FIG.2: TIME SPIRAL - FOLD IN TIME

'This dip,' I said, 'is a fold in time. Now, a fold like this can be super tiny, like on the quantum level: this is what the author thinks happens when we experience déjà vu. As we sleep, we pass through a tiny fold in time and glimpse the future.

'*Larger* folds in time, however, allow for much more.

'This, I think, is what our tunnel is,' I said proudly. 'Its two doors, when each is opened by a gem, give access to and from a section of the future that folds down into our present, allowing us to move between the two times.'

'You're saying the future—a time roughly twenty years from now—has folded down into our present?' Red said. 'And the portals allow us to access it?'

'Exactly!' I said. 'On top of that, it seems that the fold itself is moving along with the passage of time.'

'Whoa, wait, what?'

'Let me put it another way: *the fold itself is moving up the spiral of time*,' I said. 'It's like what we were talking about the other day when we discussed how our New York and the future New York appear to be overlaid temporally: if we're in there for an hour, an hour passes here. Likewise, if we stay here for a day, a day passes there.'

'Okay,' Red said. 'How about this: can we *change* the future? You know, like they do in the movies?'

I nodded at the book by the Caltech guy. 'Dr Maguire says no. If we could change the future, he says, that would mean that there are *multiple* futures and Maguire thinks that's not the case.

'He maintains that there is only *one* timeline of history. If, by virtue of a fold in time, you got to glimpse the future, he says you would be glimpsing *the one and only future*, the future that is going to happen no matter what. Maguire doesn't believe in changeable futures and he thinks multiverses are horseshit. So, no, we can't change the future. It's set, at least according to him.'

'All right, last question,' Red said. 'The portals only allow people of a certain *age* to pass through them. How do you and your genius buddy explain that?'

I held out my hands. 'Come on, give a girl a break. Have I not *opened your mind* here? I don't know why the tunnel has an age–limit. Or why it only works in the winter months. You're gonna have to find a Time Lord like Dr Who to answer that, if, of course, the world doesn't end first.'

'Yeah,' Red said gloomily.

As it turned out, the rest of New York City was less perturbed by the impending end of the world than we were. Despite the scientists now appearing almost daily on TV, the late-night hosts were openly mocking the coming cataclysm and most regular folk just carried on with their lives.

This included the elite of Manhattan society. They had lunches to host, parties to attend and most of all, that Saturday night, March 3, they had the East Side Cotillion to stage.

THE COTILLION

As the morning of Saturday, March the 3rd dawned, I was contemplating a quiet night at home. After our group run the previous weekend, I was still feeling keyed up and needed to decompress a little.

As it happened, the day before, Red had come down with a nasty virus which had mutated into full-blown Man Flu. An evening on the couch eating popcorn, sipping tea, and watching something on Netflix sounded like just the ticket for both of us.

But then came the call at eleven in the morning from Last Minute Staff and Events asking if I could work that night at triple-time rates from seven till eleven.

On any other Saturday, I would have done it just for the money—hey, it was *triple*-time pay rates—but on this occasion I said yes just so I could see Jenny. I still felt bad about not standing up for her in the common room and, if nothing else, I wanted to make sure she was okay. Besides, what use was triple-time money in a world that would end soon anyway?

And so I left Red on the couch, coughing and sniffing and feeling sorry for himself, and went to work.

It wasn't until I met Jenny—also dressed in black trousers, black vest and white shirt—at the back entrance to The Plaza Hotel that evening that the thought dawned on me: just what event were we working at? What event could require extra servers at such late notice and be prepared to pay such exorbitant rates for them?

Of course, Jenny knew and she thought it was hilarious.

She grinned. 'That's right, Cinderella. You're going to the ball, only you're not going with Prince Charming, in a beautiful gown and glass slippers. You're going as the hired help!'

And that was how I ended up attending the East Side Cotillion, the most exclusive debutante ball in America: as a waitress.

The Plaza's upper ballroom, already an amazing space with panoramic views of Central Park, had been dressed up to the max: a forest of orchids, state flags and dining tables ringed a broad dance floor.

The elite of New York society sipped Dom while they chatted—distinguished-looking men in tuxes, hand-some women in designer dresses and diamonds, and, of course, the thirty debutantes in their virginal white gowns, gripping bouquets of pink and red roses, and hanging off the arms of their cavaliers.

It was, I must admit, every girl's dream.

Jenny hadn't been far off the truth: this was the modern world's version of Cinderella's ball. For one night, every one of those girls was a princess and the focus of society's undivided attention.

I glimpsed Misty conversing amiably with the mayor, her white-gloved arm linked through Bo's elbow. Her hair had been professionally curled and her make-up was perfect. She looked great.

Around her neck, beautifully complementing her dress, was her figure-eight necklace with the amber gem embedded in it.

Her mother hovered nearby, happily accepting compliments about her daughter. Starley Collins wore a glimmering gold dress that hugged her slim, aerobicised physique perfectly. Her diamond earrings glittered.

Then I noticed her necklace.

Mrs Collins was wearing a necklace that was identical to Misty's: a figure-eight-shaped pendant also with a yellow gem in it.

The second gem.

I was pleased to discover that my assigned area of the ballroom did not include Misty's table. It didn't feel right to be serving drinks to my schoolmate.

And so I glided through the pre-dinner crowd with a tray of champagne flutes, quietly taking people's finished drinks and offering them new ones, happily earning my triple-time rates, until the moment I emerged from the bar area with my tray reloaded and I found the way blocked by Misty and her mother.

'Skye!' Misty exclaimed, hugging me. I can't imagine how it looked: me in my plain black-and-white waitress clothing and her in her extravagant white dress, embracing. 'I thought it was you! How *embarrassing* for you to see me like this.'

I wasn't so sure she felt it was *she* who should be embarrassed.

She indicated her mother. 'I don't know if you've met my mom, Starley Collins. Mom, this is Skye Rogers, Todd Allen's stepdaughter.'

'Why, of course we've met!' Mrs Collins exclaimed. 'At the building.'

Her gaze wandered over my shoulder, searching for someone more important to talk to.

I didn't mind. I took the opportunity to examine her neckpiece up close. It appeared to be exactly the same as Misty's.

When she finally turned her full gaze back to me, Mrs Collins caught me looking at her necklace and she smiled knowingly. 'These two necklaces have been in our family for a very long time. It's so nice to wear them in public knowing that no-one else knows their secret.'

'I feel privileged to be in on it, ma'am,' I said.

She smiled briefly before her searching gaze found someone and she said, 'Oh, there's Hilda. Please excuse me.'

When she was gone, Misty said to me, 'I asked my mom today if she had ever gone up and out of the well back when she'd done her runs. She said no, back then the well had been covered over with a layer of vines and thornbushes, so they couldn't even see the sky. My mom and her friends didn't even try to get out of the tunnel. They knew something weird was going on, though, because the entry cavern was different. With us, it's all covered in dust in the future; for them it also looked different. But by going out into that other New York, we're doing something they never did.'

At that moment, Bo appeared at Misty's side with a couple of drinks.

'Misty, they're asking for everybody to be seated. I got us some dri—' He cut himself off, seeing me. 'Skye? Hey. What are you doing here . . .?'

I felt my face go hot as I blushed bright red. 'Just, you know, working on a Saturday night.' I flicked a stray strand of hair over my ear self-consciously.

I felt stupid. Stupid and underdressed in my vest and trousers, while they stood there in their finest formal wear. I may have lived in a wealthy building with a wealthy stepfather and gone to the same wealthy school as they did, but tonight they were in a different league.

I don't know if Misty saw something more in my discomfort, but when she hooked her arm in Bo's, her eyes locked onto mine, flashing with a definite sense of ownership.

Oh, she saw it, all right.

'I'm sure we'll see you later,' she said as she led Bo away to their table. I caught him glancing back at me a little helplessly as they left and I just rolled my eyes in a wry way that said, as best as I could, *Never mind, it's okay*.

All in all, I can't say the East Side Cotillion really did that much for me.

It turned out to be just another ball.

Sure, it had a short half-hour where the debutantes were 'presented' to society and that was kind of nice. Misty's eyes shone as she strode up the aisle, all on her own, while the master of ceremonies announced her name.

At her family's table, I saw her sister, Chastity, and her little brother, Oz, clapping. Her parents positively beamed. Her mother actually leapt up from her chair and gave Misty a one-woman standing ovation.

But after the presentation segment of the evening, well, the guests did what guests do at any other ball, wedding or gala: they got drunk.

As the well-dressed men began to indulge in shots of whiskey and bourbon, they sloughed off their bow ties and loosened their shirts.

The dazzlingly-dressed women began to drop their champagne flutes, breaking them. One woman slapped another. I even caught a sixty-something matron— unable or perhaps unwilling to find the distant ladies' room—hitching up her dress and peeing into a potted tree in a side corridor.

As Jenny and I bent down with matching dustpans to sweep up two more smashed champagne glasses, Jenny said, 'Welcome to the world of the rich and well bred.'

'Is it always like this?' I asked. 'Or do you think they're indulging more because of the gamma cloud?'

Jenny said, 'No, society functions are always like this. They start off all ceremonial and stately, and then they descend to this. Have you said hello to your buddies on table two?'

She nodded at Misty's table.

'I've seen you and your brother hanging out with Misty and her people lately,' Jenny said, a little sadly. 'Be careful.'

'What do you mean?' I asked.

'Just be careful. That family is weird. Got a mean streak. Misty, obviously. Her little brother, Oz, is odd. And her sister, Chastity, well. Last year, a lot of people thought Chastity was going to be named Belle of the Ball at the Cotillion. But Becky Taylor got the tiara instead. Chastity was so pissed.'

'Becky Taylor?' I said, trying to remember where I'd heard that name. Then it clicked. 'Wasn't she one of the girls from Monmouth who went missing?'

'She was indeed. Disappeared on this very night last year,' Jenny said. 'After the Cotillion finished, she went out into the night in her white debutante's gown and never came back.'

'You think Chastity had something to do with it?'

'I'm just saying, be careful.' Jenny headed back to the kitchen, while I continued to brush shards of glass into my dustpan. When I was done, I stood up and found myself standing face-to-face with Bo Bradford.

'Hi,' he said.

'Hi.'

'Didn't expect to see you here.'

I did a mock curtsey. 'Musta left my gown at home.'

'You look great,' he said with a smile. Then he looked around, as if to check if anyone was nearby. 'Listen, I'd really like to restart our little study sessions at the Met. I enjoy them a lot. Things have got a little, I don't know, crazy lately.'

I smiled. 'I'd like that, too.'

'Like what?' a voice said from behind me and I spun to find Misty right in my personal space. She was staring intently from me to Bo and back again, as if she'd caught us in bed together.

Bo saved me. 'I was saying that all this talk about the end of the world just gets to you after a while. I said I'd just like it all to stop.'

Misty seemed to evaluate this explanation for a moment, and then she blinked, accepting it, and smiled tightly.

'That's my Bo,' she said. 'Always seeing the emotional side of things. I'm far more pragmatic. If the world's gonna end, just end, already.'

At that moment, Jenny emerged from the kitchen and stopped abruptly, almost bumping into Misty.

'Jenny,' Misty said slowly. 'So good to see you. I was just thinking I needed another drink. Can you run along and get me—oh, I don't know—something bubbly?'

'Get it yourself,' Jenny said. She held up her watch. 'It's eleven o'clock. I just clocked off. I don't work here anymore.'

But Misty wasn't done. 'That's okay. I don't want to be too hard on you, Jenny. I mean, I wouldn't want you to, you know, harm yourself or anything like that.'

Jenny froze. I did, too.

I could see Jenny's mind working, wondering how Misty could possibly know about her history of self-harm.

And then, just for a second, Jenny glanced at me and for a horrifying moment I thought she might think *I* had told Misty about her suicide attempt.

Then Jenny straightened, maintaining her dignity. 'Misty, there's one thing you haven't figured out about me, something I would've thought you'd have got by now. No matter what you say, no matter what you do, *you cannot hurt me.*'

And with that mike drop, she strode off.

I wanted to chase after Jenny, to assure her that it hadn't been me who had given up her secret, but Misty grabbed my arm. 'Hey, Skye. The ball is over but the night is still young. Want to go for a little celebratory run?'

A LATE-NIGHT RUN

We arranged to meet behind the Met in an hour, so that Misty could go home and get changed. When I arrived at the conservancy garden, I expected to find all the other runners there—Bo, Verity, Hattie, Dane, perhaps Griff—but Misty stood there alone.

It was just her and me.

'I thought we should spend some quality time together, just us girls,' Misty said lightly.

I nodded even though I was a little unnerved. This had never happened before. Apart from the incident in the locker room with her period, we had never actually done anything on our own before.

Jenny's warning echoed in my mind: *Be careful*.

Misty's debutante gown had been a two-piece affair, so she had swapped out the billowing lower half for some jeans and her Golden Goose sneakers. She'd thrown a jacket over the upper half: a white sequinned strapless bodice that actually went quite well with the jacket and blue jeans combo.

Arriving in the entry cavern, Misty grabbed a small backpack from the corner and slung it over her shoulder. It was the pack containing the grappling hook. After we had gone exploring as a group, it had been decided to leave the pack here for future use.

Then she placed her gem in the slot in the low pyramid, the rippling curtain of purple light appeared, and in we went.

MISTY AND ME, ON THE INSIDE

Misty talked all the way down the tunnel, gossiping about the attendees at the Cotillion, what they'd worn, who they'd gone with, how thrilled she'd been to bump into me there, and Bo.

'I don't want to sound like some silly love-struck fool, but I just adore him so much,' she said wistfully. 'And I know he loves me. It'll sound weird, but we just have a *connection*. I've known it since I was little. My mom and Bo's mom talk about it all the time. They're convinced he and I will be married by the time we're twenty-three.'

She said this as we arrived at the trash heap beneath the well, the site of my second—and most amazing—kiss with Bo. Of all the places in the world, this was not the best one for me to contemplate Misty and Bo being together forever. And listening to Misty talk so weirdly about connections and the like, I was very glad she didn't know about that kiss.

I peered up the well shaft as Misty hurled the grappling hook up into it. I was thinking about Screaming Bald Guy. This was his time of night.

After several tries, Misty succeeded in securing the grappling hooked and we scaled the knotted rope.

We emerged from the well inside the Central Park of the future.

It was past midnight. The moon was high, bathing the park in dim silver light.

All was silent.

A faint wind rustled through the trees.

No bald man. Thank God.

'This way.' Misty headed off toward the Swedish Cottage. I hurried after her.

She pushed westward, striding with purpose, following the Bridle Path for a while before she veered abruptly onto a narrow dirt trail. Clearly, she had a plan, somewhere she was intent on going.

My mind whirred.

Why has she brought me here? And not one of her closer friends, like Verity or Hattie? And alone?

Then we stepped out of the park onto Central Park West and as I beheld Misty's destination, I finally realised why she had brought me along alone.

Our destination loomed before us, twin pointed shadows stabbing the night sky, the ghastly gigantic vandalism on them visible in the moonlight: the two towers of the San Remo building.

'After we saw Verity's place and the school,' Misty said, 'I wanted to go to our building to see what happens to our families. I figured we should go together, just the two of us, in case it's, you know, gruesome. I plan to do the same with Hattie.'

I couldn't fault her logic. It was actually quite considerate.

Like me, she had seen Verity's shock at seeing her parents' message on her bedroom wall. And that had just been a message. What if, like at the school, we discovered the long-dead bodies of people we loved in our homes? That was definitely best done with a single companion and not the larger group.

And so we crossed the grassy field that was Central Park West and stood before the San Remo building, with the two hateful messages scrawled in giant letters on it.

This time, I was able to look more closely at the figure hanging from the noose on the face of the building.

It was a man.

His features had long ago been eroded by the weather and whatever remaining birdlife there was, but his clothes were still intact. Indeed, the rope around his neck had been tied around the collar of his overcoat, which was how he had remained hanging for so long.

Seeing the figure up close for the first time, I suddenly recognised the overcoat: black with purple sleeves.

The man hanging in front of my building was Manny Wannemaker, the firebrand radio host.

'They hanged Manny . . .' I gasped.

Misty just shook her head and together we entered the San Remo building.

We went to Misty's place first.

Our footsteps echoed as we climbed the internal fire stairs, guided by the flashlights of our smartphones. The stairwell smelled musty: the odour of abandonment.

We came to the 21st floor and emerged from the stairwell into a dark corridor. The lone window at the end of it had been shattered, allowing rain to enter. The carpet stank of mould and mildew.

The front door of Misty's apartment was ajar.

It squealed as Misty pushed it open.

Looters had been through here. There were muddy bootprints all over the expensive white carpet.

But they had been selective. Some drawers had been pulled open, yet the furniture had not been damaged at all. It was the work of treasure hunters not indiscriminate vandals.

Wind whistled through the broken windows, making the curtains billow.

The vines of a few potted plants had spent the last twenty years creeping toward the windows, seeking sunlight and rain. They looked like snakes draped over the chairs and couches. They made my skin crawl.

Walking slowly and warily behind Misty, I scanned the apartment.

The bookcase in the living room was intact, its neat rows of books untouched for twenty years. Their tops were covered in a layer of moist dust but their spines were visible.

It was the classic 'Republican Voter's Bookshelf': the entire Tom Wolfe collection, including an original hardback of *The Bonfire of the Vanities*; everything ever written by Ayn Rand; *Free to Choose* by Milton Friedman and his wife, Rose; and a bunch of books written by Fox News hosts like Bill O'Reilly and Glenn Beck.

I smiled wryly when I saw one particular book hiding on the bottom shelf: *Living History* by Hillary Rodham Clinton.

'I'm guessing that was a gift,' I said to Misty, nodding at it.

Misty snorted derisively. 'Yeah. It's even autographed: "To Starley, from Hillary". My uncle Morty gave it to my mom for her birthday, just to get a rise out of her. It certainly did that. Uncle Morty's a left-wing liberal asshole. My mom got the last laugh, though, when Hillary lost the election.'

Misty's parents—or at least their bodies—weren't there.

'Maybe they made it to the Retreat,' Misty said.

Moving through the empty apartment, I came to Oz's bedroom.

Stepping cautiously through the doorway, I saw all the Rangers paraphernalia on the walls again—the posters, pennants and framed jerseys—only now their vivid red, white and blue colours had been paled by age and dust. And then I noticed.

The goalie's mask was gone.

Oz's signed Rangers goalie mask, the freaky one that had been decorated with the American flag.

In the spot where it had stood back in the real world, I now saw a bare circle in the dust—like the pale patch left on a wall after you removed a painting that had hung in the same place for many years.

I frowned, thinking.

Someone had been here recently and taken the goalie's mask.

Bang! The door behind me slammed shut.

I whirled, my pulse rate spiking.

Had it been the wind? Or something else?

I was reaching for the doorknob when a faint clinking sound made me spin back to face the bedroom.

It had come from inside Oz's closet.

My eyes went wide. My heart began to—

Then with a loud crash the door to Oz's closet burst open from within and three dark figures exploded from it, fists raised and shrieking, the leader clutching a kitchen knife and rushing at me with pure unadulterated rage.

ATTACKERS

I screamed as they threw me back onto Oz's bed.

The first of the three attackers leapt on top of me. He was a large man and I felt his immense weight as he landed astride me. He shrieked as he raised his knife and then thrust it down at my chest.

I raised my hands in pathetic defence, squeezed my eyes shut.

Yet nothing happened.

No searing pain. No bloody wounds.

Then, slowly, the man's shriek became a cackle, then a laugh, a deep wicked laugh that I recognised: Griff O'Dea's laugh.

I opened my eyes to see Griff kneeling on top of me. He was dressed in a dark tracksuit and a black ski mask. He yanked off the ski mask, allowing his frizzy orange hair to spring outward and revealing a broad grin on his freckled face. Behind him, Verity and Hattie wore similar tracksuits, beanies and grins.

'Boo!' Griff said. 'We got you.'

A moment later, Misty opened the door (which she had evidently slammed shut) and joined us, smiling apologetically.

'Sorry, Skye. We couldn't resist the opportunity for such a good prank,' she said.

Gradually, my pounding heart slowed and I returned her smile, albeit weakly.

The fact that I accepted the prank graciously seemed to go down well with the group and they each patted me on the back as they headed out of Oz's dusty bedroom.

As she went past me, Hattie took a swig from a little bottle of Moët and burped. She was wearing her black and gold Lululemon tracksuit. I'd been ambushed by a girl in designer athleisure wear.

I shook my head and followed them.

Of course, Misty had planned it all.

Before I'd met her above the entrance cavern, she'd already sent Griff and the girls ahead, into the other New York, using her mother's gem.

Bo and Chastity joined us in the apartment a minute later. They had come in with the others earlier and had been waiting upstairs while the prank had been executed. Bo had considered it too mean and had said he wouldn't be a part of it. Chastity, on the other hand, had thought it was inspired. As the butt of the joke, I agreed with Bo, but then I had to admit it had been kind of clever.

And so now this was Misty's exclusive Cotillion afterparty, held in her own private alternate New York.

We hung out for a while in Misty's abandoned apartment, drinking and smoking—both cigarettes and pot; I didn't partake in either—before everyone decided to head back.

'You wanna check out your apartment?' Misty asked as we walked out her front door.

'I don't know—' I began.

It was the truth. Having seen Verity's experience, I felt

I was better off not knowing what my family's future held.

'Let's go see my place!' Hattie burst between us, her piggish nose red from drinking. 'We're so close. It's only a few floors down.'

The group voted with their feet and within minutes we had descended the darkened stairwell and gathered outside Hattie's apartment on the 16th floor.

The door was locked. Hattie was reaching for her key when Griff just kicked the door in.

'Don't need keys in this New York,' he snorted.

Then he stepped aside allowing Hattie to stumble past him through the doorway, still gleefully drunk.

She stopped instantly.

Her mouth fell open in horror, her drunkenness abruptly vanishing.

I saw the blood immediately.

On the walls, on the furniture, on the curtains.

Then I saw the bodies: Hattie's parents lay face-down on the floor of the living room. Like Hattie, they were both overweight, and it looked like they had died in the act of crawling: Mr and Mrs Brewster each had a large kitchen knife embedded in their backs and each knife was surrounded by many more bloody stab wounds.

'Jesus God in Heaven,' Verity whispered.

'Damn . . .' Misty said.

'What happened here?' Griff said.

Hattie just stood there motionless and speechless.

I swallowed. It looked like something out of a slasher film . . . or a slaughterhouse.

The knives in Hattie's parents' backs also served another purpose. The killers had used them to pin identical notes to the corpses, written in Spanish:

NO HAY GENTE RICA
EN EL CIELO

Hattie stammered, 'Wh—what does it mean?'

Griff translated. 'It says, "There are no rich people in heaven."'

Hattie's breath began to come in faster and shallower gasps.

And then we saw the third figure, half-hidden beyond the kitchen doorway, seated, it appeared, at the table in there.

Hattie hurried into the kitchen.

I reached out to hold her back. 'Hattie, wait—'

But it was too late.

She froze in the doorway.

I joined her.

The figure appeared to be seated calmly at the kitchen table, hands in her lap, head bent as if in prayer.

Then I saw the ropes. She was tied to the chair. Before I saw the figure's face, I knew who it was. I could tell by her chunky dark-haired frame and the (now slightly burned) black and gold Lululemon tracksuit she wore.

Hattie knew it, too.

It was her own dead body.

As I stood there watching this impossible moment—Jesus Christ, they were both wearing the *same* outfit—my mind raced.

I mean, did this amount to some kind of time paradox? I'd seen time-travel movies. Was it permissible for someone to see their own corpse in the future?

Or what if you *met* yourself in the future? Would that

cause the universe to end? *Back to the Future* would say yes. *Star Trek* (at least the Abrams version) would say no.

I decided that since none of us was killing our own grandfather in the past, it was probably okay.

I was ripped from these thoughts when Hattie began hyperventilating.

Coming around the table, I saw that the dead Hattie's face was blackened and charred, horrifically burned. The skin had either melted or sloughed off, revealing her hideous screaming skull.

A thick rag (presumably doused in some kind of flammable liquid) had been jammed into her mouth—it was still there—and been set alight.

Hattie had been burned alive.

Or rather, *would be* burned alive.

For good measure, a meat cleaver had been jammed into her heart.

Misty gasped.

Verity said, 'What . . . the . . . hell . . .?'

Bo just blinked repeatedly.

I glanced at Hattie. I couldn't imagine what she was thinking right now. To see your dead future self was one thing, but to see that you had been *murdered*, and so horrifically, well, that was beyond comprehension.

The blade in her chest also held a note in place. It read:

LIMPIAR SU PROPIO
BANO, PERRA

Griff translated it in a low voice: "'Clean your own toilet, bitch.'"

And suddenly it all made sense.

I recalled Hattie's awful comments about her household staff, the ones she called 'lazy Mexicans', the ones she and her mother bullied mercilessly.

In the free-for-all before the gamma cloud, it seemed, when the lines between employer and employee—between lower class and upper class—had vanished, her staff had taken their revenge.

I watched Hattie watching herself.

It was like seeing someone go insane right before your eyes. At first she just stared blankly at her own corpse. Then she began coughing, gagging, choking . . .

. . . and then she vomited explosively.

And then, worst of all, her mouth flecked with her own vomit, she began to laugh, a hideous, insane, tear-filled laugh.

'Fuck me,' Misty said. She turned to Bo and Griff. 'Get her out of here. Take her home.' The foul discovery had evidently sucked the fun out of her run and she wasn't happy about it.

Bo and Griff hustled Hattie out of the apartment and down the stairwell. Misty, Chastity, Verity and I stepped out into the corridor in grim silence.

'Let's go back,' Verity said.

'Yeah, night's over,' Chastity said. She and Verity started to head off.

But Misty wasn't done. She turned to me. 'Wanna go check out your place?'

'Oh, I don't think so—'

'Come on,' Misty said. 'We all did it. And we're so close.'

She was right about that. My apartment was on the 20th floor of the north tower, only a few minutes away.

Verity saw us pause. 'What's the problem, kids?'

Misty said, 'Skye doesn't want to check out her apartment but I think she should.'

Verity frowned. 'After *that*?'

'Somehow, I don't think Skye's been tormenting her household staff. Or have you, Skye?'

'No.'

'Come on, the rest of us have done it. You and I can do it together, just the two of us. We can catch up with the others at the exit. I got your back.'

I really didn't want to go, but I felt socially cornered. If Red had been there, I might have had a better chance of deflecting Misty's entreaties, but alone, wanting to be part of the group, a group that had seen their fates, I just couldn't hold her off.

'Oh, okay,' I relented.

Misty and I arrived at my apartment a short time later. Verity and Chastity had gone off after Bo, Griff and Hattie.

The front door was closed.

Locked. Bolted. And covered in splintered hack-marks, the kind made by axes.

Todd would have been pleased. He'd told me once that our front door, while looking like it was crafted from wood, was actually made of plate steel underneath. And the deadbolt required a laser-cut key that could not be copied.

I had my key from the 'real' New York in my pocket and since there was no reason it wouldn't still work, I lifted it toward the lock.

I hesitated for a moment, unsure whether I should do this, but then I took a deep breath and slid the key into the lock.

It turned easily.

The damaged door unlocked and I pushed it open and the instant I did, I forever wished I hadn't.

THE FATE OF MY FAMILY

They were hanging from the ceiling, side by side, their heads bent forward, their necks broken.

My mom and Todd, or what was left of them.

The nooses Todd had fashioned were good ones. The knots had stood the test of time. Birds might have pecked out my mother and my stepfather's eyes, and the skin on their faces might have sloughed off due to exposure, but their skeletons still hung there, twenty-plus years after the event.

Misty saw my face go pale. 'Oh, Skye . . .'

Then another thought hit me.

Red.

He wasn't in the living room. I wondered if his body was somewhere else in the apartment.

It was then that a second thought came to me.

What if *my* dead body was somewhere here, like Hattie's? I tried not to think about that.

I cautiously stepped inside.

Even though my relationship with my mother was complicated, as I gazed up at her hanging body, I couldn't help but feel sorry for her.

There was a note on the coffee table below the two bodies. It was written in my mother's compulsively neat handwriting and it read:

Dear Skye,

We are trapped in here.

It is now March 17. The city has been in uproar for three full days now.

After that horrid siege at the University Club, riots began downtown, but they seemed to be isolated there.

But then Manny Wannemaker criticised the rioters on his radio show (he called them 'free-loading welfare losers'). Word went out on social media to get him. They found out he lived in the San Remo and they surrounded our building.

The siege began on the 14th, I think, then the mob forced their way past the police and inside. They have been working their way upward ever since, ransacking apartments as they go and killing the occupants.

They broke into Manny's last night and hanged him from the window of his apartment. The crowds massing outside cheered.

We sent Red ahead to the Retreat earlier on that first day but we got trapped here and so we missed the last chopper.

Now we cannot get out.

The gamma cloud is going to arrive in a few hours and we have decided to kill ourselves rather than die at the hands of the cloud or the murderers banging on our door right now.

We don't know where you are or where you have gone, and are hurt that you left without saying anything. We will see you on the other side.

Mom and Todd

She hadn't even signed off 'Love Mom'. And she couldn't resist the final emotional barb that she felt hurt that I'd left without telling her where I'd gone.

My mother. She had forged her way in the world the only way she knew how: with her looks. It had got her the life and lifestyle she wanted. And I imagined that, in her mind, in doing it all, she felt she had been heroically providing for Red and me when our father had gone nuts.

As for Todd, he hadn't been a bad guy or a good guy. He'd loved my mother, which was a good thing, I supposed, even if he'd been largely indifferent toward Red and me, but maybe that had just been his way.

I gazed up at the two hanging bodies and shook my head. They had died here having not been able to make it to their rich people's hideaway at Plum Island. Their money hadn't been able to save them.

'Sorry, Mom,' I said to her corpse.

I dropped the note and checked the other rooms to be sure Red wasn't there.

I looked in Red's bedroom first. It was untouched—the Cadillac couch, the R2-D2 fridge, even the stupid hammock was still there—all covered in twenty years' worth of damp dust.

No Red.

I went to my room next, edged open the door.

I glimpsed my framed posters—Green Day, The Killers, Eric Burdon and the Animals—but there was something wrong with them. There was something *on* them, paint or mud or something. I pushed the door open fully.

Giant letters were spray-painted across the wall *and* my posters:

I'VE BEEN WAITING
A LONG TIME FOR YOU, SKYE!

My blood turned to ice.

What the hell? Waiting for me?

I recalled my toy kangaroo in the tunnel, with the note in its pouch that read, *HE IS WAITING FOR YOU.*

Misty appeared behind me and for a moment I relaxed. It must be another prank.

'This isn't very funny,' I said.

But Misty's face was flat. 'We didn't do this, Skye,' she said in a low voice.

Fear came flooding back.

I blinked hard, trying to regather myself. My original instincts had been right: I should never have come here.

Thankfully, I did not see my own dead body anywhere. I don't know how I would've taken that.

But now I was in the same boat as Verity: I knew what the future held for my mom and my stepdad, but my future—and my brother's—was still unknown.

It was time to go.

With a final look at the grisly message on the wall of my bedroom, I slammed the door and left the apartment.

As Misty arrived at the stairwell, I walked a short distance behind her down the hallway, head bowed in thought.

'Skye . . .' a male voice said softly.

At first I thought I'd imagined it. Someone saying my name.

'Skye . . .'

I turned.

A figure, a man, stood at the far end of the long hallway. He stood dead still, backlit by the broken window behind him, thirty yards away, staring right at me.

His face was shrouded in shadow, but from the outline of his head I could tell that he was wearing a helmet of some kind.

He just stood there watching me.

For all I knew, he had been watching us from the end of the hallway the whole time and neither Misty nor I had noticed him.

He took a step away from the window and in the shifting light, I saw his helmet.

He was wearing Oz's New York Rangers/American flag goalie mask. It concealed his face.

And then he revealed a loaded crossbow from behind his back and said, 'Hello, my pretty,' and I dashed into the stairwell and ran for my life.

Verity and Chastity got the message pretty fucking fast when they saw Misty and me burst out of the stairwell, screaming, 'Run! Get back to the well! There's someone up there!'

We bolted out of the San Remo building and across Central Park West and as we hurdled the stone fence and entered the darkness of the park, I risked a glance behind me.

The figure in the mask emerged from the San Remo, only he wasn't running. He was strolling casually, twirling his crossbow.

We ran headlong through the park, crossed the Transverse, dashed around the Swedish Cottage, clambered down the well, retrieved our rope and exited the tunnel in record time.

★ ★ ★

We emerged from the portal to find Bo and Griff waiting for us, still holding Hattie between them. Bo saw the fear in my eyes immediately.

Misty came out last of all, still dressed in her jacket, debutante bodice and jeans.

She bent down and removed the yellow gem from the pyramid and turned to face us with a wild-eyed grin.

'That,' she said, 'was the most messed-up run we've ever done.'

PART V

THE MISSING GIRLS
OF MONMOUTH

**Three may keep a secret,
if two of them are dead.**

BENJAMIN FRANKLIN

THE DAYS BEFORE THE EVENT

I don't really remember going home after that run. I only recall staggering into my bedroom, falling into bed, sleeping deeply and waking up around midday the next day.

Still in my pyjamas, I padded out into the living room—the same living room I had seen in the future with my mom and Todd hanging dead from the rafters, the windows cracked, the apartment a dust-covered cave.

That morning, however, the apartment shone, lit by brilliant sunshine. The beige carpet was spotless, the curtains were pulled back from the windows and all my mom's carefully selected pieces of modern art were polished and shining.

Red was there, eating Cheerios for lunch and looking much better than he had when I'd left him the previous night.

'Where are Mom and Todd?' I asked.

'Gone to Southampton for a few days,' Red said with his mouth full. 'Said they'd be back on Friday. Although I reckon they've gone a little further than Southampton: I think they're going to Plum Island, to check out the Retreat. After all, it'll be home in a little over a week.'

Only they would never get to the Retreat. Here was

where they would die, in this apartment, trapped like rats with an angry mob banging at the door.

I hesitated for a moment, wondering if I should tell Red about it. Screw it. I told him.

I told him everything I'd seen the previous night: Mom and Todd's hanging bodies, the note, and also what had happened to Hattie.

'Damn . . .' Red gasped. 'What should we do? Should we tell Mom and Todd to stay away from New York? To *not* come back? Can we do that? Can we change the future?'

'I don't know,' I said. 'I mean, it depends if the future we've been visiting is the *only* future. According to Dr Maguire from Caltech, it is, and even if we told them to stay away, it wouldn't make any difference. Fate would conspire to put them in that room at that time. There's no way to know.'

Red said, 'Blue, I know you and Mom don't always see eye to eye, but we've got to at least try. Let's ask her and Todd if we can all leave the city before March 14. We have to at least do that.'

'Okay,' I said. 'Let's do it together when they get back on Friday night.'

On Monday, all the talk at school was about the recently held Cotillion.

Misty—despite all the horrors we had seen on our run after the Cote—was in her element, basking in the attention.

But her mood visibly darkened the moment she saw Jenny the following day.

Their heated exchange at the Cotillion was clearly still on her mind. I got the impression that it wasn't often that someone got the better of Misty Collins in a verbal spat, but Jenny had and Misty didn't like it.

'How's your dad doing, Jenny?' she asked airily in the corridor on Tuesday. 'After the divorce, do you think you'll live with him or with your mom and the tennis pro? I hope you're okay, though. I wouldn't want you to run out of Xanax and slash your wrists in despair.'

Jenny visibly stiffened, but she didn't take the bait. She just rolled her eyes at Misty.

But then she turned to me.

It wasn't a fleeting glance this time.

The withering look Jenny gave me was far worse than the one she'd given Misty. It was the look you gave someone who had breached your trust. Shit. I was going to have to talk to her.

But for some reason, Jenny didn't show up for school on Wednesday or Thursday, so I didn't get the chance.

And then on Thursday I experienced a different kind of conundrum.

At lunchtime, in the space of five minutes, I received *two* invitations: Bo asked me to meet him after school at the Met to study and Misty asked me to join her and Griff once again after school at The Plaza for high tea.

I didn't know what to do. I really wanted to see Bo, alone, in our private place, but I didn't want to upset Misty. I especially didn't want to decline her invitation and have her ask, 'Well, what are you doing instead?'

I decided to go to The Plaza and hurry over to the Met afterward.

When I arrived at The Plaza's private tea room, Misty and Griff were already there, in their usual seats by the fireplace. They were, however, engaged in intense conversation. Not wanting to interrupt, I waited behind a lattice screen nearby.

Griff was saying, 'Only fifteen families got invited to the Retreat and mine wasn't one of them, so I'm screwed unless my brain is in the 0.5% that survives the cloud. You gotta give me your gem when you go. Then I can hide inside the tunnel when we pass through the gamma cloud and come out after.'

'I thought your dad had money?' Misty said.

She said it with serious judgement. She might as well have said, 'I thought you were one of us.' (With his renovated-townhouse-garage, I thought Griff's father had money, too.)

'Not in fucking cash,' Griff said. 'He's a theatre producer. He spent all his cash on our apartment and the garage to keep up appearances. Most of it he borrows against his intellectual property rights. You know how it is: asset rich, cash poor.'

'Oh,' Misty said. She clearly didn't know how it was at all. You were either rich or you weren't.

'So can you leave me the gem?' Griff asked.

Misty paused. 'Okay. Everyone going to the Retreat is supposed to leave by helicopter on March 15, but knowing what I know, I'm going to make sure my parents leave before then. Be here on Sunday the 11th at noon. I'll bring the gem or I'll send someone with it.'

Griff fell back into his chair. 'You're a lifesaver. Thanks.'

'Anytime,' Misty said.

I took that as my opportunity to join them and I stepped around the screen and said my hellos.

Ninety minutes later, I hurried to the Met where I found Bo in our café. Only he wasn't studying, he was staring up at a television on the wall, transfixed.

Everyone in the café was.

'Check it out . . .' Bo said.

I looked up at the TV.

It was tuned to CNN and showing footage of a siege of some kind.

The ticker tape at the bottom of the screen read: BREAKING NEWS: ATTACK AT UNIVERSITY CLUB, NYC.

A female reporter was standing on the street, speaking urgently into a microphone: '—six kitchen employees armed with AR-15 assault rifles took control of the exclusive University Club an hour ago. After barricading all the exits, they vandalised the outside of the building. Then the shooting started and they began tossing dead bodies of members out the upper-floor windows. The police have now surrounded the building but they don't have many options: the assailants are entrenched, well armed and not likely to come out anytime soon—'

A sudden burst of gunfire made the reporter duck. The camera filming her skewed wildly, tilting up in time to show a bloodied body come sailing out of a window.

Screams of horror. Shouts from the cops.

The camera remained on the building and I saw the graffiti on its limestone face, written in bright red paint:

YOUR MONEY
CAN'T SAVE YOU!

Similar incidents were occurring around the world, an inordinate number of them in Europe.

Why the collapse of social order began in Europe, no-one really knew.

Perhaps it was because the scientists there had been more in agreement about the catastrophic effects of the gamma cloud (almost all of them had declared with grim certainty that the world was going to end, whereas American scientists continued to offer mixed views depending on which cable news channel they appeared on). Then again, maybe it was because of the centuries-old and highly visible class distinctions in Europe that had long divided the Old World rich from the desperately poor.

Whatever the case, acts of violence by the low and middle classes against the wealthy began to spread like a contagion around the world.

A three-thousand-strong mob of unemployed young Muslims from the projects in Paris had stormed some mansions in the 7th arrondissement.

An even larger crowd of migrants living in a squalid tent city near Calais overwhelmed the gate guards, knocked down the fences and flooded into the Channel Tunnel, walking en masse down the car lanes and train tunnels toward England.

Gangs of masked British hooligans—whipped into a frenzy by social media—invaded homes in the posh London neighbourhoods of Belgravia and Mayfair. There were far too many of them for the police to stop.

Similar events occurred in Germany, Italy and Spain, and in wealthy tax havens like Monaco.

Countries that had in the past been oppressed by

colonial powers—like India, Brazil and South Africa—saw even more shocking incidents of violence against the homes and symbols of the old elites.

Whether the attackers believed this was their final chance to upend the socio-economic order, or whether they just saw an opportunity to unleash their baser instincts even if the world didn't end, it didn't matter.

In the face of the end of all things, the boundaries of civilisation were no longer being recognised. The pent-up rage of the poor and middle class was being explosively released.

And with the bloody siege at the University Club in New York—where the minimum-wage staff had risen up against the elite membership—the contagion began to spread in America.

That was when the chaos began, in the days before the event.

One more thing would occur that week and it would shake my world even more.

On Friday morning Ms Blackman called a school assembly and informed us all that Jenny Johnson had disappeared.

ANOTHER MISSING GIRL

All the adults in my world immediately jumped to the same conclusion about Jenny: kidnapping.

After the siege at the University Club, the wealthy of New York City were on their guard for assault, attacks and abduction. Many feared their own staff and servants.

Women carried pocket-sized tasers and stun guns in their purses. Men now carried pistols in holsters under their jackets.

Misty's mother, Starley, bought a gun. (Of course, in true Collins style, it was the height of fashion: it had a white pearl grip, gold screws and a gleaming silver barrel.)

But the kidnapping theory had one major hole in it. No-one had demanded any kind of ransom from Jenny's father. No-one had contacted Ken Johnson at all, let alone sent Jenny's fingers back to him one at a time.

And there were no signs that Jenny had run away: she had not packed anything from her room. She had simply left for school on Wednesday and vanished.

Jenny Johnson had disappeared into thin air.

For those keeping count, that made her the fourth girl connected to The Monmouth School to disappear without a trace in the last two years.

Immediately after the school assembly, as one of Jenny's friends, I was called into the headmistress's office.

I sat in a lone chair before five adults: Ms Blackman, Ken Johnson and three other school functionaries including the counsellor, Ms Vandermeer.

My heart went out to Ken. His eyes were red from crying, bloodshot with worry. The bags under them were testimony to the sleepless nights he'd had in his grand yet empty apartment. His cheating wife had moved out only days before.

I stared at Ms Blackman behind her big mahogany desk. Rapid-fire images of her in the future flashed across my mind: of her rotting corpse, in this very room, in that very chair with a self-inflicted bullet wound to the head.

'Skye,' the corpse said before I blinked back to reality and saw Ms Blackman addressing me. 'Did Jenny say anything to you about running away, anything at all?'

'No. She never said anything like that.'

'Jenny suffered from clinical depression,' Ms Blackman said. 'Did she show any signs of despair lately? Perhaps regarding all this gamma cloud nonsense.'

'No, ma'am. She seemed fine.'

As I said this, I was thinking about Jenny's altercation with Misty: Jenny's verbal wit had been perfectly fine lately. Likewise, her inner strength. I recalled her flat declaration to Misty at the Cotillion: '*You cannot hurt me.*'

Then Ken said, 'Skye, Jenny told me that you'd hurt her feelings recently. That you'd betrayed her confidence. Is that true?'

I froze. *Oh, no.*

She really *had* thought it had been me who'd blabbed to Misty about her suicide attempt and she'd told Ken about it.

But what could I say? That Misty had gone to the future, rifled through Ms Vandermeer's filing cabinet and gleefully read Jenny's confidential medical file?

Damn.

I stammered woefully. 'That . . . that was a . . . misunderstanding.'

The look Ken gave me broke my heart.

I could only bow my head.

As I left Ms Blackman's office, my reputation as a good friend irreparably shattered, my mind raced.

As every adult in that office knew, in the modern world it was very hard to vanish completely without a trace. Cell phone towers, security cameras at train stations and airports, ATM records: *something* always gave away where you were.

Yet at The Monmouth School, *four girls* had done just that. What was it about the school that could make such a thing happen? What secret did it hold?

I knew the secret.

If you carried someone through a portal to another time and left them there, that would do it.

And suddenly I found myself thinking about the missing girls of Monmouth and the connections they'd had to the secret runners.

The first girl to disappear, Trina Miller: smart, pretty, a sophomore. She'd been friends with Misty . . . only for Misty to freeze her out socially when she'd started tutoring Bo Bradford. She'd vanished soon after.

I knew nothing about the second girl, the special-needs student, Delores Barnes, the one with Down Syndrome.

And then there was the third girl, Becky Taylor.

She had been a year older. Popular, beautiful and clever, she'd beat out Chastity Collins for the title of Belle of the Ball at the Cotillion last year . . . and had then disappeared that very night.

Becky had also been the leading contender to be Head Girl at Monmouth this year, but after her disappearance, Chastity took that title.

So both Trina and Becky had clashed with the Collins girls—girls who had more than a little ruthlessness in them and who had access to their own private time portal.

I recalled Jenny's words at the Cote about the Collins clan: *'Just be careful. That family is weird.'*

And now, after a particularly venomous confrontation with Misty—following months of smaller skirmishes dating back to the first school assembly—Jenny was suddenly gone.

Could Misty and her friends really be that spiteful, that malicious? That *evil*?

I liked Jenny. I liked her dad, too, and I hated seeing him in such pain. In this world of unreal wealth, superficial friends and casual entitlement, Jenny and Ken Johnson were grounded, real, decent.

My runs with Misty's crew were adrenaline hits, not friendship.

But Jenny, with her similar wrist scar and our shared job, was the closest thing I had to a true friend. And wherever she was, she hated me right now.

I had to do something about this.

But to take action was to cross a line—like it had been back in Memphis—except that the danger in defying Misty was far greater than it had been in defying Savannah. Here it could be deadly.

Screw it, I thought.

I knew what I had to do.

GETTING INSIDE

I found Bo at lunchtime on the rooftop basketball court.

I'd sought him out to see if I could convince him to venture into the portal with me later that day, but as it turned out, I didn't have to.

'I want to find out what happens to *my* family,' he said firmly. 'I have to know. But I don't want to do it with the whole group. Will you come with me?'

'Sure,' I said. 'I want to check out a couple of things myself. How about we go today after school?'

Bo nodded. 'I'll ask Misty for the gem. Meet me at the Met at five.'

At 4:59 p.m. I was standing on the front steps of the Met dressed in hiking boots, a North Face jacket and jeans, when my phone buzzed.

It was a text from, of all people, my dad down in Memphis.

> HEY BLUE!
>
> GREAT NEWS. THEY'RE LETTING ME OUT ON MONDAY (I THINK THE COMING END OF THE WORLD HAS MADE THE POWERS THAT BE AT THE HOSPITAL A LITTLE MORE LENIENT).

I'M BOOKED ON A TRAIN TO NYC ON TUESDAY.
I'LL BE ARRIVING AT PENN STN AROUND 3:00 P.M.
ON THE 14TH. CAN'T WAIT TO SEE YOU.
   (P.S. I HOPE YOU'VE BEEN EATING YOUR VITAMIN
SUPPLEMENTS AND SARDINES!)
   LOVE, DAD

I was both pleased and horrified. I wanted to see my
dad more than anything, but I also had foreknowledge
that on March 14 total societal breakdown would
begin in New York. My dad would be riding that train
directly into the chaos.

I was lifting my phone to call him when Bo ascended
the steps of the Met, dressed in sneakers and his lacrosse
tracksuit.

With a smile, he held up the gem. He'd got it from
Misty without any fuss.

'I was honest with her,' he said. 'I told her I wanted
to see what's going to happen to my family without the
larger group.'

'Did you mention that I was going with you?' I asked.
'I think Misty has more than a little crush on you.'

Bo grimaced uncomfortably. 'Yeah, I've kinda noticed
that. And, no, I didn't mention you were coming.'

'Okay, then. Let's do this.'

THE INVESTIGATION RUN

It was about 5:30 p.m. when Bo and I climbed out of the well inside the other New York.

Bo lived at 960 Fifth Avenue, another very prestigious address in New York. Unlike the San Remo or the Dakota, celebrities did not bother to apply at '960', as it was known: it existed solely for the ultra-wealthy elite who delighted in their wealth *not* being seen. The last apartment to be sold there went for $70 million, in cash.

It was also a block away from Monmouth, which suited me fine, because that was my destination.

We came to the entrance to 960.

I gave Bo a solemn nod. 'I hope it's all okay in there. I'll go to Monmouth while you check it out.'

'Thanks,' Bo said. 'Oh, wait.' He pulled something from his pocket and quickly looped it over my head: Misty's necklace, with the gem attached to it.

'Here, take this. If something happens to me, you'll be able to get back home.'

'But what if something happens to *me*?' I asked. 'What will you do?'

'I'll find you,' he said. 'I promise.'

With a final nod, he went into his building.

When he was out of sight, I hurried up Fifth Avenue and dashed into the ruins of The Monmouth School.

★ ★ ★

I went straight to Ms Vandermeer's office, the one in which Misty and Hattie had read through the confidential files of Jenny and who-knew-how-many other students.

In fact, the files they had been reading were still spread out messily on the floor where they had left them.

I went straight to the filing cabinet, slid it open and flicked through the files till I found the one I was looking for:

COLLINS, MELISSA (MISTY)

I'm not sure what exactly I was looking for in Misty's file or what I expected to find. Perhaps some mention of the missing girls, some link to them.

And there it was, right near the front of her file, a report from January of last year:

PSYCHIATRIST'S REPORT

Psychological appraisal following incident with Ms Trina Miller at The Monmouth School

Misty is a troubled young woman. She displays both sociopathic and narcissistic tendencies. In her social interactions, she is controlling and manipulative. Or in less formal terms, she likes to get her way.

The altercation with her fellow student, MS KATRINA (TRINA) MILLER, on January 4 is illustrative.

Ms Miller, it appears, asked a male student at the school, MR BEAUREGARD (BO) BRADFORD, on a date to Tavern on the Green. Misty, it turns out, harbours feelings for Mr Bradford and she confronted Ms Miller, her friend, about asking Mr Bradford out. Insults were exchanged before Misty slapped Ms Miller across the face, an act which resulted in Misty receiving a brief suspension from school and an appointment to see me for this psychological evaluation.

In our session, Misty showed not the slightest sign of remorse for striking Ms Miller. She declared that they would no longer be friends. She said this matter-of-factly and without emotion.

RECOMMENDATIONS:

Medication is not the answer for Misty. Her problems are not of the kind that can be addressed with drugs. She is self-involved, controlling and entitled, but she is not psychotic. It is simply the case that when she doesn't get what she wants, she reacts aggressively.

It is my professional opinion that regular and continued cognitive behavioural therapy sessions that challenge her world view would be the best treatment for her.

Dr Vivienne Freeman, MD PhD PsyD

A second sheet was paper-clipped to the report:

PSYCHIATRIST'S REPORT

Addendum following disappearance of
Ms Trina Miller

I have been asked to report on whether or not Ms Misty Collins might have been involved in the disappearance of her fellow student at Monmouth, Ms Trina Miller, two weeks ago.

While it is true that Misty and Ms Miller were involved in an altercation shortly before Ms Miller's disappearance, I find it very difficult to believe that a girl of fifteen, even one with Misty's psychological profile, could have carried out someone's total disappearance so comprehensively.

Hmmm. I couldn't say I agreed with the good Dr Freeman. But then Dr Freeman didn't know about Misty's secret portal through time.

It was then that I glimpsed another report behind the first one.

It caught my attention because the label on it did *not* read, COLLINS, MELISSA (MISTY).

It was marked, COLLINS, OSCAR (OZ).

I opened it and read it:

PSYCHIATRIST'S REPORT

Psychological appraisal of Mr Oscar (Oz) Collins [copy for insertion into file of Melissa (Misty) Collins]

Mr Oscar (Oz) Collins was referred to me after his mother discovered several searches on his smartphone relating to pornographic material.

It is my assessment that Mr Collins is an average teenage boy with the curiosities of an average teenage boy. Having spoken to Oz about the issue, I told his mother not to worry. Such searches—which are easy to do these days—are normal for a teenage boy curious about the opposite sex.

Interestingly, however, when I pressed him on the matter, Oz vehemently protested his innocence. He maintained, even though he could not prove it, that it was his sister, MELISSA (MISTY) COLLINS, who had stolen his phone and made the pornographic searches on it. She had done this, he said, as an act of vengeance after he had informed their parents that she had gone out when she had been grounded.

Oz informed me that, as punishment, his parents have decided to send him to a military camp for the summer. At this news, he says that Misty taunted him, 'Fantastic. Now I get to enjoy the summer without having you around to spoil it.'

I stared at the file.

Poor Oz. Misty had set him up so he'd be shipped off to military camp for the summer. And then for good measure she'd told everyone at school about it and trashed his reputation. What a bitch.

I returned the file to its drawer, lest Misty came here looking for it.

Now very curious, I sought out another file and found it:

MY LITTLE SISTER PROGRAM

BARNES, DELORES

Delores was the second girl to disappear, the one with Down Syndrome who, while not a student at Monmouth, had been connected to the school via the My Little Sister Program.

I opened the file and after flipping through some pages, found something relevant to my search:

STUDENT INCIDENT REPORT

Incident with Henrietta (Hattie) Brewster

Delores was involved in an altercation with Henrietta (Hattie) Brewster on the sidewalk outside school this morning.

It seems to have started innocently enough. As she arrived at Monmouth to participate in the My Little Sister Program, Delores tripped on the sidewalk and spilled her hot chocolate onto and into Ms Brewster's new handbag.

Ms Brewster, naturally, was not amused. According to several girls who witnessed the incident, Delores was instantly apologetic. Unfortunately, Ms Brewster was not in the mood to forgive and she expressed her anger at Delores with some epithets that are not, shall we say, the Monmouth way. According to those witnesses, she said to Delores, 'You stupid fucking Mongoloid idiot! I don't know why we have to babysit you retards anyway. Shouldn't you be doing some basket-weaving course or something?'

Ms Brewster was counselled about her language and forced to apologise to Delores. Delores continues to be upset by the incident. She has offered to pay for a new purse for Ms Brewster numerous times and continues to apologise to

**Ms Brewster whenever she comes to our school
for the My Little Sister Program.**

I read the report with increasing dread.

Poor Delores. By the look of it, she had accidentally bumped into Hattie on the street and spilled her hot chocolate all over Hattie's new and no doubt expensive handbag.

Of course, Hattie—mannish, belligerent and gunning for a fight—had let fly with a barrage of insults.

And, shortly after, Delores Barnes had vanished from the face of the Earth.

A chill slithered up my spine.

The pattern was clear, at least to me. Three girls who had offended Misty's clique of runners—one who had challenged Chastity; one who had crossed Misty; and one who had angered Hattie—all mysteriously disappeared soon after.

The cops and the school's FBI investigator had clearly not suspected Misty's gang in the three disappearances. And why would they? They were too disparate, too disconnected.

Even if the investigators *had* put the incidents together, they couldn't possibly have been expected to figure out that Misty's crew had a secret location—in another time—to which to dispatch those girls who had displeased them.

This, I figured, had been Jenny's fate, too.

But where could she be? And how could I possibly find her?

I closed the file, slid it back into its place and slammed the drawer. It was time to leave.

As I made to go, I stepped on one of the files on the floor, left there by Misty and Hattie.

I wouldn't have taken any notice of it had I not recognised the name on the spine.

O'DEA, GRIFFIN (GRIFF)

It lay open. To another psychiatrist's report.

PSYCHIATRIST'S REPORT

Psychological appraisal following incident at Barneys on June 12

This shoplifting incident highlights Griff's significant and strict medical needs. If Griff does not take his medications, his manias will reveal themselves very quickly.

First, there will be more cleptomaniacal incidents like this. When he is not medicated, he is a compulsive stealer. He likes what other people have.

But if Griff is deprived of his medications for a longer period of time, we will see more violent and impulsive incidents like those that occurred in his youth: the torture of pets and small animals, and disproportionate acts of revenge on people he feels have slighted him (I refer to the recent incident where he cut up his mother's favourite dress with scissors after she refused to buy him some designer sneakers).

This incident is a timely reminder for all of us involved in Griff's mental health to keep a close eye on his medication schedule. I would, accordingly, like to increase his dosages of Risperdal and Clozaril. He is lucky that after his

**parents paid for the items he stole, the store chose
not to press charges.**

So Misty had been reading up on Griff. And while it sure
made for interesting reading, I had more important things to
do right now.

I threw down the file. I had to figure out where—

'Hey, Skye. Thought we might find you here,' a voice said
from behind me.

It was Misty's voice.

I turned.

Misty, Hattie, Verity and Chastity stood in the doorway,
their eyes deadly, blocking the exit.

TRAPPED

I just stood there in the school counsellor's office, wearing Misty's necklace, looking like a burglar caught red-handed.

There was a moment of silence as we all assessed each other.

Verity and Chastity glared evenly at me. Hattie's eyes darted excessively: a facial tic she'd developed since she'd seen her own dead body. Her mind was gone.

'What did you do with Jenny?' I said.

Misty's lips curled into a thin smile. 'Like with the others, we took her someplace that'll have special meaning just for her.'

'The others? You mean Becky, Trina and Delores?'

'It started with Trina,' Misty said, 'because Trina betrayed me. It was the best way to get rid of Becky. As for the retard, well, we just did that for fun because she ruined Hattie's new Birkin bag.'

'I loved that bag . . .' Hattie drawled, still blinking weirdly.

I said nothing but I was thinking: *Holy shit.*

Misty spat. 'Fucking Trina. You know, I thought she was my friend. And then she went and asked Bo out on a date. My Bo! On a date! At fucking Tavern on the Green. Jesus Christ, what a cliché.'

Misty's heavy-lidded stare became harsher. She threw something at me and I caught it.

Her phone.

On the screen was an mpeg video. I pressed the triangular 'Play' icon . . .

. . . and saw the high heap of trash in the tunnel underneath the well. Faint light came down the well, illuminating the space. It was the signature fish-eye view of a GoPro camera.

Then two figures entered from the right, both holding phones as flashlights.

Bo and me.

On our first private run, when we had gone up and out of the well to explore the world of the future for the first time. I watched as, on the screen, Bo tried several times to hurl his grappling hook up into the well until at last it caught.

And then—to my horror—I saw Bo hold me in his arms and kiss me tenderly.

I remembered the moment vividly, only now I looked at it through Misty's eyes.

Oh, shit . . .

It was then that I recalled my very first run with the larger group, when Misty had fiddled around among some crevices in the left-hand wall of the tunnel near the trash heap.

She had been planting the GoPro.

Misty snatched the phone from me. 'You can't imagine how furious I was with Trina when she went behind my back and tried to steal Bo from me. *She was my friend*. And now you, Skye. *Kissing* him! I thought you were my friend and now I see you trying to take him from me.'

I spoke slowly, calmingly: 'Listen, Misty. There's nothing going on between me and Bo—'

'Bullshit! I saw you at the Met together! One afternoon after school, Hattie saw you both go in there! She followed you and called me.'

I glanced at Hattie. She looked like a prison guard.

Verity just shook her head disapprovingly.

Chastity was inspecting her fingernails, bored.

I tried a different tack. 'Misty, I didn't know there was anything between Bo and you—'

'Bo and I love each other!' she screamed at my face, spittle flying, and in that moment I knew for certain that Misty was a psychopath.

She caught herself, took a deep breath. 'Bo and I have a *connection*. Through our bloodlines, through our souls. We are meant to be together. After I saw this'—she nodded at her phone—'I wanted to fucking tase you right away, drag you in here, tie you to a streetlight like we did to Becky and leave you to the crazy scavengers of this time. But the girls here talked me out of it, said it was too close to Becky's disappearance. They convinced me to wait till it got closer to the end of the world, till things got bad, till now, when another disappearance or two wouldn't be followed up.'

Verity smirked. 'Don't thank us all at once.'

Misty said, 'In the meantime, I had to content myself with messing with your head: taking you to your apartment and showing you how your parents killed themselves.'

I frowned. 'You knew how they died?'

'Of course I knew. I'd already been through your apartment. I got in via the balcony to your parents' bedroom. Honestly, you don't think you and Bo were the first people to leave the tunnel and explore this world, do you? Granted, I didn't think to burn a hole in an oak tree to figure out just how far into the future this place was, like your brother did.'

At the mention of Red, I turned to Verity.

Verity cocked her head. 'Don't worry, we'll tell him that

you came here alone with Bo and the crazies got you. Have no fear, I'll take good care of your brother after you're gone.'

Misty said, 'When we dumped Becky in here, we went to the trouble of writing a text on her phone to cover our tracks. We won't even bother doing that for you.'

She added, 'You really did me a favour, coming in here now with Bo. Meant I didn't have to go to the trouble of luring you to the conservancy garden outside, tasing you and then hauling your ass in here.'

'What are you going to do to me?' I said warily.

Misty smiled tightly. 'I'm guessing you came here to find Jenny, so we're going to give you what you want. We're going to take you to her.'

Then Misty's hand whipped out from underneath her track top and I briefly saw a Taser C2 stun gun in it. She pulled the trigger and I glimpsed the plastic gun's twin electric-shock probes rushing at me before everything went black.

BOUND

'Wake up, sleepyhead! Wake up!' a distant voice cooed at the edge of my consciousness.

Then, *whack!* Somebody slapped me, hard.

I opened my eyes to see Hattie's broad heavy-set face right up close to mine.

'She's awake,' she snorted and stepped away to join Misty, Chastity and Verity. Misty, I saw, must have taken back her gem while I'd been unconscious. She now wore it around her neck.

I was outdoors, sitting with my back up against the base of a post of some kind, my hands wrapped around and behind it, tied together at the wrists with a plastic garbage-bag tie.

Only this was no ordinary post.

It was painted hot pink.

It was the tall pink crucifix on the roof of the Met that I had seen unveiled by Jenny's father, Ken, at the announcement event in January; the sculpture by the British artist Clivey named *The Price of Feminism*.

The buildings of the Upper East Side loomed over me, stretching away to the north and south. It was early evening, the sky almost fully dark. While I had been knocked out, the sun had gone down.

I guessed I had been out for about thirty minutes. Just

above the roof's waist-high rail, I could see the tops of the trees of Central Park—

A groan from above me made me look up.

'Oh, God . . .' I breathed.

Jenny hung on the back side of the crucifix, Christ-like, a mirror image of the sculpted woman on the front face of the cross.

Jenny looked asleep or semi-conscious. Her head was bowed, her eyes closed. Her arms were stretched wide, tied with rope to the crossbeams while her legs were bound to the stem beside my head.

Across her forehead, written in red lipstick, was one word:

BITCH

Jenny was drifting in and out of a tormented sleep, groaning and shouting in her nightmares.

Her clothes were dirty, her hair was pressed down against the sides of her head, sodden from exposure to rain and wind. I guessed she'd been out here for at least two days and nights.

Directly across from her was a simple chair with a white placard resting on it. On the placard, written in black marker, were the words:

YES, JENNY, I <u>CAN</u> HURT YOU.

Misty had made her point.

Not only had she left Jenny for dead, she'd left her for dead hanging from the arty fibreglass crucifix her own father had caused to be installed on the roof of the Met.

Misty smiled at me. 'Time for us to go. But we're not going to leave you all alone. We're going to do for you what we did for Trina and Delores and Becky. Send out a call for the crazies.'

She placed a pink Jambox portable speaker on the rail and hooked it up to my phone. She swiped through my playlist.

'Fuck, what a totally lame list. Oh, here we go, Most Frequently Played . . . look at that, The Animals.'

She selected 'The House of the Rising Sun' by Eric Burdon and The Animals, hit play, turned the volume way up, and with a curt nod to the other girls, turned and left, leaving me on the roof of the Met with the unconscious Jenny, bound to the bright pink crucifix.

BAIT

'There is a house in New Orleans . . .

'. . . they call the Rising Sun . . .'

The first haunting lines of the famous ballad blared out from the speaker at full volume, echoing across the deserted park.

The song's melancholy organ line, combined with Burdon's deep foreboding voice, was unnerving at the best of times, but when played so unnaturally loudly, the effect was multiplied. If I was going to die to any song, this was not the one I'd choose.

And if there was anybody out in the park, they would hear it for sure.

'. . . It's been the ruin of many a poor . . .'

I struggled against my bonds. But the plastic garbage-bag tie was thick and unyielding. I couldn't sever it. I tried banging against the fibreglass crucifix, attempting to break it, but got nowhere. It was too strong.

'Jenny!' I called above the music. 'Jenny, can you hear me?'

She groaned.

'Jenny, wake up! We gotta figure a way out of this—'

And then I heard them, over the music, and I froze.

Two calls in the distance.

'Weeee-oh!' then 'Oooh-we!'

Call and answer, like I'd heard in the abandoned subway station with Bo. Hunting calls.

Someone was down in the park.

At least two someones.

Drawn by the loud music.

Eric Burdon's voice rose to a howling wail:

'. . . The only time he's satisfied . . .!

'. . . is when he's on a drunk . . .!'

I began to breathe faster.

I tugged uselessly at the plastic tie. I craned my neck to try and see over the rail into the park.

This was all getting to be too much.

I was losing my shit.

The wall of sound and my whole sorry predicament was bludgeoning my mind—the song's rambling organ solo blared in my ears; my wrists were now bleeding; the hunting calls kept coming, getting closer.

Misty had put the song on a loop and it played through twice. As it came to the booming crescendo at the end of its third run-through, despair overcame me.

'. . . I'm going back to New Orleans . . .!

'. . . to wear that ball and chain!'

As the song began again, I looked up and called to Jenny, trying to rouse her, which was why I never heard him approach me from behind, not until his hand landed roughly on my shoulder and spun me round and I screamed in terror.

HIM

It was Bo.

At the realisation that it was him and not some axe-wielding maniac, I slumped with relief and started bawling my eyes out.

Bo reached over and turned off the music. Blessed silence.

Then he knelt before me and pressed his hands to my cheeks, his eyes locked on mine.

'Skye, it's okay, it's me,' he said. 'I went back to the school but you weren't there. I wandered around searching for you and then I heard the music.'

He looked quizzically from my bound wrists to Jenny above me. 'What the hell happened here?'

'Misty and the other girls,' I said. 'I think it's safe to say Misty is unhealthily in love with you. Like, *we-have-a-connection* in love with you.'

He reached into his pack, looking for his pocket knife. He pulled it out, unfolded it.

'Cut Jenny down first,' I said. 'She's been up there for a while.'

Bo stood and began sawing away at the ropes binding Jenny to the pink cross. He freed her legs first, then her left arm. With that arm free, she flopped down onto Bo's shoulder.

'Wha—what's going on . . .?' she moaned, her eyes still closed. But at least she was waking.

Bo began sawing at the final set of ropes tying her right arm to the crossbeam.

When his pocket knife cut through the last bit of rope, Jenny came away completely from the pink cross. As she dropped fully onto his right shoulder in a fireman's carry, Bo smiled encouragingly at me just as something sharp and pointed sprang out from his chest, spitting a tiny gout of blood as it did so.

At first, Bo didn't seem to feel it. He just froze on the spot, frowning as if confused. Then his eyes glanced down at the bloody arrow-tip protruding from his chest.

It had entered through his back and emerged right through his heart.

Then his eyes met mine—the expression in them desperate, loving, horrified and helpless at the same time—before they drained of all life and he dropped flat onto his face, not even attempting to cushion the fall.

'Bo!' I screamed.

But as Bo dropped I was suddenly able to see the man who had shot him, standing there on the roof twenty yards away.

'You . . .' I said.

He was again wearing the American-flag goalie's mask. This time I saw that he also wore a dirty New York Rangers hockey jersey as well. And he was gripping an expended crossbow.

'Hello, pretty girl,' he called.

I was still tied to the base of the garish pink cross. Bo lay dead before me, with Jenny's limp body draped on top of him. Jenny groaned, blinking back to life.

America Face advanced slowly toward us.

'I've been waiting for you, Skye . . .' he said. 'I've been waiting a long time. Why didn't you come back for me?'

I swallowed.

The message on my bedroom wall.

'Who are you!' I yelled. 'How do you know me?'

As he walked, he calmly began reloading his crossbow.

I was now totally freaked out. My mind was a churning mix of raw grief for the loss of Bo and sheer terror at my new predicament. I felt sick to my stomach and panicked in the extreme.

And then I saw it.

On Jenny's wrist.

Jenny had fallen in such a way that her right hand had come to rest not far from my hips and her ugly black watch was now close to my bound hands.

Clarity returned. For now, survival trumped grief.

I didn't waste a second. I shimmied sideways and, with my hands still behind my back—still pinned behind the vertical stem of the cross—I grabbed hold of Jenny's watch.

I didn't need to unclasp it: I just had to withdraw the little two-inch blade hidden inside it, the blade designed for a kidnap scenario.

America Face clearly didn't know what I was doing. He was still cranking on his crossbow as I got the blade out of the watch and began using it to saw through the plastic garbage-bag tie binding my wrists.

After a few hurried sawing movements, I cut through the plastic tie and my hands sprang free.

I leapt to my feet and took in the situation.

America Face was twenty feet away; Jenny was at my feet, her eyes opened fully now.

America Face seemed shocked that I was up. He was even more shocked when I snatched up Bo's fallen pocket knife and hurled it at him.

It wasn't a great throw, but it was good enough. The knife sliced across his left forearm, causing him to swear and drop the crossbow momentarily.

I seized the moment.

With a final sad look back at Bo's dead body on the ground—as much as I wanted to, I couldn't mourn him now—I grabbed Jenny, looped one of her arms over my shoulder, took three bounding steps toward the rail and in a moment of total desperation, with no other options available to me, I decided to test the thoughts I'd had at the unveiling of the crucifix and leapt over the rail, off the roof of the Met.

FLEE

Jenny and I landed on the sloping glass wall below the roofline and immediately began sliding down it.

We slid wildly for about forty feet, creating crude black slashes in the dust-layer, before we rolled to a halt on a flat section of roof that preceded another sloping glass wall.

'Don't stop,' I gasped, pushing Jenny to the next edge and down that slope we went, sliding down it on our asses before the sloping glass wall suddenly went vertical and became a sheer drop and before I could do anything about it, we sailed out into thin air.

We fell through the wild overgrowth of vegetation that had swallowed the park-side of the Met building, the many vines and branches of the trees slowing our fall before we landed with twin thumps in some bushes at the base of the tangle, bruised but okay.

Now Jenny was fully awake. A couple of death-defying slides will do that to you.

She looked at me with wide eyes. 'What the *fucking hell* is going on?'

I glanced up at the roof. America Face peered down at us. He waved tauntingly.

'Just run,' I said. 'We might be able to catch Misty and the others at the well. I'll explain as we go.'

★ ★ ★

We raced through the park.

At one point, we stopped to drink some rainwater from a wide puddle on a path. After two days on that roof, Jenny needed it, and we weren't too proud to kneel down and drink like animals from the ground, scooping water into our mouths.

'What is this place?' Jenny said as we resumed our run.

'We think it's the future,' I said. 'About twenty years into the future. The world after the gamma cloud wiped out most of the population. It's a long and weird story, but there are two portals that link our time to this one: you come in through one and go out through the other. We're trying to get to the exit now, before Misty and her bitches close it and shut us in.'

I turned as I ran.

'Jenny, I swear I didn't tell anyone about your cuts or your parents. Misty and the others went to the school in this time and read your file.'

Jenny threw me a wry smile. 'If I had a dollar for every time someone used the they-went-to-the-future-and-read-your-school-file excuse, I'd be a rich woman. It's okay, Skye. I believe you. When you wake up on the roof of the Met, crucified to a pink fibreglass cross, looking at a taunting placard and seeing the ruins of New York all around you, you develop an open mind.'

We dashed around the Shakespeare Garden toward the Swedish Cottage.

I was hoping that our rather direct method of exiting the Met—sliding down its sloping glass roof—might have helped us gain on Misty and her gang, and it had.

I raced around the Cottage, arriving at the dirt clearing that contained the well—

—and stopped in mid-stride.

Verity sat with her back pressed against the low well, her left foot caught in some horrible-looking metal contraption. She whimpered as she tugged vainly at her leg.

As I cautiously approached her, I saw what the contraption was.

A bear trap.

My mind raced: where did someone get a goddamn bear trap in New York? Then I realised: it was one of the six bear traps from the gruesome exhibit at the Met.

I scanned the ground surrounding the well and saw the other five bear traps from the museum arrayed around it, hidden underneath a carpet of dead leaves and branches.

Someone had laid them here.

To catch us as we tried to leave.

I immediately thought of America Face.

Poor Verity had stepped on this one and its spring-loaded metal jaws had clamped around her ankle with shocking force, and now she was hopelessly caught in its grip.

At that moment, Verity saw me. 'Skye! Oh, Skye! You gotta help me! You gotta fucking help me get this off! Misty and the others left me behind—'

I can't say I felt very inclined to help her. Fifteen minutes earlier, when she'd had me at her mercy, she hadn't been offering to help me.

I bounded past her and jumped up onto the rim of the well.

'Sorry, V,' I said. 'I gotta catch your friends before they shut us in here.'

I dropped into the well, using the knotted rope that Misty hadn't bothered to take with her, and slid down its length before dropping onto the trash heap.

I bounced off the heap and peered down the tunnel.

MATTHEW REILLY

I saw three running shadows racing away into the darkness: Misty, Chastity and Hattie, bolting for the exit.

I hurried after them, but I knew in my heart that they had too great a head start.

I ran for about two hundred yards before I saw the exit portal spring to life, abruptly silhouetting the three girls in rippling purple light. I couldn't be certain, but I thought I saw Misty turn and see me.

Then they jumped through the shimmering curtain and my horror was complete when, a few seconds later—as Misty removed the gem from the pyramid—the square of purple light winked out.

I stopped, alone in the tunnel.

I was now stuck here, stranded in the future.

THE UNCERTAIN FUTURE

I rejoined Jenny at the top of the well.

It was fully night now in the dead city.

My mind was reeling. Bo was dead, we were stuck here, and my own personal nemesis, America Face, couldn't be far away. Oddly, it entered my mind then that I hadn't called my father back; he'd be on his way to New York soon and I wouldn't be able to warn him of the coming anarchy.

I felt entirely overwhelmed. I didn't know what to do. In my wildest dreams, I'd never contemplated this.

Jenny touched me on the shoulder. 'Hey.'

She had just rubbed the word '**BITCH**' off her forehead and she handed me her pocket make-up mirror and a tissue.

I frowned, not understanding. Then I held the mirror up to see my own face and I saw two words written in lipstick on my forehead:

MAN THIEF

A final taunt from Misty. I wiped the scarlet letters off with the tissue. 'Thanks, Jenny.'

Man thief, I thought. *And the man I was supposedly stealing from Misty: Bo.*

'Oh, God,' I said. 'Bo. He came to rescue us and then . . . and then that bastard—'

My voice caught in my throat. I clenched my teeth, biting back the tears that were forming. 'He wasn't like the others,' I said.

Jenny wrapped a comforting arm around me. 'I know, Skye. I'm sorry.'

A few feet away from us, Verity was still whimpering as she struggled with the bear trap gripping her left ankle.

She looked up at Jenny and me, her eyes pleading. 'Skye, Jenny. I'm so sorry for what we did to you. Please, please help me.'

I blinked back to my senses and stared at her. 'Misty closed the exit portal. You're stuck in here with us.'

'Goddamn, Misty—' Verity spat as there came a faint whooshing noise—something fizzing through the air—and suddenly an arrow lodged deep in Verity's chest and she was thrown back against the well like a rag doll, killed instantly.

I spun.

America Face stood at the edge of the tree line, his crossbow levelled.

I grabbed Jenny's hand and yelled, 'Run!'

Fleeing through the undergrowth with Jenny, branches slashing against my cheeks, the sounds of America Face stomping through the brush behind us, my mind was screaming.

Think, Skye, think!

We jumped down onto the bramble-covered 79th Street Transverse and raced across its width, heading west.

'Where are you going, pretty girls!?' America Face's voice echoed from behind us.

How can we get out of this time? I thought.

Jenny was evidently thinking the same thing. 'Skye. If we're in another time, how do we get back home?'

'The only way back to our time is through the exit portal in the tunnel,' I said. 'It's under a private garden behind the Museum of Natural History.'

'And how do you open that portal?'

'With a special gem,' I said. 'An amber gem. There are two of them. Misty's got one, her mother has the other. You place a gem in a little pyramid at the exit portal. That'll open the fold in time and get us home. What we have to do is find one of those gems in this time.'

'All right, then,' Jenny said. 'How are we going to do that?'

As we clambered up the other side of the sunken Transverse, I thought about that.

And it suddenly occurred to me that maybe there was a way to do it.

This was the future, created by our past, and I knew some things about that past.

I looked at Jenny. 'Follow me.'

Minutes later, we crossed the rambling field of grass that Central Park West had become and stood before the San Remo building.

Jenny stared at the graffiti scrawled across the twin towers and the hanging body of Manny Wannemaker.

'What happened here?' she breathed.

'Before the gamma cloud hit, the world went nuts.' I checked the street behind us before we went inside: no sign of America Face. He must still be in the park.

Up the internal stairs we went.

'Where are we going?' Jenny said. 'Your place?'

'No,' I said. 'Misty's.'

We came to the 21st floor and hurried down the hall to Misty's apartment.

I kicked open the front door and went straight to Misty's bedroom.

'I know where Misty kept her gem,' I said.

I marched over to her bookcase.

I didn't dare use my phone's flashlight—it could be seen from afar—but fortunately the moonlight was strong.

All the books on the bookcase were in the same places they had been back in our time, only now they were covered in moist black dust.

I knew the book I was looking for.

War and Peace.

It was still there. I grabbed it, flipped it open and smiled triumphantly as I saw its hollowed-out core.

Then my smile went flat.

The book's secret core was empty.

'Damn it,' I said. 'This was where Misty kept her gem. When she fled the city before the riots, she must have taken it with her. Fuck.'

Fuck-fuck-fuck-fuck-fuck.

Jenny took the book from me. 'Kinda smart of Misty to keep her valuables in a hollowed-out book like this. I didn't think she was that clever.'

'She isn't that clever,' I said.

'What do you mean?'

'Misty didn't come up with the idea of hollowing out a book by herself,' I said. 'She learned it from her mother.'

My eyes snapped up.

'Her mother,' I said, rushing out the door and down the hall, back into the main lounge. Jenny followed, confused.

I stood before the large bookcase that dominated the lounge of Misty's apartment, scanning the Collins family's book collection.

It was the same Republican Voter's Bookshelf I'd seen before: all Ayn Rand and Fox News.

I said, 'Misty's mom taught her to hide stuff in a hollowed-out book. But she told Misty it had to be a book you were happy to eviscerate.'

And my eyes landed on it.

Living History by Hillary Clinton.

Hiding down there on the bottom shelf, a gift from a cheeky uncle, covered in twenty years of grime: a book that had no place on any Republican Voter's Bookshelf and one that Starley Collins would have happily gutted.

I snatched the Clinton book from the shelf and opened it, and my eyes lit up at the sight of the deep square hollow that had been cut into its pages.

My joy was short-lived.

Like Misty's book, this hollow core had nothing inside it. Its emptiness mocked me.

I slumped into the lounge chair behind me, suddenly overcome by fatigue, my brief rush of hope now completely and comprehensively crushed.

Jenny was still trying to catch up.

'No luck?' she asked.

'No, no luck,' I said bitterly. 'You and I are out of options. We are officially stuck here.'

PART VI

THE DEAD WORLD

[The Mayan] kings were preoccupied with their
own power struggles. They had to concentrate on
fighting one another and keeping up their images
through ostentatious displays of wealth. By insulating
themselves in the short run from the problems
of society, the elite merely bought themselves
the privilege of being among the last to starve.

JARED DIAMOND

NEW YORK CITY AND SURROUNDS

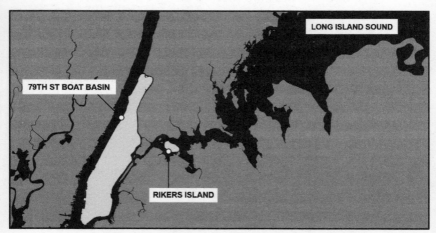

MANHATTAN ISLAND AND SURROUNDS

THE BITTER FUTURE

Angry, frustrated and forlorn, I didn't want to stay in Misty's apartment.

For that, and for one other reason, I took Jenny to my apartment over in the north tower.

'A word of warning,' I said as I went inside, 'this isn't pretty.'

As Jenny entered the apartment behind me and saw my mother and Todd hanging from the ceiling beams, the full weight of the end of humanity hit her.

'Good God,' she breathed. 'You saw this? Before?'

I nodded. 'Misty brought me here. To needle me. To get under my skin. She didn't realise that I don't care all that much for my mother. My dad, though, is a different story, as is my brother.'

That was the other reason I had returned to my apartment: Red.

I knew what would happen to Mom and Todd but I didn't know what would happen to Red during the chaos preceding the gamma cloud.

My mom's note had mentioned they'd sent him ahead to the Retreat. I hoped I might find some evidence at the apartment suggesting this had been the case.

Moving through it, I saw my own room again, my bed, my books on their shelves, and the terrible message scrawled over the wall and my poster frames:

I'VE BEEN WAITING
A LONG TIME FOR YOU, SKYE!

I hadn't forgotten my fate, at least as it was recorded in Mom and Todd's note: they didn't know where I was when they died. I figured I was in here—now, trapped in the future—when they had returned from their trip to the Hamptons and searched for me.

I entered Red's bedroom, the pop-culture boy cave. It was unchanged from the last time I had seen it—the red Cadillac couch, the R2-D2 fridge, the rope hammock by the window, all of it covered in a thick layer of dust.

I looked in his closet. His large travel suitcase was gone, as well as some clothes.

That was a good sign. Maybe Mom's note had been right.

I peered around the room.

Red may not have been the world's finest student, but he was clever, street-smart. He knew about the tunnel and he grasped time travel. If I suddenly went missing, he might suspect I was in this time. But what would he do?

I rummaged through his desk and his drawers, looking for some kind of message, but found nothing.

As I stood in the middle of his bedroom, frowning, my eyes fell on his R2-D2 fridge.

Its silver domed 'head' was covered in filthy dust.

On a hunch, I opened its front door.

The fridge was empty . . .

. . . except for a white envelope sealed inside a clear Ziploc sandwich bag on the top shelf.

The envelope was labelled: **BLUE**.

★ ★ ★

I tore it open and read it.

> *Dear Blue,*
>
> *It's your big brother here, coming to you from twenty-odd years ago. How weird is that?*
>
> *I'm not sure where you are but I'm guessing you're 'inside'. Assuming no-one finds this note first, it should still be here in twenty years.*
>
> *It's March 14 and things have got totally crazy here in NYC, even though the gamma cloud is still three days away. The whole city has become a war zone.*
>
> *I'm leaving the apartment now. Mom and Todd just called me from across town and told me to go to the helipad on the East River now. I tried to convince them to meet me at the helipad, but they're insisting on coming back to the apartment. They want to collect some bags and clothing (and some cash that they want to bring).*
>
> *When you get back to the present, find me at the Retreat.*
>
> *Stay safe, little sis.*
>
> *R*

I stared at the note, tears of relief trickling down my cheeks.

I was so pleased Red had got away safely.

My feelings for my mom and Todd were more mixed: their final trip back to the apartment—to get their suitcases, clothes and some money (for what, in a destroyed world?)—had been their death sentence. My mother's vanity and belief in a class system based on wealth had been the end of her.

I noted that Red's attempt to alter their future hadn't worked.

Then it struck me and I said aloud, 'Oh, Red. Thank you.'

Standing behind me, Jenny said, 'What? Why?'

I spun to face her. 'My brother just gave me an idea. There's one more place we can look for the gems, and while we're at it, maybe we can find out what happened to him.'

We hurried out of Red's bedroom into the hallway.

'What place?' Jenny asked, chasing me.

I turned as I ran. 'We have to get to the—'

'You're not going anywhere,' a deep voice said from the other end of the hallway and I looked up to see America Face standing there, crossbow in hand, blocking the way.

'Hello, Skye,' he said. 'I've been waiting a very long time for you.'

THE MAN IN THE MASK

'Who are you!?' I demanded.

Slowly, the tall figure reached up with his free hand and unclipped the strap of his red, white and blue goalie's mask.

The facemask fell to the floor and I saw him.

He looked totally different with his wild frizzy hair shaved off. He was also twenty years older than the seventeen-year-old I knew, but his freckled features were unmistakable.

It was Griff.

Age had given his face creases and he had filled out. This 38-year-old Griff was a man, full-grown and powerfully built.

And angry.

'Misty told me you'd meet me, Skye,' he said flatly. 'She said you'd bring her gem to The Plaza so I could ride out the gamma cloud. I waited and waited but you never came.'

I began to see what had happened. 'Griff. Please. Let me explai—'

'I waited for you!' he shrieked. '*I waited while the world burned and you never came!*'

Jenny and I both took an involuntary step back.

It was then that the full impact of Griff's fate hit me: Misty had lied to him—she had never told me anything about getting the gem to him and probably had no intention of ever getting it to him.

And so he had *not* been able to avoid the coming of the gamma cloud and the collapse of society that had accompanied its arrival.

When it had come on March 17, he had been one of the few to survive it, probably, I realised now, because of the many medications he'd been on.

And then he had waited—in this empty ruined world, for twenty-some years—for the secret runners to emerge from the well.

'You've been waiting all this time?' I asked.

The older version of Griff nodded.

'For me?'.

He nodded again. I saw his hand regripping the crossbow . . . and suddenly I recognised that, too: it was Verity's dad's $4,000 crossbow.

Lines from Griff's medical file came to me: how he had to keep taking his meds; cleptomania; disproportionate acts of revenge against those who slighted him. He'd clearly helped himself to Oz's hockey mask and Mr Keeley's crossbow . . . and he'd been stewing *for twenty years* to unleash his vengeance on me.

Griff said, 'When we did our runs, I knew that the tunnel transported us roughly twenty years into the future. So I kept track of the years and the seasons. For the record, your brother was right: the tunnel took us twenty-two years into the future.

'I wanted to be here when you emerged, so, not long after the coming of the gamma cloud, I parked that yellow cab over the hatch leading to the entry cave. I also drove a garbage truck over the exit hatch behind the Museum of

Natural History and deflated its tyres, too, so the only way you could get out was through the well.

'Since then I've been coming back to the well every year at this time to watch and wait for you and the others. I was the one who cleared the area around the well and set up camp there.

'A few months ago, I saw the others inside the tunnel, saw the lights on their phones. After that, it was only a matter of time till you emerged, Skye.'

'Griff,' I said, 'Misty did this. She manipulated you. She lied—'

'SHUT UP!' Old Griff yelled. 'SHUT YOUR FUCKING MOUTH! *You* did this! You left me! You have no idea what I've seen in the last twenty-two years! What I've had to do to live!'

I fell silent.

'Do you know who survived the cloud?' he said softly. 'I'll tell you, because I saw it all happen in real time. I saw every normal person drop dead where they stood. Who kept standing? Every crazy-assed psycho with a warped brain, that's who. Seems the mistimed electricity in every psychopath's and schizophrenic's brain made them immune to the gamma radiation.

'Whack-jobs in mental hospitals; bipolar and borderline personality disorder sufferers; the mentally ill on the streets. They survived. So did most of the psychos in prisons and county jails. In other words, everyone who howls at the moon.

'Somewhere in the chaos before the gamma cloud, someone decided to blow open the gates to the jail on Rikers Island so now there are all sorts of bad mother-fuckers running around. The Bible was wrong. The meek didn't inherit the Earth. The insane did.'

He shook his head, looking down at the crossbow in his hand.

When he looked up again, I saw madness in his eyes.

'I've had twenty-two years to think about how you left me for dead, Skye. Left me to live in this shithole of a world. Twenty-two years to think about how I was going to kill you. I'll tell you now: slow. I'm going to shoot you with this crossbow and while you're alive, I'm going cut off each of your limbs and eat them in front of your dying eyes.'

Then, right there in the hallway outside my brother's bedroom, he raised the crossbow and fired it at me.

AWAY

The arrow shot through the air but by the time Griff fired it, I'd yanked Red's wooden headhunter's shield off his door and held it up in front of my face.

The arrow struck the shield . . . penetrated it . . . but not all the way through. Its razor-sharp tip stopped an inch in front of my nose.

Griff's eyes blazed with fury.

I shoved Jenny back into Red's bedroom and we fell through the doorway together. I quickly slammed the door shut and toppled my brother's bookcase in front of it. A second later—*bam!*—the door shook violently, hit by Griff from the other side.

I turned to face the room.

'There's no way out of here,' Jenny said.

She was right. My don't-die plan had only gone as far as using Red's shield to fend off that first arrow. It hadn't extended to getting out of the apartment.

Bam! The door shook again.

'I'm coming for you, Skye!' Griff yelled. 'I've waited a long time for this and I won't be denied!'

My eyes scanned the room and found the window . . . and Red's Balinese rope hammock suspended in front of it.

There was no time to be subtle.

I grabbed his R2-D2 fridge and threw it through the window.

Glass exploded everywhere and the little droid fridge fell three floors straight down the face of the north tower before it struck the 18th floor crossover terrace, bounced off it, and fell another eighteen storeys and smashed into a thousand pieces on the sidewalk of Central Park West.

The window gaped before us.

I didn't stop moving. I still had Jenny's anti-kidnapping blade and I used it to saw into Red's rope hammock, cutting it in such a way that its back-and-forth lengths of rope were released to form one long stretch.

The hammock was about six feet long, but when unwound in this way, six feet became twelve, then eighteen, then twenty-four, then thirty.

I left one end of the hammock anchored to the ceiling and tossed the other end—the thirty-foot length of rope—out the window.

'Are you kidding me?' Jenny said.

'We don't have to go all the way down the building, just to the crossover, and then we run. Go! Go!'

Jenny didn't need to be told twice.

Out the window she went, gripping the rope like an abseiler, and in a moment she was out of sight.

Bam! The door behind me shook again and this time the bookcase shifted and I saw Griff squeeze his face through the gap—then replace his face with the crossbow.

He fired it.

I ducked.

The arrow whizzed out the window behind me.

Then I grabbed the length of rope that had been my brother's hammock and leapt out the window.

With my feet pressed against the outer wall of the San Remo building, I lowered myself down the face of the tower, the giant blood-coloured letters blaring '**WE ROSE UP!**' surrounding me.

Three floors below me, Jenny stood on the 18th floor crossover, looking up.

'Jump!' she yelled.

I let go, falling the last ten feet.

Jenny caught me and we sprinted away to the south tower, charged inside it and descended its fire stairs as fast as we could—knowing that Griff was at that very moment racing down the identical stairs in the north tower.

As we hit the bottom of the stairwell, Jenny said, 'Skye, where do we go now?'

My face set itself into a resolved grimace. 'Same place I was going to say earlier: we go to the Retreat at Plum Island.'

'Plum Island is a hundred miles away, at the far end of Long Island. How are we gonna get there?' Jenny asked.

'I have an idea for that,' I said. 'Follow me and don't stop till I say so.'

And so we ran.

Out of the San Remo and then westward through the deserted weed-covered streets of the Upper West Side.

Leading the way, I made sure we zigged and zagged, lest Griff spot us, but I always made sure we were tracking westward.

As we raced down 79th Street, I heard a cry and I turned to see Griff bounding down the decrepit street a hundred yards behind us, crossbow raised.

'Don't stop!' I yelled. 'Keep running!'

A minute later, we burst out of the building-lined street into a wildly overgrown park flanking the Henry Hudson

Parkway: Riverside Park. Beyond it lay the broad expanse of the Hudson River.

'The river?' Jenny said, perplexed.

'Not the river,' I panted. 'This way.'

We cut across the abandoned parkway, hurdling its guardrails, and beheld the near shore of the river. On it was our destination, the only boat marina on the entire island of Manhattan: the 79th Street Boat Basin.

Still parked in their slots on the basin's docks, abandoned by man and time, were several dozen recreational boats.

I instructed Jenny to grab as many gas cans as she could find while I jumped into the most basic motorboat I could see.

I wanted something simple and gasoline-powered, a vessel with no electrical circuit boards that could have been fried by the gamma cloud twenty-two years ago.

I found one: a little utility dinghy with an outboard motor, the kind of runabout rich people used to ferry themselves out to their bigger boats.

Thankfully, I'd driven little boats like these back in my sailing days with my dad. I primed the outboard motor, working the choke, and then I yanked hard on the starter cord.

It didn't start.

'*I see you, Skye!*' Griff's voice cut across my consciousness like fingernails on a chalkboard.

He was standing up on the parkway, looking down at me from a hundred yards away. He fired the crossbow but the distance was too great and it sliced into the water three feet from me.

Griff leapt over the guardrail.

I kept yanking on the starter cord.

Jenny joined me in the dinghy, dumping a few cans of gasoline onto the floor and untying the ropes. Suddenly the little boat's engine caught and with a smoky bang, the outboard motor sputtered to life.

I almost screamed with relief. After a few seconds, it was chugging with a regular rhythm and that was good enough for me.

'Let's go, Skye . . .' Jenny urged.

'Wait!' I said, jumping out of the boat and onto the deck, where I yanked a laminated map of greater New York off a noticeboard. It showed Manhattan Island, Connecticut and Long Island.

Then I leapt back into the dinghy and gunned the engine and we peeled out of the 79th Street Boat Basin at speed, racing out into the vastness of the Hudson River.

I turned to see Griff arrive at the shore, swearing and gesticulating with rage.

At first, I took us north—my plan was to go up and around Manhattan Island via the Harlem River and then cut through to Long Island Sound—but as I peered northward into the moonlit gloom, I saw that the George Washington Bridge had collapsed, blocking our way.

And so I banked the boat around and took us south down the Hudson. It would take a little longer going around Manhattan this way, but we could still make it.

It was only when we were a full mile downriver that I dared to breathe a deep sigh of relief.

TO THE ENDS OF THE EARTH

Cruising around New York in our little dinghy was a totally surreal experience.

It was a still night and the river was like glass. As we glided past the empty city, gazing at it by the light of the moon, the scale of the catastrophe that had befallen the world truly hit home.

Not a single window glowed with electric light. Every one of the many towers of the city was dark. Some buildings had toppled over, others—like the Empire State Building— teetered at extreme angles.

Creeping vegetation covered everything, a deeper black in the darkness, a visible cancer slowly consuming the cityscape.

And then there were the truly bizarre sights.

A dozen container ships—left to drift when their crews had abruptly dropped dead—had washed ashore and now rested against the buildings of downtown. One big oil tanker had managed to wedge itself fully into 14th Street up against the Standard Hotel. Moss and shrubs had half-swallowed both the ship and the hotel, so that it was hard to tell where the building ended and the boat began.

A crashed 737 aeroplane lay on the parkway down near Chelsea. The impact had caused the parkway to collapse. On another section of the road, two enormous Staten Island ferries lay on their sides like a pair of beached whales.

We rounded the bottom of the island and saw the Statue of Liberty.

Lady Liberty's head and upraised arm were gone, evidently by explosive force, judging by the outwardly bent metal at her neck and shoulder. They now lay at the base of her podium, turning the once-great statue into a modern-day Ozymandias.

Scrawled in red paint on the front of her iconic robes was the chilling message:

SEE
YOU ALL
IN HELL!

Jenny's eyes filled with tears. 'It's all gone. All of it.'

'And it ended so terribly,' I said, 'in anger and violence. What's wrong with people?'

It was then, as we turned northward up the East River, that we beheld the bridges.

The Brooklyn Bridge was still standing but it was entirely covered in vines. The Manhattan Bridge was half broken: the suspension cables at the city-end had buckled, so the roadway at that end had dropped into the river. As for the Williamsburg Bridge, both of its once mighty towers, eaten away by vegetation, had collapsed, causing the whole thing to fall into the river.

Importantly for us, the fallen wreckage had not entirely blocked the way.

We wound our way past the colossal pieces of fallen concrete and steel, our little dinghy tiny alongside them.

As we passed Brooklyn, I saw a fire atop a warehouse and beside it . . .

. . . a crucified human being.

Jenny stared at it, open-mouthed in horror. 'What is *that*?'

Guided by the simple map I had taken from the boat basin, we cruised up the East River before we turned right at Lawrence Point, heading east toward Rikers Island, La Guardia Airport and Long Island Sound.

As we came to the point, I saw a pulsing orange glow beyond it and my heart began to beat a little faster. Then we rounded the point and the prison island came into view.

I gasped. 'Mother of God . . .'

'The world didn't end for everybody,' Jenny said flatly.

In this otherwise dead city, the prison was alive with light and movement.

Fires burned in every guard tower. Drums boomed. Shadowy figures danced and drank. I saw more crucified figures on the walls, backlit by the firelight. Masked men with guns patrolled the lone bridge that connected Rikers Island to the shore near La Guardia.

This was what Griff had said.

To survive the gamma cloud's effects on the human brain, one needed to possess either a medically-created immunity or a natural one.

A natural resistance included having dysfunctional or overactive synapses in your brain. That group included people like Griff but also others taking medication for anxiety or depression or post-traumatic stress. But, by definition, that group also included most of the psychopaths and sociopaths at Rikers Island.

Welcome to the new world . . .

I cut the engine.

'What are you doing?' Jenny whispered.

'I don't want them to hear us or see our wake,' I said.

I leaned over the side and started paddling gently.

And so it took us much longer to pass Rikers Island than I'd hoped. We clung to the Bronx shoreline to the north of the firelit prison island, eventually using the seat-pads of our little boat as improvised paddles. It wasn't until we had passed Whitestone Bridge that I dared to restart the engine.

As dawn broke on this eerie new world, we powered away from New York City, heading toward the rising sun, cruising up Long Island Sound in our dinghy, forging our way toward Plum Island.

THE RETREAT

It took us two full days to reach Plum Island.

For one thing, our little dinghy wasn't exactly the fastest motorboat in the universe; for another, well, both Jenny and I simply needed sleep.

Once we were well clear of the city and Rikers Island, we came to a remote inlet near Caumsett State Park and there we found an offshore channel marker—it was basically a hut on stilts about a hundred yards from the shore.

It was perfect. Strung out from lack of sleep and the stress of running for so long on pure adrenaline, I estimate that we both slept for close on sixteen hours, right through the whole next day. I can't speak for Jenny, but I've never slept so soundly.

After our big sleeps, we spent the following night and most of the day after it cruising along the northern shore of Long Island.

It was going on four in the afternoon when it came into view.

Plum Island.

Low and flat, with a weird cluster of white box-like buildings that were both very old and very new, the island rose up out of the horizon before us.

It was a cloudy day and already getting dark. This was the final factor in it taking so long for us to reach Plum Island:

I didn't want to go ashore at night. I wanted to see its secrets in the full light of day.

The Retreat had waited for me for twenty-two years. It could wait another night.

And so we slept on another channel marker till morning came. Then as soon as the sun rose, we brought our little dinghy ashore on Plum Island.

We landed at the island's main arrival area, a semicircular ring of docks sheltered by a pair of breakwaters.

Broken boats littered the shore; a few helicopters lay upside down beside them. Tossed around by twenty years of storms and hurricanes, the boats and choppers had smashed all the jetties and storage shacks to splinters.

I ran our little dinghy aground near a large white sign that had almost been completely consumed by weeds:

US GOVERNMENT PROPERTY
LANDING PROHIBITED

'I guess the creators of the Retreat decided to keep the government's old keep-out signs,' I said.

Jenny said, 'You don't advertise your secret hideaway for the rich and powerful.'

We walked a short way across the island until we came to its largest set of structures, a massive cluster of white-painted warehouse-sized buildings that had once been the Animal Disease Center.

Facing the waters of the Sound to the north, the compound was, quite simply, enormous. And the features that had once enabled it to keep animal diseases contained had been cleverly converted to allow humans to survive for a long time: water tanks, diesel generators, living quarters and, importantly, airtight spaces for food storage.

It was the perfect sanctuary for the exclusive few to ride out the gamma cloud.

And then I saw the damage.

'This hideaway,' I said, 'didn't stay secret.'

The damage to the white-painted buildings had not been done by any storm or hurricane.

Hundreds of bullet holes pockmarked the walls. Charred, blasted-open sections of the walls indicated the use of grenades or explosives of some kind.

A battle had been fought here. A big battle.

A lawn of waist-high grass separated the buildings of the compound from the Sound, and after a moment my scanning eyes noticed objects in the grass: dozens of small boats not unlike my little dinghy. Rowboats, motorboats, all kinds of boats lay in the deep grass. They, too, had been tossed by years of storms, but their legacy was clear.

'The public found out about the Retreat,' Jenny said. 'They wanted to get in as well, so they stormed it.'

I nodded. I could picture the scene:

A dozen wealthy families—still wearing their Armani suits and glittering jewels—staring out at an armada of poor people storming the shore in their little boats like an invading seaborne force.

With a final look back at the lawn, I stepped inside the nearest building.

★ ★ ★

Bullet holes in the walls—shattered windows—dangling fluorescent light tubes—bloody smears on the floor.

Jenny and I strode silently through the wreckage until we came to the area containing the living quarters. The doors were made of thick steel and had rubber seals. Each door also had a vacuum-sealed porthole window of double-glazed tempered glass sunk into it.

Nameplates on the doors identified the families who were to live in them.

As I peered in through the portholes, I saw how the wealthy had died.

Unable to penetrate the fortified airtight apartments, the attackers had cut off the air, suffocating the wealthy occupants. How did I know this? The messages scrawled on the porthole windows in blood or lipstick told me:

YOUR MONEY CAN'T BUY YOU AIR! DIE WITH THE REST OF US, RICH PRICKS!

I wasn't sure what was more repugnant: the image of wealthy families trapped in the airtight chambers they had paid a fortune to occupy, slowly suffocating, or the pure hatred of the poor who had caught up with them.

I guessed this was what the French Revolution had looked like.

I found the first apartment I was looking for. The nameplate on it read:

ALLEN

The door to my family's chamber was open. It was empty. No bodies. No sign of Red. No sign even of his suitcase.

I knew that my mom and Todd had not made it to the Retreat. But Red's note had said he was coming here.

I began to despair. I needed a sign, a sign that he'd made it.

And then I saw it, sitting all by itself in the back corner of the room:

A bronze-coloured Graceland baseball.

I picked up the gaudy ball, turned it over in my hand, saw the smiling face of Elvis Presley on it—

—and some handwriting.

Red's handwriting, in black marker, on the ball:

Gone to Dad's favourite beach house

I exhaled with relief.

Red had made it to the Retreat and then—I imagine when he saw the incoming attackers—he'd fled, but not before letting me know he'd got here.

'Oh, Red,' I said aloud, making Jenny spin.

She came over. 'Your dad's favourite beach house? What does that mean?'

'Race Rock Lighthouse. It's over by Fishers Island, not far from here.'

Buoyed by the hope that Red might have escaped from the Retreat alive, my thoughts returned to my own predicament and my focus narrowed.

I sought out another apartment and found it a short way down the corridor.

The heavy steel door was slightly ajar, its rubber lining holding it loosely in the doorframe.

The nameplate on the door read:

COLLINS

The Collins family did not die well.

The evidence before me was pretty clear: they hadn't died of suffocation, huddled together in their airtight apartment.

Five bodies, long decayed, lay on the floor. They still wore the clothes they had been wearing twenty-two years previously. Their bags lay in the corner, not yet unpacked.

The partial closure of the chamber's door had kept animals out, preserving the corpses somewhat. It was only the ravages of time that had decayed them: all five were shrivelled and dry, their leathery skin clinging to the bones beneath. Their fingernails, I noticed, had continued growing for some time after their deaths and looked positively ghoulish.

Mr Conrad Collins—Misty's father, successful property developer and descendant of the *Mayflower*—lay crumpled against the far wall, his face all but unrecognisable. His grey suit was riddled with bloody bullet holes. Whoever had shot him had shot him *a lot*, with an automatic weapon.

Lying beside him, still dressed in a pair of diamante-studded hipster jeans and a tight top, was the dried husk of the girl who had once been Chastity Collins. Two bullets had blown out the back of her head.

Starley Collins still wore a white-and-gold Gucci pantsuit. It too had been shredded by bullet holes.

I stepped closer and moved aside the collar of her jacket, checking her neck.

'Damn it,' I said.

'What?' Jenny said from behind me.

'She's not wearing her necklace,' I said. 'The figure-eight one with her gem in it. I was hoping she'd worn it when she came here.'

I went over to the last two bodies. Misty and Oz.

They lay face-down, one on top of the other. I shoved the top body with my shoe.

The dead-eyed faces of two strangers stared up at me. Two poor folk who had been shot during the confrontation.

They weren't Misty or Oz.

I spun on the spot, suddenly fearful.

Misty hadn't come here. Hadn't fled to the Retreat when her family had escaped the city on March 14.

The revelation rattled me. For some reason, I didn't want to stay here anymore.

I recalled Misty's taunt from before:

'*You don't think you and Bo were the first people to leave the tunnel and explore this world, do you?*'

Had Misty come all the way out here? Had she discovered what would happen at the Retreat and so had *not* gone there with her family back in the present?

I definitely didn't want to stay here anymore.

A quick search of the Collinses' luggage revealed that there were no gems here, not Misty's or her mom's. I had the distinct feeling that Misty had got the better of me somehow, that even now she was one step ahead of me.

'Let's go,' I said to Jenny.

'Where?'

I looked at her. 'Since we haven't got any other options, we follow the trail my brother left behind.'

RED'S TRAIL

Race Rock Lighthouse—my father's favourite beach house—is actually not that far from Plum Island, less than twenty miles away. But getting there can be a little hairy as you have to sail across a channel that is exposed to the Atlantic Ocean.

After loading up our little dinghy with gas cans filled with fuel, we left Plum Island and arrived at Race Rock several hours later.

Thankfully, the sea was relatively calm and we tied our boat to the little dock that serviced the fairytale-like cottage built on its tiny mount a short way off Fishers Island.

Before they had abandoned it, the last people to come to the cottage had shuttered all the windows and doors, which was why when I opened the main door, I found the interior of the lighthouse dry and oddly neat and tidy.

It was empty, except for one thing.

A lone envelope on the kitchen table, weighted down under a rock and labelled: **BLUE**.

I tore it open.

A single line in Red's handwriting was on the note inside it:

I have gone to the place where Liberty lost.

Reading it over my shoulder, Jenny frowned. 'Where Liberty lost?'

I stared at the line.

'He's being cryptic, in case someone else found this note,' I said. 'Red, my dad and I used to vacation up here in the summertime. We'd sail all over the place: to this lighthouse, over to Martha's Vineyard or up around Rhode Island.'

I thought for a moment. 'The place where Liberty lost . . .'

And I smiled. 'I got it. *Liberty* was the name of a famous racing yacht. The yacht that lost the America's Cup in 1983 at Newport, Rhode Island.'

It was nearing sunset when, a few hours later, Jenny and I arrived in our little motorised dinghy at Newport, Rhode Island.

I was shocked when I saw men armed with assault rifles standing on all the major headlands, but as I looked more closely at them, I saw that they wore jeans, boots and denim jackets: the clothes of ordinary men, not crazies or inmates or soldiers. As we sailed into the port, I noticed a heavily fortified guardhouse on the Newport Bridge.

A small police patrol boat came out to meet us and at the sight of me, the young deputy at its controls went bug-eyed and he quickly allowed us to pass.

I was very confused by all this and wanted to know more, but as we came to the city piers of Newport, all those thoughts flew from my mind as I saw him standing there, smiling knowingly, waiting for me.

It was my brother, Red.

Only now he was nearly forty years old.

OLD RED

His facial features hadn't changed—the sparkling eyes, the elfin face—but the body around them had.

No longer was Red a lean sixteen-year-old boy. He was stockier, visibly stronger. His forearms were all muscle.

His face had aged considerably: the skin around his eyes was wrinkled from squinting and browned from working long hours out of doors.

In the three days since I had last seen him, my brother had aged twenty-two years and become a man.

There was one other thing about him that I should mention: he was wearing a sheriff's uniform, complete with a shiny bronze star.

I leapt out of the dinghy and embraced my brother, tears streaming down my face.

I can't imagine how it looked to the two dozen people who had gathered at the pier to watch our little boat pull in: who was this teenage girl throwing her arms around their sheriff?

'Blue,' he said. 'I'm so glad you made it here. You found my notes? And the baseball?'

I handed him the Graceland baseball as if it were made of gold. 'I did. Boy, am I thrilled to see you.'

Red said hello to Jenny but then he noticed the crowd watching us. He also glanced awkwardly at the buildings behind him, as if checking who was behind their windows. 'Let's go to my place and get you cleaned up. Then we can talk.'

We went back to Red's home a few blocks from the piers. There Jenny and I showered—in an actual shower although the water was cold—and redressed.

By now the sun had set, and when I came downstairs, I found Red standing at the kitchen table (it was lit by candles) holding the hand of a very pretty woman and with two outrageously cute little girls in front of him.

'Blue,' he said, 'this is my wife, Tabitha, and our daughters, Katie and Skye.'

I looked down at the smaller one. I guessed she was about six years old. 'Skye, huh? What a lovely name.'

In response, the girl hid behind Red's leg.

His wife seemed most perplexed by all of this. Her expression was half-jealous, half-confused—my likeness to Red must have thrown her, but she was clearly thinking: *Who the hell is this girl?*

Dinner followed.

Red told Tabitha that I was the daughter of a cousin who had been thought lost in the chaos of the gamma cloud's arrival. He'd left a message for my family in New York and instructed his deputies to keep an eye out for me if I ever arrived. It wasn't the best cover story in history, but it was better than saying your sister was a time traveller.

After dinner, Red, Jenny and I adjourned to his study. Red closed the door.

He smiled wryly. 'You had to arrive just before dinnertime, didn't you?'

'Sorry,' I said. 'Talk to me, please. Tell me about all this.'

Red sat in the chair behind his desk. 'It's been twenty-two years, but I remember the day you disappeared like it was yesterday. I figured you'd gone inside—with Bo and Verity, who also never came back—but then I had to go to the Retreat. For some reason, Misty didn't go and wherever she was, she must have taken her gem with her, and I couldn't do anything to come get you. Then the city went crazy and, oh, Blue, I'm so sorry I left—'

'Red,' I said. 'Forget it. As far as I'm concerned, it's been three days. And I haven't spent a moment of it hating you for not coming to save me.'

He bowed his head. The timelines of our lives had literally gone down separate paths. What had been three days for me was a lifetime for him and this had clearly weighed on his mind the whole time.

'Tell me about the world in 2040,' I said. 'And that.' I jerked my chin at his sheriff's star. 'Can't say I expected to see you as the sheriff.'

Red gave a small smile. 'The gamma cloud wiped out humanity all right. By our reckoning, less than 0.5% of the population survived.

'And most of those survivors are people with what our doctors call "atypical hypersynaptic brain function". Which is another way of saying that most of them are not exactly friendly individuals: criminals, murderers, rapists, antisocial aggressive types plus the clinically insane.

'A much smaller percentage of the survivors are folks like me: people who happened to be on the right medication at the time or who just took the right vitamins or ate the right foods. Many, strangely enough, were on anxiety medication, which means they're the exact opposite of aggressive. They're modest, humble people who somehow survived with all the assholes. It's like the cloud wiped out the middle and kept only the extremes of people. We've tried to gather all the decent ones on this island.'

So Griff wasn't entirely correct, I thought. Some of the meek *had* inherited the Earth.

'What happened after the cloud?' Jenny asked.

Red said, 'In the years after the gamma cloud, the whole eastern seaboard was a mess. Empty cities. Roaming gangs of prisoners. I went to the Retreat—Mom and Todd never made it—but I saw the writing on the wall when it was attacked the first time on March 16 by about fifty of the "Angry Poor" as the wealthy were calling them. I figured a lot more angry people would come later, and they did.

'So late on March 16, I left my baseball there with the message for you, stole a little motorboat and hightailed it out of there. I rode out the gamma cloud alone at Race Rock Lighthouse and somehow survived. I guess Dad's diet and vitamin regime worked.'

He stared off into space, remembering. It was so strange to see my brother, my twin brother, looking and acting so grown up. His weary eyes now held half a lifetime of hard experience behind them.

He shrugged. 'I couldn't stay at the lighthouse. So I ventured out, looking for people like me, people who would want to rebuild. How do you rebuild society? One brick at a time, I guess. I met some good people—also met a few bad people. I've also killed quite a few people. But the good folks and I rounded up more good folks and we settled here on Rhode Island.

'It's a great spot to start rebuilding society because it's big enough to have a couple of power stations and its own water supply, yet it's only accessible by three road bridges. It's defendable. We guard all those bridges 24/7, plus all the sea approaches.

'After that, well, we identified the people a new society needs most: doctors, electricians, plumbers. Funny, a new community doesn't need hedge-fund managers and investment bankers. We've managed to restart one of the power stations and get some electricity online again—at least for a couple of hours a day—plus the water mains which allows for flushing toilets. Trust me, the world's better with flushing toilets.'

'A new town also needs a good lawman,' I said. 'An honest man, someone who won't favour one person over another, someone who can be trusted to enforce the law.'

Red bowed his head modestly.

I smiled warmly. 'You always had it in you, Red. I knew that.'

'I do my best,' he said softly. He snuffed a rueful laugh. 'I always teased you that I was older than you. By two minutes. Now I really am older. What about you? What happened?'

I told him everything: how Misty and her clique had been responsible for the missing girls; how they had brought Jenny into the future and left her for dead; how we had battled the furious Griff and fled New York with him on our tail; and how we had gone to the Retreat not only to find out Red's fate, but also to acquire Starley Collins's gem. Without a gem to place in the exit portal, we were stuck in this time.

'But her gem wasn't there,' I concluded.

As I finished speaking, I looked at my brother—now thirty-eight years old, a father and a sheriff—and a great sadness came over me. My trials over the last few days paled in comparison to the years of danger, fear and terror he had endured since the cloud.

And I realised: this world was now his world. It was not mine. He had lived in it, fought in it, *earned* his place in it over twenty-two years. I hadn't.

And in my heart of hearts, I felt I couldn't stay. Twins we may still have been, but we were not the same anymore. I wondered if we could even live together in this time.

Red's aged eyes met mine and I could see that he was thinking the same thing.

'There's also another problem,' I said. 'Dad. He sent me a text just before I made this run. He's going to arrive in New York City—alone and unprepared—right in the middle of all the chaos. I have to find a way back to help him.'

It was then that a peculiar look crossed Red's face.

'I've got something for you,' he said as he reached down and slid open his desk drawer. 'Something I've been holding on to for a long time.'

He pulled an envelope from the drawer and handed it across the desk to me.

Written on it in a teenager's hand were the words:

FOR SKYE
DO NOT OPEN TILL 2040

My eyes snapped up. 'Who—what is this?'

Red said, 'When I was leaving Plum Island just before the gamma cloud hit, someone ran into the water after me, chasing my boat, begging to come with me. It was Oz Collins.'

'Oz?' I said.

'Yeah. I'd chatted with him on the first day I arrived at the Retreat. He wasn't as bad as the other kids said. I'd heard he was a weirdo, but he wasn't like that at all.'

'Misty made up all that stuff,' I said. 'Set him up.'

'Hmmm,' Red said thoughtfully. 'Oz asked about you and I said you were missing, but in those times a lot of people were missing. He gave me a kind, almost distant smile and wandered off. Next time I saw him was when he chased me out into the water as I was fleeing Plum Island on March 16. He also knew it wasn't a safe place to stay.'

'I thought you said you rode out the gamma cloud at Race Rock alone?' I said.

'I did,' Red said. 'Oz asked me to drop him back on Long Island. He didn't say why. He said he was going back to the city. So I dropped him off, but when I did, he gave me this envelope.'

I took the envelope and stepped into the corner of the office to read its contents privately by the light of a flickering candle.

There was a note inside it and it read:

Dear Skye,

I know you don't know me very well, but I feel I know you. You were kind to me on two occasions that I have always remembered: that time you defended me after my magic act at the talent show and when we talked about our costumes at Verity's birthday party.

Some people think I'm weird, but I'm not. I'm just shy. I find it hard to talk to people which is why it was so nice when you chatted with me.

This may surprise you, but I know about the tunnel and how it works. I visit the other world sometimes.

I looked up from the note.

'No way . . .' I said aloud.

Both Red and Jenny looked at me questioningly but I held up my hand and kept reading.

Like every little brother in the world, I watch my sisters constantly, especially when they sneak out at night. This is how I discovered the tunnel.

Sometimes, I would steal my mom's gem and use it to enter the tunnel. Other times I'd take Misty's.

(I saw you once when I was inside: I was up on the roof of the National History Museum but I was wearing my hood, so if I were spotted I wouldn't be recognised. Another time, I shrieked at your brother down the well. Sorry about that. But I found that screaming crazily at someone was the best way to scare them off.)

I know Misty is unhinged. She can hate like no-one else. Because of her, I spent a whole summer at military school and everybody thinks I'm a porn-addicted freak. And she hates you because Bo likes you. This is why—I suspect—you are missing now: she has left you stranded inside.

I also overheard her talking to Griff on the phone, telling him that you would get a gem to him. This was obviously a lie, since I imagine you're in the other New York. I have encountered Griff there, an older Griff with a shaven head, lurking around your apartment, waiting for you, I guess.

(I actually tried to warn you about Griff, with a message in your toy kangaroo, which I grabbed in the future. But maybe that was a bit too obtuse or perhaps you never saw it.)

As I leave Plum Island today, I am taking with me one last thing: my mother's gem.

I am going to leave it for you in a secret place so you can find it in the future, open the exit and get back to the present. If I can help you get back and mess up Misty's plan for you, it would make me very happy indeed. My final revenge on her for that summer at military school.

I can't tell you in this letter where I will leave your gem, lest it fall into the wrong hands. All I can say is that I have left it in a place that only you will notice and know.

I'm not sure where—or when—I will see you again, Skye, but I wish you luck, and I thank you for being nice to me at a time in my life when few others were.

Best wishes,
Oz Collins
March 16, 2018

I stared off into space, thunderstruck.

Oz had taken his mother's gem with him when he'd fled the Retreat.

There was a way out of here.

A place only I would 'notice and know'.

I handed the letter to Red and Jenny. They read it as I thought some more.

Oz had been the figure in the hoodie. Like Red, I'd assumed the shadowy figure in the hoodie and the shadowy bald man—Griff—had been the same person. But they hadn't. Oz had worn the hoodie, while Griff, having shaved off his mop of red hair, was the bald guy.

When she'd finished reading the note, Jenny came to the crux of the issue right away. 'Why does he say a place you would *notice and know*, not just one you would *know*?'

'That's the question,' I said.

What would I notice that no-one else would? What did Oz know about me—from our few interactions—that he could utilise in such a way?

And then I got it.

'Stephen King,' I said aloud.

'What?' Jenny said.

'If we want to get back to our time, we have to go back to the city,' I said firmly. 'Back to my apartment. Back to my bedroom.'

BACK INTO THE DARK WORLD

The next morning, after a glorious sleep in a clean bed under a solid roof in a quiet house, Red helped us load up the dinghy with extra gas and food.

It was sunny for now but black clouds loomed on the horizon.

'A big storm's coming,' Red said, handing us a pair of plastic ponchos. I thought I saw him glancing at one of the warehouses beside the dock as he spoke.

'Thanks,' I said, stowing the ponchos on the boat.

I turned to Jenny. 'Are you sure about this? You could stay here, you know, in this time.'

Jenny said, 'First of all, if my dad's going to die, I don't want him doing so thinking I went missing. If I can, I want to find him so he knows I'm safe, and then see out the gamma cloud with him. If you're gonna face the end of the world, you want to do it with the people you love.'

She shrugged. 'I also wouldn't mind seeing Misty again so I can slap her in the face.'

We boarded the dinghy. Red's family—still clearly curious and confused—watched from a distance.

Red handed me a pistol. 'Just in case you run into some of the nastier survivors out there. I wish I could give you both a gun, but this is all I can spare.'

'I appreciate it.' I jammed the gun into the back of my jeans.

Then I looked my brother in the eye. Wherever I went now, in place or time, I didn't think I'd ever see him again. He knew it, too.

'You've done well for yourself, Red,' I said. 'I'm proud of you. Proud of what you've become.'

'Thanks.'

'Good luck with this place. Bring civilisation back. Someone has to.'

'We'll try,' he said. 'You take care of yourself, Blue. If you get back and find Dad, tell him that I did okay.'

'I will,' I said.

We embraced one last time and then I hopped in the dinghy and, with Jenny by my side, we powered away from Newport, leaving its armed citizens and fortified bridges behind us. Red stood on the dock watching and waving until we disappeared behind the headland.

Our journey back was slow and tough.

It began to rain not long after we left Newport, and when the storm hit and the Sound became too choppy, we had to take shelter at an inlet and stay there for the night.

The rain continued throughout the next day, but the wind died down a little, so we were able to work our way back down the Sound.

After almost a full day of travel, the ruins of New York City appeared on the horizon: a line of jagged skyscrapers—some of them broken—rising into the grim stormy sky.

I stared hard at them.

We were going back in.

★ ★ ★

We reached Rikers Island just as night fell.

It was still raining hard, but that actually turned out to be a blessing in disguise since the rain drove the unruly inhabitants of the prison indoors and we were able to pass by the island unseen. Although, just to be safe, we turned off the engine and paddled silently along the Bronx shore.

Then the wind came up again and another full-blown storm hit, even worse than the one from the day before: rain, forks of lightning, thunderclaps, raging winds.

Just as the river around us began to get whipped up by the wind, we pulled our trusty little dinghy in to Pier 107 on the eastern shore of Manhattan and climbed out. We would go on foot from there, trekking back to the San Remo via the Upper East Side.

The wind blasted down the canyons of the city and the rain flew sideways as we came to Central Park.

We crossed the park and eventually my home came into view: the San Remo building.

With a final look at each other, Jenny and I went inside.

HOME

The hallway outside my apartment was dark and dank. Rain poured outside, drumming against the broken window at the end of the corridor. The occasional flash of lightning lit up the space like a strobe.

We approached the front door cautiously.

It was ajar.

It wobbled slightly, buffeted by the wind entering the apartment through its shattered windows.

Gripping my pistol tightly, I pushed open the door with its barrel.

The hinges squealed loudly. I swore inwardly: if anyone was here, they would have heard—

A hand shot out from the darkness and grabbed my wrist, dislodging the gun from my hand. It clattered to the floor.

I spun to see Griff standing right beside me—no longer wearing his Stars-and-Stripes hockey mask and gripping his crossbow in his spare hand!

'Hi, Skye,' he said before he punched me in the face and I fell to the floor, my nose gushing blood.

'I thought you might come back here,' he said. 'Trying to find a way out, I imagine. But if I couldn't get out, neither can you.'

He stood astride me, aiming his crossbow down at my face just as Jenny came bursting through the doorway and crash-tackled him, bumping his crossbow just as he fired it and the arrow—a twelve-inch-long ultra-stiff carbon-fibre bolt—slammed into the floor with a powerful *whump!* one inch from my right ear.

It quivered, sticking up vertically from the hardwood floor.

Griff grunted as he hit the ground with Jenny on top of him. They separated and began to stand but Griff was faster, and as he rose to his knees, he backhanded Jenny with one big fist, knocking her out with a single blow. Jenny crumpled to the floor.

I took the opportunity to leap onto Griff's back and wrapped my arms around his neck, trying to break it. Fat chance. He just dropped us both backwards, slamming me back-first onto the floor underneath his bulky frame, knocking the wind out of me.

Then he knelt on top of me and in that moment I knew that unless I did something right then, something lethal, I was dead. Kill or be killed. Nothing more, nothing less. And so I did the only thing I could think to do.

I kicked Griff in the balls, grabbed him by the back of the neck, rolled sideways and, with all my strength, slammed his face into the floor.

Did I aim for the arrow sticking up from the floor? It's hard to say. I definitely saw it out of the corner of my eye in the split second before I did it.

As Griff's forehead hit the floor, the blunt end of the arrow was thrust up into his left eye and he screamed in a way I had never heard a human being scream before.

The arrow penetrated Griff's eye socket, shot up through his brain and then came bursting out the back of his skull, spraying blood and brains as it did so.

Face-down on the floor, both arms limp, Griff's body

shuddered gruesomely, spasming involuntarily before it finally went still. A pool of blood oozed out from under his face. It looked like his head had been nailed to the floor by the arrow.

I rolled away from his body to check on Jenny. I shook her gently and her eyes fluttered open.

'Did we . . . did we get him?' she asked.

I nodded at Griff, face-down in the pool of his own blood, the arrow—with flecks of blood and brains on it—sticking out the back of his head.

'Oh, we got him all right,' I said.

When I was sure Jenny was okay, I hurried into my bedroom.

I saw the books on the shelves, my eyes zeroing in on my prized Stephen King collection—arranged in order of publication, the one truly personal thing that Oz Collins knew about me, the one thing that he knew I would *notice*.

And there it was.

Misery.

As Oz knew, it was my favourite Stephen King novel, and it was wedged between *Rose Madder* and *The Green Mile*.

Only that was the wrong spot.

Its usual place, earned by order of publication, was between *The Dark Tower II* and *The Tommyknockers*.

Something only I would notice and know.

I grabbed *Misery* and opened it . . .

. . . to find the pages of my favourite novel hollowed out and inside the void that had been created . . .

. . . was a single amber gem.

Starley Collins's gem.

'Oh, Oz,' I said aloud, 'thank you.'

★ ★ ★

Jenny and I dashed out of the San Remo and headed directly for the private conservancy garden behind the Museum of Natural History.

I figured we could go to the exit cave there, stand in the short section of tunnel behind the portal, place the gem in the pyramid and then simply step back through the portal to the present.

But when we arrived at the conservancy garden, I stopped short.

I'd forgotten that Griff had been here.

The fence surrounding the garden had been flattened and the thing that had toppled it—a garbage truck, driven here long ago by the vengeful Griff—lay directly on top of the hatch in the garden.

Its tyres had indeed been deflated, causing the huge rust-covered vehicle to lie flat on the hatch. There was no way on God's Earth we could move it.

Twenty-two years of unchecked shrub growth had climbed up and around the garbage truck, making it part of the garden and actually hiding the hatch even more comprehensively than it had been hidden before.

'What do we do now?' Jenny asked.

'The well,' I said. 'We go back to the well and get into the tunnel. We'll be able to get to the exit portal and our time that way.'

We raced back into the park, across the Transverse and around the Swedish Cottage.

We pushed through the bushes surrounding the clearing and beheld the low brick well.

Verity's body still lay slumped against it, her lifeless eyes open in a stupid stare, one leg still gripped by the bear trap and the arrow still lodged in her heart.

On the ground around her and the well, still partially concealed by a carpet of brown leaves and twigs, were the other five bear traps from the Met exhibit.

'Stay back,' I warned. 'Let me find a safe path between the traps.'

Jenny hung back as I edged carefully forward, cautiously pushing the carpet of leaves aside with my toes until I arrived at the well . . . just as a figure rose up from behind it and aimed a pearl-handled pistol directly at my heart.

Misty.

Misty's eyes were deadly. She held her mother's gun with a firm assured grip.

'I've been coming here the last few days,' she said. 'Just for a couple hours a day. I saw you in the tunnel, Skye. I don't know how you got away from that roof but you did. So I've been coming here to check up on you.'

'Have you told Griff yet that I'm going to bring him your gem?' I said. 'Have you lied to him yet?'

'I have,' Misty said. 'And he gets so angry, Griff. So angry. And in case you're getting any ideas, my gem is hidden in a crevice in the tunnel—one of the thousands of tiny crevices in there—so you won't find it and get out using it.'

I'd had enough. 'Listen, bitch, I've travelled way too far for way too long to play stupid games with you now. If you're gonna kill me, just kill me, okay?'

'Okay,' she said lightly, re-aimed the pistol and pulled the trigger.

★ ★ ★

Nothing happened. The gun didn't fire. It just clicked.

Misty frowned but I knew what had happened.

She didn't have a round in the chamber.

Classic city-girl error. Any girl who'd grown up in the South or in a hunting family would never make that mistake, but a spoilt rich kid from the Upper East Side—especially one like Misty who had probably learned everything she knew about guns from the movies—clearly would.

I wasn't going to let her rectify the situation. As Misty frowned quizzically at her pistol and reached for the slide, I bounded forward, leapt over the well and threw myself at her.

We went tumbling to the leaf-covered ground, and as we did, a cluster of brown leaves exploded upward as I inadvertently clipped one of the bear traps hidden underneath them and—*snap!*—the trap's metal jaws sprang shut with terrifying force inches from my hip.

But Misty still had the gun, and as we landed in the carpet of leaves, she yanked on its slide, chambering a round, and suddenly that gun was live.

I grabbed her gun hand with both of my hands, holding it at bay. I glimpsed Jenny over on the other side of the clearing, too far away to be of any help.

Her arms shaking, fighting against mine, Misty began to bring the gun around toward my face.

I tried to resist but whether it was exhaustion on my part or just sheer strength on hers, Misty was too strong, and the gun's barrel came closer and closer.

I clenched my teeth as I struggled against her, but it was no use. In a few seconds, Misty was going to shoot me in the face.

Fuck it, I thought, and I shifted my weight suddenly, rolling the two of us across the leaf-covered ground—rolling and rolling—until Misty's head came down in the middle of a pile of brown leaves and *clang!* the leaves erupted, fluttering upwards, and a pair of steel jaws came blasting out from under them, wrapping around her head, clamping down on her neck in a single brutal instant.

There came a sickening crack and Misty's body slumped immediately.

That she was dead, there was no doubt.

The powerful clamping mechanism of the bear trap had almost torn her head from her body, its steel teeth almost biting all the way through her neck. Mercifully, the leaves that Griff had used to conceal the trap shielded most of the grisly sight from my view.

Blood dripped onto the gruesome necklace of leaves that were now pinned to Misty's throat. Her eyes stared up at the sky, unblinking, lifeless.

Jenny picked her way carefully over to my side.

'Fucking hell,' she gasped, looking at Misty's body. 'Now, *that* is what she deserved.'

I just shook my head. 'You got that right.'

A few minutes later, Jenny and I sat on the rim of the well.

We had pulled as many branches and stalks as we could over to it and laid them across it, trying to conceal the well from this future world. I had also taken Misty's keys from her: the ones that opened the hatches at each end of the tunnel.

Jenny went down the well first. I lingered for a moment on the rim, giving that strange world around me one last look. I thought of Red and of Bo and of the journey I had survived.

And then into the well I went, pulling the last branches across it behind me.

Down the well and into the tunnel.

My heart leapt when I saw the exit doorway at the far end.

Jenny and I came to the ancient portal and I inserted Starley Collins's gem into the pyramid. The curtain of light sprang to life and as we stepped through it together, I closed my eyes with relief—

—and when I opened them we were on the other side, back in the present day, in the exit cave beneath the Museum of Natural History.

I led Jenny up the ladders to the surface and a few minutes later we emerged from the gardener's hatch in the conservancy garden and I heard the glorious sounds of car horns and police sirens in the night.

We were back.

Just in time to witness the end of the world.

PART VII

THE END OF CIVILISATION

**What the caterpillar calls the end of the world
The Master calls a butterfly.**

RICHARD BACH

MAYHEM

New York City was in meltdown.

It was indeed March 14—the night of March 14, to be precise—and the city had descended into chaos, chaos that would only get worse over the next three days.

Police cars and ambulances sped every which way, lights flashing, sirens wailing. Looters laid siege to buildings; hooligans threw Molotov cocktails into shop windows. Fires blazed everywhere.

Jenny and I split up to find our respective fathers, arranging to meet later.

I passed the San Remo building: a giant crowd of rioters was massed in front of it, held back by police. They chanted, 'We want Manny! We want Manny!'

I couldn't have got in if I'd tried.

Red would—thankfully—have already left for the Retreat. But somewhere in there, huddled and afraid, were my mom and Todd, as well as the radio host, Manny Wannemaker, who had inflamed this very crowd. And that wasn't even mentioning the shocking murders that would happen—or may have already happened—in Hattie's apartment.

I didn't linger.

I raced downtown to Penn Station where, amid the heaving throng of people trying to escape the city on trains, I finally found my father sitting quietly and patiently on a suitcase at our usual meeting place by the escalators.

He had waited eight hours for me. We embraced and hustled out of there.

The next three days went by in a blur.

There was no point returning to my apartment. I couldn't get in anyway. Mom and Todd would die by their own hand and Red, as I knew, was already gone.

I desperately wanted to tell my dad about the portals and my travels through time. Open-minded as he was, I knew there was really only one way to do it, and that was to take him to the entry cave and show him.

That cave turned out to be one of the safest places in the city and a good spot to lay low during the uproar.

I showed my dad how the portal operated: placing the gem in the pyramid, initiating the curtain of purple light and stepping through it.

Because of the age restriction on travelling through the time-tunnel, I had him dash overland through the park to the exit portal on the west side and sure enough, I popped out of that portal soon after to meet him. After that, I showed him the well behind the Swedish Cottage.

He was, of course, amazed.

But once the initial shock wore off and I told him about the theory of time I had found, his analytical mind took over and he started talking animatedly about time spirals, Einstein Bridges and folds in time.

I told him everything. About Misty and the runners and the missing girls, about Misty's feelings for Bo, about Bo and me, about being tied up on the roof of the Met with Jenny and about Bo's horrific death there. And I told him about Red's future: how I'd found Red twenty-two years from now as the sheriff of a fledgling community on Rhode Island.

'Red's always been a big kid,' Dad said, 'but I've long believed that he'd mature well. I'm pleased to hear that.'

When I showed my dad the photos Bo had taken of the cave paintings in the tunnel of priest-like figures holding coloured gems, my dad said something odd: 'What are those *other* gems they're holding? The red and green ones?'

I hadn't noticed them before but there they were: the priests held not only two yellow gems, but two red gems and two green ones as well. I told my dad I'd never seen any red or green gems in the flesh, just the yellow ones.

My dad shrugged. 'If the yellow ones create a twenty-two-year fold in time, what do the red and green ones do? If you find them, maybe they *also* initiate these portals, but in different ways. They might create different kinds of folds. Longer or shorter ones or ones that go *back* in time.'

'That's enough, you!' I said, smiling. 'I've already done more time-travel thinking this past month than I ever thought I'd do. I'm just glad I could share it with you.'

As March 17 drew near, my dad and I met up with Jenny, who by then had found her father, Ken.

We decided we would all find a nice quiet place to face the gamma cloud together, somewhere away from the disintegrating city.

Ken, it turned out, owned a small waterfront cottage on a remote inlet on Long Island called Bullhead Bay, out near the famous golf courses, Shinnecock Hills and the National Golf Links of America. Typical of Ken, it was not ostentatious or obviously opulent. From the outside, he said, it looked like a shack.

And it was accessible only by boat or seaplane. Sounded good to me.

Since we couldn't hope to reach Ken's seaplane, parked at its marina in Jersey, we just found a car—there were plenty of abandoned ones—packed it with supplies, and drove eastward, out of the city, out past JFK and along the Long Island Expressway till we came to the turnoff for Bullhead Bay.

A rowboat took us the rest of the way. I loved the cottage: you could hardly have found a more remote—or beautiful—place, except perhaps Race Rock Lighthouse.

On March 17, as Dr Harold Finkelstein had predicted, the world swept through the gamma cloud.

When the hour drew near, the four of us gathered in the living room of the cottage and sat on the floor in a circle, holding hands.

The first thing to go off was the radio, then the refrigerator, then the lights. The gamma cloud was knocking out the electricity.

And then, as he held his daughter's hands in his, Ken Johnson's eyes rolled up into his head and he slumped to the ground, dead. The last thing he saw was Jenny's kind, loving face.

As for Jenny, thanks to the regimen of anti-depressant drugs she'd been taking over the last few years, she survived the passage through the cloud.

I did, too. The peculiar diet of vitamins and sardines my father had suggested got me through, as it had with Red.

My dad also survived, in all likelihood because of the various medications he had been on while he'd been institutionalised in Memphis.

We buried Ken in the garden down by the shore. I held Jenny as she sobbed into my shoulder.

Over the next few days, the world went still. Still and quiet.

We saw no planes in the sky overhead. No cars or trucks on the roads. We heard none of the familiar sounds of suburbia, no lawnmowers or leaf blowers.

On the third afternoon, my dad took me aside.

'Blue, thanks for finding me at Penn Station. It's been so wonderful to spend this time with you. But listen to me. Over the next few years, this world is going to be a hard place, a dangerous place. It won't be safe for a sixteen-year-old girl and it certainly won't help if you have to watch out for your silly old dad during that time.'

My brow furrowed. 'What are you saying?'

He bit his lip for a moment.

'I think you should go through your portal,' he said. 'You and Jenny.'

'What?' I said. 'And leave you here?'

'Blue.' His voice was calm. 'That portal offers you

and your friend a golden opportunity to avoid the worst of humanity. No father who had a chance like this would pass it up. If you go through that portal and come out in twenty-two years' time, the world will have had a chance to settle down and rebuild, like you said Red will do at Rhode Island.'

'I can't leave you!' I said, tears welling in my eyes.

'Yes, you can, and, yes, you should,' he said kindly. 'I probably should have made you go through the portal before the gamma cloud arrived, but I—I don't know—maybe I was selfish. I think I *wanted* to be with you during it.'

'But what will you do?' I said.

'I'll be okay,' he said. 'Might find myself a yacht somewhere round here and sail around for a while. I'll give it a few years and then head on up to Rhode Island and find Red, maybe join his community as a doctor.

'I won't tell Red everything I know about your travels—it's probably best he meets you in the future without any foreknowledge—but if you don't mind, I might hide somewhere when you turn up at the Newport pier twenty-two years from now. I wouldn't want to freak *you* out when you get there. From everything you've told me, I imagine you'll already be in quite a state.'

'Thanks,' I said, and in my mind's eye I recalled Red's odd looks at Newport, when I'd caught him glancing at the warehouse beside the dock. My spirits lifted. Had this been what was going on? Did it mean my dad made it there?

My dad looked me square in the eye.

'This isn't negotiable, Skye,' he said. It was so odd to

hear him use my actual name, but it had the effect he desired. It added serious weight to his argument.

'Today is March 20,' he said. 'Since nothing's going to be working and survivors are going to be edgy, let's give ourselves two days to get back to the city from here. Then at, say, 6:00 p.m. on March 22, you and Jenny will step through your portal and emerge from the well in Central Park twenty-two years from now. I'll keep a close eye on the calendar, and unless something happens to me between now and then, I'll make sure I'm waiting at that well at 6:00 p.m. on March 22, 2040, when you come out.'

I didn't know what to say. It was a huge sacrifice for him to make, to spare us twenty-two years of hell.

'Please, Blue, it's for the best,' my dad said. 'As your father, it'll make me feel a whole lot better. Please do this.'

I buried my face in his chest and cried while he just held me tightly in his arms.

My dad was right about getting back to Manhattan. It took a while; almost two full days.

The roads and expressways were empty; all the traffic lights were off; trigger-happy survivors were already guarding their homes with shotguns; any car moving on the roads was instantly noticeable.

But we made it back and, two days later, on March the 22nd, just before 6:00 p.m.—carrying backpacks stocked with food, and wearing sturdy hiking boots and stout clothing—Jenny and I arrived at the conservancy garden behind the Met accompanied by my dad.

I said my final teary goodbyes to him there in the garden before I tore myself away and Jenny and I dropped down through the hatch and closed it behind us.

Even though I knew that in the not-too-distant future Griff would park a yellow cab right on top of that hatch, both sealing it and hiding it from the world, I locked the hatch from the inside with Misty's key anyway.

Minutes later, standing in front of the ancient stone doorway down in the entry cave, I placed the amber gem in the pyramid and the curtain of rippling purple light appeared.

I looked at Jenny. 'Ready?'

'As I'll ever be,' she said, taking my hand.

And together we stepped through the portal, out of our broken world and into the future.

Ten minutes later, I poked my head up out of the well and saw my father standing there in the bare clearing around it.

Even though only minutes had passed for me, he was twenty-two years older—now in his late sixties—leaner, wirier, more tanned, and he bore some pale scars on his face that hadn't been there before.

And by his side stood my brother, Red, in his sheriff's uniform.

And they were smiling.

THE END

AN INTERVIEW WITH MATTHEW REILLY ABOUT *THE SECRET RUNNERS OF NEW YORK*

SPOILER WARNING!
This interview contains
spoilers from
The Secret Runners of New York

Well, Matthew, you've given us dragons, hovering cars and ancient wonders—and now, finally, time travel! You're a well-known Back to the Future *fan (most of us know about your DeLorean). So what made you want to write a time-travel story?*

Since I was a kid, I've always loved time-travel stories, especially *Back to the Future* and *The Terminator*. I particularly love the idea of planting clues in one time and revealing them in another.

To my mind, *Back to the Future* did this amazingly well. In that movie, one key gag was the fact that Marty McFly and the viewer *knew the futures* of all the characters Marty encounters in 1955. That made it very funny. (The DeLorean made it legendary!) With *The Secret Runners of New York*, I wanted to do something a little different: I wanted to write a story set in the present and also in a very peculiar future, one that is both uncertain and ugly, so that readers will be concerned about what happens to our lead characters.

Over the years, you have written two big series—the Scarecrow books and the Jack West Jr books. What makes you write a standalone novel like this one?

You know, every now and then, I just like to branch out creatively.

I get so much enjoyment out of writing the Scarecrow and Jack West Jr novels. I love the characters and inventing new and wild plots for them. And writing a sequel—whether it's the second book in a series or the fifth like my recent book, *The Three Secret Cities*—is its own kind of challenge (the key part being: giving readers all the characters and pace they enjoy but with a new and refreshing take).

But then, sometimes, I just have an idea which works for a single story. *The Great Zoo of China* (dragons in the present day battling tanks and fighter jets) was like this, as was *The Tournament* (a sweet teacher–student story about how a young girl becomes a great queen, set during a wild chess tournament filled with cheating, poisonings and murders) and *Hover Car Racer* (a super-fast thrill-ride with hovering cars that was ultimately about brothers and families).

And I must say, my fans are very good about this! While they let me know how much they like the ongoing series, they also allow me to try new things. This is great, because by writing *Great Zoo*, *Tournament*, *Hover Car* and now *Secret Runners*, I become a better writer, which means the next instalment of Jack's or

Scarecrow's adventures will be better, too. So I thank my fans for that.

In the end, it's all about creativity.

Do you consider The Secret Runners of New York **to be a Young Adult novel?**

Hmmm, that's a tricky one. Because its lead characters are teenagers, some people have called *The Secret Runners of New York* a Young Adult or 'YA' novel. Now, while I know that this sort of labelling is unavoidable, to be honest I don't really see the novel as a YA title.

In the end, I think *Secret Runners* is a novel, plain and simple, and that readers of any age can enjoy it.

It's also very much a 'Matthew Reilly novel': it's fun; it's big; the lead characters are thrown into wild and frightening scenarios; it's set during a chaotic present and a frightening future; but most of all, it's *fast*! That, to me, is a Matthew Reilly novel, no matter how old you are.

What do you think is the key to a good time-travel story?

For me, the key to a good time-travel story is establishing the 'rules' of time travel in your tale.

In *The Secret Runners of New York*, for instance, I decided that if Skye was in the future for a day, then she would be away from our present *for the same amount of time* (unlike, say, in *Back to the Future*, where Marty can be away from 1985 for a few days but return to the exact moment he left).

The second key is to have cool and intricate twists. I loved the idea of hiding precious objects in hollowed-out books so that they could be rediscovered, untouched, in the future twenty-two years ahead. That gave me many opportunities to hide fun things in those books and to also indulge my love of books.

And yes, I have hollowed out books in real life myself. I'm not sure if that is good karma for an author to do, but, hey, I admit it!

How did you come up with this 'rule' for how time travel works in **Secret Runners***?*

Many years ago, I read about time being an upward spiral rather than a straight line. It was so long ago, I've forgotten where I read it. I like the idea that dips in that time-spiral would account for déjà vu (that notion that you have seen some place or encounter that you are currently experiencing sometime in the past; I have definitely experienced this myself).

I thought this notion of a time-spiral would be a good explanation for time travel. The rest actually wrote itself: once you accept the notion that time is a spiral, then it's quite an easy jump to my main rule mentioned above: that the present and the future move along at the same speed, so if Skye is in the future for a day, she is missing from the present for the same amount of time.

This gave me the rather sinister possibility of missing girls actually being stranded in the future by nasty individuals.

Can you give us any more clues about the tunnel—who might have built it, and why?

In my mind, I think the tunnel was found—whether intentionally or not—by members of the Mayan civilisation. Seeing that it worked only for young people of a certain age, they then used it as an initiation rite for young members of their community: a test which, when passed, allowed teens to advance into adulthood.

The idea of sending kids into another time or dimension from which they might not return struck me as pretty scary, and I figure if it scares me, it'll scare my readers.

The carvings of wolves or dogs chasing the young initiates suggests that perhaps wolves or dogs were sent in after the teens to stop them trying to turn around and force them to go towards the other end.

In other novels, you've had some amazing moments where the world has almost ended. But in Secret Runners, *you actually show us* the end of the world! *Can you discuss that a little?*

First, let me say this: I didn't want to end humanity with a virus! I've seen that in too many movies and

TV shows. For my story, I wanted something that would kill *nearly* everyone on Earth and also knock out most technology. My solution was the gamma cloud.

As for why I wrote about the end of the world, I actually did this for several reasons.

First, I love the idea of empty cities, cities devoid of human life. I just think they're visually really interesting and I wanted to set a story in one.

I also honestly wondered how we would all react if a scientist told us the world was going to end in a year or so. My personal answer—which, as you now know, I also put in the book—is that after some initial hysteria, people would just get on with life, at least until 'doomsday' came upon them.

What made you decide to set the novel in New York?

If you're going to set a story in an empty city, New York is the one. Not only is it the most visually interesting metropolis on Earth, importantly for me, it's also instantly *recognisable*.

Everybody knows the New York skyline, even if they haven't been there. From the Empire State Building to the Brooklyn Bridge and Central Park, readers generally know New York's main features, so they don't need to be introduced to it. That allowed me to get on with my story at a quick pace.

There's more new territory for you in this book—high school drama! What inspired you to centre the novel around teenagers, in particular Skye Rogers?

I find high school fascinating. We've all been there. We all have our memories. Many of us didn't enjoy the experience, many did.

I find high school in 2018 even more fascinating. I just wonder how teenagers handle it: with camera phones, Instagram, Facebook and all that.

And most fascinating of all: *high schools in 2018 for wealthy kids.*

I think that we in the developed West are living in an incredibly delicate time: a time when the rich are *really, really* rich. Unfathomably rich. Maybe too rich. French Revolution rich.

Don't get me wrong: I have nothing against rich people. I'm just saying—sincerely; objectively—that we are living in a time of *enormous* wealth inequality. Society can handle some of its members acquiring wealth and status. But if the top 1% acquire *too much* money and it is *not* spread enough to the regular folk who work for them, you end up with Marie Antoinette saying 'Let them eat cake' and suddenly you have guillotines in the middle of Paris.

For a few years now, I've wanted to do a novel about this topic, and when I was thinking about the idea of

The Secret Runners of New York, it occurred to me that a good way to tackle it was through two lenses: (1) amid the tumult of the world ending and (2) through the eyes of ultra-rich teenagers, kids who have known nothing else but obscene wealth.

For I honestly think that when people see the end of the world come into view, they will not respect walls or fences or mansions. And they may settle old scores (as Hattie discovers in one of the scenes I like most in the novel).

How did you find writing Skye compared to other younger characters you've written, such as Jason Chaser, and female protagonists, such as CJ Cameron and Princess Bess?

You know what the answer to that is: I love writing, I really do, and every now and then, I like to try my hand at a new narrator's perspective.

My big Scarecrow and Jack West Jr novels are written from what's called *a third person omniscient observer's perspective*, which is necessary for those kinds of novels, because it allows me to bounce around the world to check up on different characters in different countries.

The Tournament and *The Secret Runners of New York* are told exclusively from a first person perspective, which is entirely different.

When I write a book from a single character's perspective in the first person, it's actually a bit like acting. I try to become Skye, to see the world through her eyes, to use her language.

This is what I did with Princess Bess when she narrated *The Tournament*. It was the same for those parts in *Temple* that were written by Alberto Santiago, the runaway Spanish priest in that book.

To be able to write convincingly from Skye's point of view meant doing research and two great sources for me were a couple of young ladies I met who had attended elite private schools on the Upper East Side of Manhattan. I got fashion tips, language tips and even tips for the names of kids in that world.

And it's nice to see that my list of female protagonists is growing: CJ Cameron, Princess Bess and now Skye Rogers.

What element of this story was the most fun to write?

The mind-bending stuff. Especially the parts where characters like Griff or Red—during and just after the chaos of the gamma cloud's arrival—leave messages for Skye to read twenty-two years in the future; or where Oz leaves the kangaroo in the tunnel in the future for Skye to see in the present. I love all of that kind of stuff!

Hiding the gems in books was also fun—including inside a Hillary Clinton book. And if you know your

Stephen King, then of course, you saw that twist right away! (I love Stephen King: not just for his books, but just for being him. I think he should win the Nobel Prize for Literature for his body of work and his contribution to reading. But I don't know if literary types are brave enough or open-minded enough to do that. The man is a legend!)

We have to know, what's your next book about?

I have to take Jack through to the end. *The Two Something Somethings* is up next.

And how is LA?

Things are great here. I've been writing up a storm, both books and screenplays. There are possible TV shows in the works and feature films as well—as many of my fans know, I've had several projects fall through for all kinds of silly Hollywood reasons (director got fired, senior executive left the studio, Writers Guild went on strike).

Some very interesting news is that there is a chance that I could direct an original screenplay of mine—something I have long wanted to do—but I don't want to get ahead of myself (I'm writing this at the end of 2018; I'll know more when this book is released in late March 2019, and as I well know, in the movie business, anything can happen by then).

As always, more than anything, I just hope *The Secret Runners of New York* took you away from the world for a few hours or days. I hope you liked it because, hey, you never know, Skye may return . . .

Matthew Reilly
Los Angeles
November 2018

Matthew Reilly

Matthew Reilly is the internationally bestselling author of many novels, including *Contest, Temple, Ice Station, Area 7, Scarecrow, Hover Car Racer, Seven Ancient Wonders, The Six Sacred Stones, The Five Greatest Warriors, Scarecrow and The Army of Thieves, The Great Zoo of China, Troll Mountain* and the *Sunday Times* bestseller *The Tournament*.

Matthew's books are published in over twenty languages and have sold over 7.5 million copies worldwide. Sony Pictures have optioned the movie rights to his book *The Great Zoo of China*.

Matthew lives in Los Angeles, California. To find out more visit www.matthewreilly.com or follow him on Facebook (@ OfficialMatthewReilly), Instagram (@matthewreillyofficial) and Twitter (@matthew_reilly)

Want to read
NEW BOOKS
before anyone else?

Like getting
FREE BOOKS?

Enjoy sharing your
OPINIONS?

Discover

READERS FIRST

Read. Love. Share.

Get your first free book just by signing up at
readersfirst.co.uk

Thank you for choosing a Hot Key book.

If you want to know more about our authors and what we publish, you can find us online.

You can start at our website

www.hotkeybooks.com

And you can also find us on:

We hope to see you soon!